MW01132646

THIS TIME FOR SURE

BOUCHERCON ANTHOLOGY 2021

BOUCHERCON ANTHOLOGIES

Murder at the Beach (Long Beach CA, 2014)
Murder Under the Oaks (Raleigh NC, 2015)
Blood on the Bayou (New Orleans LA, 2016)
Passport to Murder (Toronto ON, 2017)
Sunny Place, Shady People (St. Petersburg FL, 2018)
Denim, Diamonds and Death (Dallas TX, 2019)
Where Murder is a Capital Crime (Sacramento CA, 2020)
This Time For Sure (New Orleans LA, 2021)

THIS TIME FOR SURE
BOUCHERCON ANTHOLOGY 2021

HANK PHILLIPPI RYAN, EDITOR

DOWN&OUT
BOOKS

Down & Out Books
3959 Van Dyke Road, Suite 265
Lutz, FL 33558
DownAndOutBooks.com

Cover design by Zach McCain

ISBN: 1-64396-211-6
ISBN-13: 978-1-64396-211-5

TABLE OF CONTENTS

INTRODUCTION
HANK PHILLIPPI RYAN

You know you have wished for it. In your moments of regret, or frustration, or disappointment. In the moments when someone else got the money, or the prize, or the sweetheart, or the happiness. In that moment when your nemesis whirls and walks away—while you're still trying to come up with the perfect thing to say.

We imagine, we envision, we concoct that memorable comeback. That elegant cutting remark. We replay each decision in our minds, creating new movies of what might have been. If only we had done it differently. If only we had made a different decision. If only we had it to do over. If only we had a second chance. Traveled, for once, the *other* road. *This time for sure,* we think.

I have researched the desire for revenge, and it's a fascinatingly bitter emotion. And a complicated one. Scientists say that in their studies of those who have attempted revenge, one of the key elements to "success" is that the victim knows who has gotten back at them, and precisely why.

Random unspecified unpleasantness and discomfort is not sufficient. The perpetrator of the revenge only feels satisfied when the victim has that exquisite moment of realization—that gasping shocking reality that their dastardly deed will, indeed, go punished.

So what would you do if you had a second chance? How far would you go to get back at your bête noire? And would you

1

agree with the scientists—you'd want to see it happen? You'd want your target to know you'd ultimately triumphed?

I put this proposition to nine invited authors, and to the mystery-writing community at large: tell me a story about revenge. Redemption. Second chances. Do overs. Instant replay. Tell me about evening the score, turning the tables, making things right.

And, fine. Because we are crime fiction authors, turned out there was a lot of murder involved. Hey, it's fiction.

But what was most fascinating to me were the roots of the revenge. High school, hilariously, never seems far from the surface. Steve Shrott's prom queen who got away. Andrew Welsh-Huggins' girl who married the other guy. What might a grown-up—an adult who has never quite forgotten or let go of the past—do about those simmering slights, all these years later? And if you went to high school with Edwin Hill's protagonist, you should still be very afraid.

Love and marriage, of course, are high on the list of regrets and second thoughts. Seething animosity and spousal duplicity wind their way through several of these wonderful stories— Elizabeth Elwood's bitter road trip, Elisabeth Elo's unappreciated (but calculating) wife, and the determination of Alan Orloff's returning suitor. Lucy Burdette's Key West dating scene made me laugh out loud, and what about retribution via a love podcast? Alexia Gordon shows how that can work. Or—not.

Devotion, too, led some of these characters to go farther than they've ever imagined. A crime of passion in Sharon Bader's storied Florence museum, or G. Miki Hayden's finale of justice in the streets of Warsaw.

Relationships. A loving mother and her vulnerable son in Damyanti Biswas's truly haunting "Fat Mother." And the teenager who escaped Karen Dionne's deadly Marsh King—ever wonder what happened to her? And what she might do now?

Double-crossing bad guys are ripe candidates for retribution. Whether in Alex Segura's duplicitous Miami, Gabriel Valjan's perfectly-styled 1920's New Orleans, Martha Reed's twisty tale of the Boston art underworld, or Clark Boyd's touching and poignant story of Providence. Each of them will surprise you. Friendship gone wrong—or right—is a critical element, too. David Heska Wanbli Weiden's high school best friend inspires a character to do something that profoundly changes his life— "Turning Heart" is a treasure of brutality and philosophy. Kristin Lepionka's unlikely allies in "Remediation" made me stand and cheer, and I simply had to close this anthology with Ellen Clair Lamb's chilling and disturbing meeting on the "Night Bus."

One of the absolute joys of editing an anthology like this is opening each little prize package of a story. Our contest judges— bless every single brilliant. talented, skilled, and generous one of them—went through hundreds of anonymized submissions and chose the final pool. From that, we chose ten of the very most irresistible. I will never forget when I finally got to open the manuscripts to reveal the authors of the stories I had read so carefully. Some dear friends, some absolute strangers, some never-before-published writers.

Besides our invited authors and contest winners, our roster of Bouchercon guests of honor hit it out of the ballpark, too. Every one of them, in their own distinct and unique voice, provided a treasure of a story. No one but Craig Johnson could have written the wry and knowing "Music Appreciation," no one but Charles and Caroline Todd could bring us such an elegant murder mystery in 1919 London, and no one knows the secret history of New Orleans like Heather Graham.

We have been through a lot over the past year, haven't we, dear friends? We have lost those we love, and we mourn strangers, and wondered what would happen on the other end. We cannot change the past, but we can learn from it. And one thing I learned this year? It is always safe inside a book.

We are so honored to provide this one for you. It comes with irony and humor, and some danger, some terrific twists—and a warning. One you will perhaps learn as you read these marvelous stories: Though everyone deserves a second chance, beware of retribution and revenge. Like the twists in these brilliant tales, attempting revenge is another thing you might regret.

Or—maybe not. *This time for sure*, you say. Good luck.

MUSIC APPRECIATION
CRAIG JOHNSON

"They moved him."

Lowering the mask from over my nose and mouth, I stood there at the reception desk of the Durant Home for Assisted Living feeling the world being slipped out from under me like a cheap carpet. It wasn't the first time. There had been others, and I could rattle them off like a carnival prize wheel, the emotional clacking like strikes against my heart. "Say again."

"They moved him to the ICU over at the hospital."

I stared at Mary Jo Johnson, hoping against hope that I'd heard her wrong or that she'd misspoke or was talking about some other resident of the Durant Home for Assisted Living.

Vic reached up and touched my sleeve. "Let's go."

Standing there for another instant, I turned without another word and walked out. Behind me, I could hear my undersheriff talking to Mary Jo as the heavy glass door swept closed, leaving me alone, standing at the top of the ramp looking out into the velvety darkness of a June night.

The Miller moths were swirling around the streetlight in the parking lot, pausing in their yearly migration to the mountains, the lowly Army Cutworm having grown gossamer, magically dust-covered wings.

I became aware of someone standing beside me. "They travel

5

over a thousand miles, some of them." I sighed. "Oasis Effect—they're following the nectar of budding plants; as the summer gets drier, they move toward the mountains for food, trying to survive."

She stepped past me, lowering her mask down onto her chin and looking at them. "Why do they call them Miller moths... because some guy named Miller discovered them?"

"No, it's because the dust on their wings are like the flour that settled on grain millers back in the day." There must've been a thousand of them bustling around the light. "They use the moon and stars to navigate, but then...they...they get confused."

She nodded. "I've got a goose-neck lamp with a bucket of soap suds below it to confuse about a hundred of them a night."

I nodded and then started off toward my truck. "C'mon."

We piled in and fastened our seatbelts as I fired up the engine and wheeled out of the parking lot, Vic reaching for the toggles. "Lights and siren?"

"It's not an emergency."

"One of ours is down." She flipped the switches. "The hell it's not."

Howling through the night with the red and blue lights chasing each other, we were at Durant Memorial in a few minutes, pulling under the canopy and parking next to the building.

There was a young woman sitting on a bench a little way from the front door with a surgical mask hanging limp around her neck. She was smoking a cigarette. Lana Baroja was Lucian Connally's discovered granddaughter; one he hadn't known he'd had until much later in life. She was the owner of the little restaurant/bakery on the east side of town where she made Basque pastries, most of which I truly enjoyed but couldn't pronounce.

"Hi, Lana."

She looked up at me with a sad smile. "Hey, Walt."

"I didn't know you smoked."

"Haven't for about ten years, but I am tonight."

Vic joined me. "How's he doing?"

"Not so good." Lana flicked some ash away. "They say that if they don't see some improvement, they're going to have to put him on a ventilator." Wiping her eyes, she looked up at the ceiling of the portico where more moths flittered across the smooth surface trying to find the moon. "...He won't survive that."

I placed a hand gently on her shoulder. "He survived taking a medium-sized bomber off of an aircraft carrier, bombing Tokyo and crash-landing, and being captured and almost beheaded."

She looked up at me with a sad smile. "He wasn't approaching a hundred years old."

I nodded, staring at the scuffed toes of my boots. "How's the accordion player?"

"Oh, that little prick is fine—he's twenty-two years old."

Stanley Dean, a musician with a local cowboy/polka band, had attended a Cowboy Gathering in Pocatello, Idaho, and had returned to Absaroka County thinking he was asymptomatic. A part-time plumber, he'd repaired a broken toilet in the old sheriff's bathroom, and it was only discovered two weeks later that he had acquired Covid-19 and had ultimately infected Lucian, resulting in two of the three cases in Absaroka County.

"Maybe he'll surprise you." Squeezing her shoulder, I pulled up my mask. "Go home, I've got this." Entering the hospital with Vic in tow, I spotted Ruby's granddaughter at the receptionist desk. "Hi, Janine. Who's here?"

Her eyes peered over her own mask and were red, I assumed, from crying. "Both Isaac and David in the ICU. They're the only ones there—no other patients in that wing."

I nodded, pushed through the two swinging doors to our left and continued down the hallway where two men stood in conversation. As I drew closer, they both turned to me in masks like bank robbers, neither looking me in the eye. "Well?"

Nickerson was the first to speak. "He's stabile, but even with prompt triage and isolation protocols…"

Bloomfield added, "If his acute respiratory distress continues, we'll have no choice."

I stood up straight, towering over both of them. "Ventilator."

They both nodded.

"And what are his chances of surviving that?"

Isaac pulled at the lower lip under his mask, something I'd seen him do my entire life when there was a dire circumstance. "Considering his age and cardiac history—not good."

Vic leaned against the wall. "Walt played chess with him last Thursday."

Isaac glanced at me. "Have you been tested?"

"Yes, negative."

He nodded and then stared at the closed door beside him. "Cytokine Storm; what happens is the immune system overreacts and causes inflammation in the lungs. His body is trying to fight it off, trying too damned hard, actually."

"Well, isn't that just Lucian."

We all nodded.

"Can we see him?"

Isaac glanced behind him at the nearest door. "Yes, but I'm afraid he's relatively unconscious and might not even realize you're there. He comes and goes…"

"Would it do any good if he did?"

"Always. There's generally a point where the patient begins giving up, and if you can find some way of motivating them it's possible that they can be saved in spite of themselves."

"Talk to him?"

"Absolutely, audible stimulation is usually the best. They say it's the last sense that remains when all the others are gone. I'm sure your voice would be a welcome relief."

I became aware of a young man in a hospital gown standing in a doorway next to Lucian's. Nickerson and Bloomfield turned to see him, a skinny, red-headed individual with a straw cowboy hat who gave out with a weak wave.

Holding a plastic cup with a straw and full of ice, he rattled it and spoke. "I was wondering if I could get some more water?"

David glanced at me and then started toward him. "Back inside; I'll get that." We watched as Nickerson all but bounced the young man back in his room and closed the door behind him, his voice muffled from inside. "...We assumed as a plumber you would've recognized the faucet over here."

We moved toward the closed door beside us as Isaac turned the lever and opened it. The room was dimmed with only a singular light on at the bedside, most of the illumination provided by the LED screen on the wall and a strange contraption with more displays lodging shelves of oxygen.

I pointed toward the piece of equipment I'd never seen. "What's that?"

"That's the ventilator. We thought it best to have it here and ready."

The old sheriff's mouth was covered with an oxygen mask and the blanket was pulled up to his chest, his arms uncovered at his sides, a cardio cuff and IV attached.

Never a large man, he looked even smaller there in the hospital bed.

Isaac stood at the door with Vic, a clipboard in his hands, and stared at the floor. "Did he complain of any symptoms when you saw him on Thursday?"

I thought about it. "Shortness of breath; he may have coughed a few times...I didn't think anything of it."

The Doc nodded. "Nor should you; who would've thought an accordion-playing plumber would be carrying the virus."

I shook my head. "He always hated the accordion."

Bloomfield couldn't help but smile. "Really?"

"Yep, I saw him punch an accordion player at a wedding once."

The Doc shook his head, but then he just looked sad. "I'll leave you two with him."

The door quietly closed behind us, and we both stood there, both knowing and not knowing what to do. We'd been in this same situation so many times, but this time it was different. There are people in your life that you don't know what you'll do without until you have to.

I grazed a hand across the back of Vic's arm and then walked over, pulling the guest chair from beside the nightstand and straddling it. She came up behind me, gently laying her hands on my shoulders. "How old were you when he hired you?"

I smiled, looking at the wrinkles and crags in the portions of his face that weren't covered by the oxygen mask; they looked like erosion marks steadily chiseled into granite. "Younger than you."

She squeezed my shoulders. "Now, don't take this the wrong way, because I can't think of anyone other than you that was more born to be a cop; how'd he become the sheriff anyway?"

I studied his chest, watching it rise and fall. "An egg."

"Excuse me?"

"Lucian had just gotten back from the war, World War II, and I guess he was hell on earth." I adjusted my hat and then rested my chin on the back of my gun hand. "I guess a lot of 'em were like that, just hellraisers with nowhere to do it once they got off the battlefield." I smiled, thinking about the story that had become legend in Durant. "He was drinking at the Century Club one night there on Main Street, and he and some other fellow got into it over who was the better horseman. Well, Lucian had ridden his horse into town, and it was tied up right outside the bar. So, they made this bet that he couldn't pick up an egg at a full gallop."

"You're kidding."

"Nope. So, they take this egg and they stand it up out there on the centerline in a shot glass. Lucian goes out about thirty yards and wheels Pinky, this little cow pony he had around, and blisters down Main Street, leaning out of the saddle and scooping that egg up with one hand just as gentle as you please. Then he walks Pinky back over in front of the bar where the other cowboy accuses Lucian of cheating, and that it was a hardboiled egg."

She came around to my side to look at the old man. "What happened?"

"Lucian reached out with one hand and cracked the egg over top of the cowboy's 10X hat."

She made a face. "How did that make him decide to be a sheriff?"

"It was the current sheriff that he cracked the egg on. He got arrested for drunken disorderly and disturbing the peace, and the next day when they let him out of the cell, he went into the Courthouse and filed to stand for Sheriff of Absaroka County."

She shook her head at him, and I watched as her face grew sad. "I'm going to go get a cup of coffee and leave you two alone for a little while."

As the door slowly closed, I listened to the machines that were attempting to keep the old sheriff alive. "Not the first time you've had machines trying to keep you going, huh, ol' man?" His eyes remained closed, but I thought I could detect movement under the lids. "You in there, Lucian?" I scooted my chair closer and reached out, placing my hand on his arm. "You need to pull the stick back and wheel her around; it ain't over yet. You're not going to let some little bug knock you out of the game, are you? I thought you had more fight in you than this…" I kept trying, but the words just sounded hollow, exactly like I felt.

I was about to start off again, but there was a strange noise coming from the wall to the left, a terrible gasping and wheezing. I stood and listened. Crossing the room, I pushed open the door, but the hallway was empty, which wasn't a surprise considering the place and the hour.

I couldn't hear the noise any longer and started to close the door when it started again.

I slipped out and gently knocked. There was no response, so

I pushed it open to find Stanley Dean seated on the edge of his bed. He was still wearing his hospital gown and his weather-beaten cowboy hat, his red-swirl-metal-flake accordion wrapped in about a half-dozen towels.

He stared back at me, his fingers still on the keys. "I'm sorry. I thought I was being quiet."

"You're playing that thing?"

"Uh, yeah. Our band has a competition in Spokane in November; we're in the Cowboy Polka Competition in the International Division and I can't afford to get rusty." I said nothing, and he continued. "I thought that if I wrapped the towels around it, I could still practice."

I pulled the pocket watch from my jeans. "It's two o'clock in the morning."

He reached over and took the glass of water from his nightstand. "I'm sorry."

I nodded and sighed. "How are you doing?"

"I'm good. A little tired, but I can't sleep..." He smiled. "How's Mr. Connally?"

"Not so good."

He sat the accordion beside him, some of the towels slipping to the tiled floor. "I'm really sorry. I mean, about everything. I had no idea I had it."

"Yep, I guess it works that way." I started to go, thinking about the long hours ahead. "If you don't mind keeping it down and maybe not playing tonight, I'd appreciate it."

"You bet."

I closed the door to find Vic standing in the hallway. She was waiting for me with a cup of coffee. "Problem?"

"No, no..." I took the cup, removed the lid, and took a sip. "I think the last thing Lucian would want is accordion music on his last night on Earth."

She nodded toward the handheld mic in her hands. "HPs say we've got an RV broken down in the middle of the road out on the edge of town."

"I'll..."

"No, I got this." She sipped her own coffee, unable to look me in the eye. "Are you going to be all right?"

"Yep."

She bumped my chest with the radio and then left it there. "Maybe a miracle will happen."

I watched her go and then pushed the door open, carefully closing it behind me and walking over to his bed where I watched the graphic display of his bodily rates. "You want some coffee?" I turned the chair and sat, continuing to study him. "I could make a run over to the Home for Assisted Living and fetch your bottle of Pappy Van Winkle's Family Reserve Twenty-Three-Year-Old—happy to do it."

I sat there listening to the machines, finally glancing at the monstrous ventilator on the other side of the bed, the heat in my face growing as the welling began in my eyes. Thumbing the moisture away, I sat back in the chair. "If you don't start talking to me, I'm going to go get the chess board and play for both of us. That ought to be enough to annoy you..."

I sipped my coffee and then looked at the floor, and then the wall to my left. Standing, I looked at him again and then went to the door, pushing it all the way open and flipping the rubber stop down with my boot.

Knocking on the next door, I adjusted my mask. "Hey, Stanley?"

There was some noise from inside, and the door opened, the kid still wearing his hat. "Yeah?"

"I changed my mind." I pulled his door the rest of the way open and blocked it, too. "If you're up for it, would you mind playing your accordion? I was thinking that it might be nice for Lucian to have something to listen to tonight."

His face brightened. "Really?"

"Yep. I'm thinking he'd really enjoy it."

I watched as he practically ran for his squeeze box, still setting on the bed, and quickly strapped it on. "Any idea what he'd like?"

"Oh, anything at all. He, um...He just loves any kind of accordion music."

"Polkas?"

"Especially polkas."

He looked at the propped open doors. "Are you sure it's all right?"

"There's nobody else in this wing, so play to your heart's content." I thought the grin was going to break his face, so I left him standing there and returned to Lucian's room. True to his word, the wheezy beginning of "Beer Barrel Polka" began to gain momentum as I sat on the chair and looked at my old boss and mentor.

The jaunty Polka segued into "All Of Me" as I sipped the rest of my now cold coffee, then placing the empty cup on his nightstand. Relaxing in the chair, I even went so far as to pull my hat down over my eyes. The exhaustion began chipping away at my reserves as I sat there listening to "Besame Mucho" give way to "Hava Nagila", "The Girl From Ipanema", and then "Lady of Spain". The last remnants of consciousness finally abandoned me sometime during "The Third Man Theme", and I was starting to get why Lucian Connally really, really hated the accordion.

I remember feeling the warmth of the sun coming through the window on my face before I opened my eyes. My hat must've fallen on the floor sometime during the night, and I lifted my head and looked around at the traces of morning.

Somebody was shaking my shoulder, and I finally turned and could see Vic there with a questioning look on her face.

I yawned, then followed her eyes and looked at the empty bed.

It took a few seconds for the thought to clarify, but then I sat up and placed a hand on the cool surface of the mattress where the sheets had been thrown back.

Panic took hold as I stood, looking around at the electrocardiogram monitor showing a steady flatline and the oxygen mask lying on the floor, the IV hanging limp on the floor. "Where is he?"

"You tell me, you were the one here."

Rushing into the hallway, I looked around finding Stanley Dean in his room collapsed on his bed, sound asleep, still holding his accordion. Coming back into the hall, I almost ran over Vic. I looked up at the digital clock. It was just after five.

"Walt?"

Starting for the nurse's station, I could see it was unmanned, so I continued toward the main lobby and found Janine doing paperwork at the admittance desk. I charged toward her, adjusting my mask and resting my hands on the counter as Vic joined me. "Where did they take him?"

Her large eyes came up to mine. "What?"

"Isaac and David, where did they take Lucian? He's not in his room."

"I don't know what you're talking about, there's been no activity all night." She grabbed the phone from its cradle, punching numbers. "Code yellow, first floor, room twenty-six."

I turned, looking around the lobby, but there was no one there either. I took a few steps toward the center of the room and spun again, or maybe it was the world that was turning, and I was just trying to stand still. "You were here all night?"

She nodded, still clutching the receiver. "Yes, except for when I went to the bathroom about two hours ago." There was someone on the phone, and she quickly brought it back to her ear. "Yes, we've got a patient missing."

I turned to Vic. "Did you see anything?"

"No." I started to go by her, but she shot a hand out and stopped me. "Wait."

Without another word, she started toward the front door and I followed, the pneumatic door springing away as she moved out onto the Emergency entryway. I followed and turned toward the bench where Lana had sat. There was a bundle of blanket, wrapped like an insulated burrito on the bench.

Glancing at Vic, I stepped over to the bench and peered at one end, carefully pulling the blanket away to reveal Lucian Connally's platinum crewcut. A few Miller moths, disturbed from their daylight slumber, skittered out and flew away, having taken refuge in the dark folds of the old sheriff's blanket.

Kneeling, I reached into the wool covering and placed a few fingertips at the side of his neck, whereupon he snorted, resettled himself and let out with a loud snore. I turned back to Vic and smiled. "I guess the accordion music must've gotten to him."

Pulling my hand back, I noticed one of the velvety Millers was clutching my forefinger. I stood, turning my hand and looking at the moth as it wiggled its antennas, stared back at me with gleaming black eyes, and then watched as it gently fluttered away.

BURNT ENDS
GABRIEL VALJAN

I found him. Track a man across five states and trace all his aliases and you hope to find him someplace you could admire, some city you could respect. Not so with Dooley. Instead, the trail led me to a port city, in mid-July, in a high swelter, humid as hell, with puddles from a recent storm in the unpaved street. The morning air stank of confederate jasmine and grease.

I calculated the ruin to my fresh pair of boots while I stood outside the barber shop. I had spent a dollar for a much-needed haircut and shave just behind me, and now it'd cost me five times as much to cross the road in front of me. The mayor lacked the forethought to order businesses to lay down plywood for crossings. I looked up and the sky promised rain. The barber had offered to slick my hair with Brilliantine but in this soup for weather, I declined and asked him where I could buy a hat.

The man pointed to a haberdasher and said the shop didn't open until ten. I read the German name in the window and decided I'd rather not. A newsie nearby was wearing a cap, but his head was too small. I ended any thought of a purchase when I spotted a boob in a seersucker suit, complete with walking stick, and a straw boater on his lid. It was better to remain hatless.

I approached Dooley's establishment from the rear, where some dark types he'd hired from the docks were unloading moonshine. They ignored me. They took the side job when and where they could find it and pocketed the leftover cash after their foreman on the pier received his tribute. The boss man already earned a kickback for picking them out of the litter of laborers who lined up at sunrise for a day's work. The understanding was that stevedores and dockers kept cargo moving from barges and trains to ocean-bound vessels on schedule. Nobody squeaked while their pockets got fat.

I used the cast-iron scraper at the backdoor to rid myself of the muck on my boots before I entered the premises. The hallway into the parlor was dark and the wood decent. The main room was full of tables and chairs, but empty. A barman worked solo at the counter. There was a block of ice on a silver tray. He was doing set-ups and polished glasses with a cloth. A Negro piano man in the corner practiced stride, his left hand thumped a beat while his right finessed a melody. He saw me, closed the cover and left. The barkeep's hand drifted south of the wood and I told him to keep it north. He eyed me, low to high, before he spoke.

"You looking to rob the joint?"

"Nope. You can keep your suspenders on."

"You talk strange. Where you from, fellah?"

"Danbury or Dannemora. Take your pick. I'm here for Dooley."

He told me Dooley was due any minute. I asked the man if I could take a seat.

"What'll you have?" he asked and set a small napkin down.

"Prohibition Sour, if it's not too much trouble."

"A dry man when the whole country's wet. I suppose you didn't inherit any vices."

"My father swam in drink and my mother coughed from smoke."

I watched him assemble the drink. He married lemon and orange syrups in a generous coupe glass after he chipped some ice with a pick and blessed everything with fizzed water. I could

18

tell from the wear on the wooden handle of his chipper that he preferred it to either the pistol or shotgun beneath the counter. I thanked him and placed my billfold on the counter. I pulled out a bill and pushed it towards him.

"Very generous of you, and is that leather?" he asked.

"Indeed. Have at it," I said. "Identification is inside."

He didn't trust me so I raised my glass. I wanted to enjoy my lemonade, a tart and tasty drink for the modern man. He opened the wallet, thumbed through the cards, and his lips moved as he read the different names to himself. I watched his peepers widen and then narrow.

"This one says you're a revenue man," he said.

"And yet your firewater out back is unscathed."

"This card here says you're a Pinkerton. What'd you do for 'em boys?"

"Busted unions."

"Got something against the working man?" he asked.

"Working man wouldn't give me a job and the other side came to me first."

"Ain't right, Mister," he said and folded the billfold and eased it towards me.

"Wasn't right I was a veteran, and the man inside the office and on the street thought I was too damaged for them to hire me. As for strikes, it's an injustice that some men won't allow another man to earn a decent wage to provide for his family. Avarice, plain and simple."

I smiled. He didn't.

"Well, we all have our troubles," the barkeep answered. "Mr. Dooley ain't most men."

"No disagreement there."

"You saw yourself, on your way in here who he's hired. Italians and Poles." His chin indicated the piano. "Negroes," and he pointed to the vacant lounge behind me. "He don't mind women neither, if they're willing to work. Hell, they got the right to vote now. I've worked for the man for years, and I can tell you Dooley is fair and he ain't greedy."

I'd finished my drink and held the glass by the stem. "I wouldn't be so sure of that."

"You saying my loyalty is misplaced?"

"The better word is misspent."

Our eyes met. I saw his hand inch towards the icepick on the tray. I said, "Don't."

His fingers curled around the shaft. His arm swung for my head. I snapped the glass against the counter's edge and drove the stem into the soft triangle of flesh under his chin. I held his shirt as he choked on his blood. He went limp and I released him. He dropped with a thud. I heard another sound, this time behind me and I grinned.

"Nice to see you, Dooley. We should talk."

He looked as cool as Gatsby in a tan linen suit and a Panama hat.

He preceded me on the stairwell to his office upstairs. We passed an entresol, a storage space where he kept mixed company of some red and white wines with bottles of bourbon and rye. I read the back of his suit jacket for straps and determined he wasn't carrying.

He opened the door and pressed the button for the overhead light. Dooley placed his hat on the desk and took off his jacket. His dress shirt in the shade of cornflower was a cake-eater's choice, but the bowtie didn't surprise me. I tried to strangle Dooley once with his own necktie. The professorial look had me wondering about tweeds in winter if he moved north. Not without manners, I sat down after he'd offered me a seat. He knew to keep his hands in plain view.

"I should've killed you when I had the chance. You made quite the mess for me downstairs," he said.

"Have your jazzman clean it up, or slip a tenner to one of your deliverymen."

I crossed a leg over. He noticed the ankle holster. "I see not much has changed."

"That's where you're wrong," I said. "My reflexes and aim have improved."

"I presume you wish to revisit our earlier talk?"

"A world war interrupted our last conversation."

"Don't forget Spanish influenza, which delayed you some, and then it took time for you to find me. You've been waiting for this, for what...four years now?"

"Five."

"You're a patient man," Dooley said.

"Patient as a baker, and I'm all out of flour now."

Dooley planted his elbows on the blotter. His hands came together to form a triangle, and his fingertips, the apex to support the chin of a pharaoh. What I had said was true about the war. The politicians said our boys would be home for Christmas. We weren't. I should've died a thousand times against the Kaiser. I didn't. Then the Spanish flu came and went and carried off millions. Not us. The pale rider passed us both.

Dooley had bought his way out of military service. "Only suckers served," he said. When Prohibition arrived, his luck was already in bloom because he supplied brothels, juke joints, roadhouses, and speakeasies with everything from absinthe to whiskey. He even sold grapes to housewives for winemaking at home. Then he stepped up. He bought himself the police and bankrolled city and county clerks, inspectors, judges, and politicians. He owned every foot of the Mississippi that bordered Louisiana and every railroad tie inside the state, thanks to his friend, the Chairman of the Public Service Commission, a lawyer and carnival sharpie by the name of Huey Long. None of that concerned me. A man had to make a living, and whichever side of right or wrong he chose was his business. There was a difference, though, between owning a man and *owning* him.

"I want Lincoln," I said.

"That old affair again?"

"Second time is the charm. You do know slavery ended fifty years ago, right?"

"Don't you mean, third time is the charm?"

"There won't be a third time, Dooley."

"A threat. You always were the confident one. Let's hear your offer."

"Two grand. Half now, and half after I see Lincoln. Tonight sound good?"

"Tonight doesn't work for me," Dooley said.

"Figured as much. Tomorrow night then?"

"You have a grand on your person?"

I touched my chest. "In my pocket."

"And what if I don't accept your terms?"

"Your piano player has another mess."

"I'm curious. Why the interest in Lincoln?"

"We've been over this. I won't play the same record twice."

"You know, I could take your money and you'd still need to survive the night and live to see tomorrow evening."

"Now, who is the confident one? Deal or not?"

"Deal. Be at The Pelican tomorrow night, after dinner."

He flicked a card with an address on it. The location wasn't important, the password for the doorman he'd written on the back was. Dooley smiled with good teeth and I placed the fat envelope on the edge of the desk and left to enjoy a brief nap.

As I ranged and harvested the night into the light of the next day and the next night, I ruminated on a verse from the Book of Job that had sustained me during the war and provided sustenance now, "For now thou numberest my steps: dost thou not watch over my sin?"

Dooley's restaurant was on the highway, on a plot of land that both time and care had forgotten until Dooley developed it into a massive two-tier eatery. Brick walls were painted white, high windows with shutters blocked out the heat and humidity during the day and opened like night-blooming cereus in the evening. Footlights on all that stark stone made the building shine as bright as an iceberg in the sunlight.

When folks thought of food and Louisiana, what came to mind were crabs, crawfish, gumbo, jambalaya, and oysters, and if they contemplated barbecue and the Bayou State in the same sentence, they might think of a whole suckling pig cooked low and slow over coals. Cochon de lait.

George Washington Lincoln was an artisan of Cajun and Creole foods, and a renaissance man of the grill and smoker, and he had mastered beef, chicken, pork, and seafood. There wasn't a type of hardwood he hadn't used. Hickory. Mesquite. Oak. He could barbecue with a simple hole in the ground, a pit made with cinder blocks, or use the elaborate grill Dooley had built for him inside the White Pelican. Whatever the meat, it melted in your mouth; and if he smoked it, the rubs Lincoln used produced a bark that kept the meat moist and tender inside. His sauces and sides were accessories to the perfect culinary crime, in that he stole both your taste buds and your money.

People paid good money for Lincoln's food. The problem was that whites didn't know a black man, a grandson of slaves, prepared their meals. The problem was that Dooley kept the man captive, chained up, and out of view. Lincoln received money, but his cash was locked up inside Dooley's safe and Dooley had the combination, like he had the key to the shackle around the man's foot.

I saw Lincoln. He didn't see me.

Lincoln was feet away from me working a brisket, engrossed in removing the point end, which he would cook and season some more for the delicacy called burnt ends. Often set aside, Lincoln made it a prized morsel.

I saw that his right ankle was fettered. What shocked me was what had been done to his left foot. At some point in his captivity, Lincoln escaped from Dooley. The first time a slave ran away, he was flogged; the second time, the master lopped off half of his foot, so he could never run again; the third time, the boss man killed him. Lincoln understood the penalties of freedom.

Lincoln's people had come from Evergreen Plantation and before that, the Constancia, before it was renamed Uncle Sam Plantation after the Civil War. Generations of his family had worked the watches, cutting and stacking sugar cane on both plantations. Lincoln, knife in hand, saw me. The staff fled the kitchen. I had not slept much and I'm certain I looked like something out of the pages from the Book of Revelations.

"You shouldn't be here," he said.

"I'm here to right the balance."

Dooley must've noticed the exodus and eased into the room. I walked over to a clean table and placed the second fat envelope there. I asked him to unlock the cuff around Lincoln's foot.

"I've always had someone else do it," Dooley said. "You think, in all these years, I'd allow myself near a man with a knife."

"You dead, and Klansmen come for him without a thought, or you dead at his feet, him chained up only makes their job easier for them."

Dooley ambled over to the table, peeked inside the envelope, smiled and tossed me the key. I tapped the table next to me and asked Lincoln to slide the knife down my way, which he did. I handed him the key and he unlocked himself.

Dooley stood there, washing his hands like a rat on his hind legs. "You think you're going to walk out of here, the two of you? You, Mr. Pinkerton, with this scrap."

Lincoln moved. "Don't," I told him and reached out and squeezed his bicep. I answered Dooley, "I do."

"You really are something," Dooley said. "Confident doesn't cover it. Vanity is more like it. And why would I allow you two to leave?"

"Because you're nothing after tonight and you have nothing," I said. I lifted my chin, to indicate the double-doors. "Nobody in this place will stop us." I pointed to a candlestick telephone behind him. "Call your heavies. Let your muscle know you're in a jam, and see who comes running. I'll wait."

"I could call Shaughnessy. He's a crazy mick," he said.

"He won't answer."

"And why is that?"

"Because he's dead, and so are the rest of your goons. You think I look the way I do because I slept at a flophouse? Go, call the police, and see what that'll do for you, assuming they answer."

"You didn't?" Dooley said, his face ashen. "You won't get away with this."

"Yes, I will, and I've already helped myself to your safe. Lincoln?"

"Yes?"

I pushed the knife back towards him.

"Don't forget your knife."

We were on the midnight train, headed out west. Dooley stocked more cash in his safe than I'd expected. His greed paid for our private car and all the Pullman porters we needed. Those men enjoyed several good meals, cognac and cigars, and all the perks, thanks to Dooley.

On the third day, I bought a paper at a stop and was reading it when Lincoln asked me why I had come back for him after all those years.

"Was it redemption?" he asked.

"Nope. You could say I'm sentimental."

"Is it because I saved you from drowning when you was a child?"

"I know how to swim, thank you very much." I snapped the paper and creased it and scanned the columns. "You don't know how to read, do you, Linc?"

He shook his head. "Never had the time."

"We need to fix that, if we're going to open a barbecue joint together. Speaking of barbecue, this article ought to interest you some."

"What it say?"

"The remains of a man were found inside a smoker. Identification deemed impossible, it says here. Wonder why that is?"

Lincoln answered, "In too long and all the meat falls off the bone."

REMEDIATION
KRISTEN LEPIONKA

It happened because Carter got a job working for the Radon King. A sign caught her eye while she waited for the bus at Broad and Wilson—*HAND OUT flyErs get paid Daily signing bonus EASY!!!!*, written in a clumsy scrawl with capital letters randomly thrown in like the human resources version of a ransom note. The situation was this: ten cents per flyer, uniform provided, a location-tracking app that must be downloaded to Carter's phone to prevent funny business. "So if you just dump the flyers in the trash, I'll know." The Radon King handed over a heinous lime-green polo shirt with a logo embroidered on the chest along with the signing bonus—twenty dollars, cash. "Use it to get a normal haircut," he said. "I don't know what that is, but I don't even know where to look."

Carter took the money and smoothed over the long side of her asymmetrical shag, which covered her one eye a bit too much. "So is it a bonus, or?"

The Radon King flapped a hand. "Do you want the job or not?"

After leaving the Radon King's office with instructions to return in the morning in the polo shirt to collect flyers for her route, Carter went to the Mobil station to see what twenty bucks could get today. One pack of Turkish Golds with enough change for a soda, half a ticket to New York on the Chinatown bus, or ten tablets of tramadol, the weakest, cheapest opiate available. She went home and gave her roommate three of them in exchange for a haircut with a pair of sewing scissors.

Her roommate couldn't stop laughing while she did it. "This haircut is legit terrible," she said, "I mean, no wonder you grew it out. Your ears are like side mirrors. And the shirt is not helping matters, no, it is not."

Carter studied her reflection in the window above their sink. Without her bangs in her face, she looked like her father, if her father had been a semi-recovered junkie flyer-deliverer instead of an abusive carpet salesman. The color of the shirt gave her skin a nuclear glow. She said, "But the question is, would you take a flyer from me?"

Carter's roommate snipped a last little bit off the crown of her head and frowned. "Maybe you could get a hat, too."

Steve Simons was not a quitter. He had never quit a damn thing in his life, except his first marriage, though that wasn't so much about quitting a relationship as it was restarting a life. He didn't quit the restaurant business despite a couple very bad years in the nineties; he didn't quit pursuing young waitresses even though they were less and less interested these days; he didn't even quit smoking despite knowing better, because smoking was fucking fantastic and, also, because Steve Simons was not a quitter.

"They can put it on my tombstone, okay, *Here lies Steven J. Simons, who was not a quitter*," he said to the guy at the third-rate bank, aware that his eyebrows were beginning to sweat, "that's how true it is. This is nothing but a momentary setback. If you see me through this, I'll tell you, you will have my business forever."

The guy at the bank did not seem impressed. "I'm sorry, Mr. Simons," he said, again. "We're unable to extend your credit line any further, as I've said a number of times now. I do wish you the best of luck with the project. Now, if you'll excuse me but..."

Which was a polite way of saying *get out of my face, you sweaty, broke loser.* Simons swallowed carefully and mopped off his forehead. So this was it. The end of an empire. He had no choice now. He could sell, but he'd never recoup what he had already put into the building. It should have been the easiest money of his life—twenty brand-new condos on the edge of the next hot neighborhood, where rents had easily doubled in the last couple years. The fringes of downtown were perfect for the influx of New Yorkers who'd chased fashion-industry jobs out to the Midwest, for suburbanites who woke up one day determined to become interesting. After two decades of helping the local economy with a string of highly successful Olde Towne East restaurants, he was finally going to get his payday. He'd gotten a no-brainer good deal on the land itself, and all Simons had to do then was build.

But the project had been cursed from the beginning. Protests from the neighborhood groups, who didn't want another high-occupancy building on Parsons, decrying him as a money-grubbing gentrifier—him! Long-time resident of Bryden Road, the Near East Side Restaurant King!; a string of mysterious thefts; two fires; a site foreman who had an actual nervous breakdown in the middle of laying brick for the elevator shaft and had to be replaced, at the last minute and at great cost. Everything went wrong, expensively. Dramatically. He had to sell some of his stake in the restaurants, then a little more, he remortgaged his own house, then re-remortgaged it, and by the latest estimate, Simons still needed eight hundred grand to get the building into livable condition. But these units would pay for themselves nearly right away, if he could just get them finished. Except now, even the third-rate bank, which at one time would have been happy to throw money at him, was saying *if you'll excuse me but* and getting up from the desk, actually leaving him sitting there alone, because that was how little he mattered.

He drew himself up to all of his five-eight-and-a-half height and strode out to the lobby, where Deirdra was waiting. She barely looked up from her phone when he walked in. She said nothing. She didn't even make a sympathetic expression. This woman, his *wife* for chrissakes, whom he hated in this moment even more than the third-rate banker, could not be bothered to acknowledge him.

He said, "Let's go."

She pressed her mouth into a thin like and kept typing away. The sound of her opal nails tap-tap-tapping was enough to make him want to strangle her right then and there.

He suddenly got a terrible, wonderful idea.

The green polo shirt was like a cloak of invisibility. Carter quickly learned that there was no better way to make people ignore you than walking around a residential neighborhood in a uniform with a stack of flyers. Nobody answered her jaunty knock. A few times, front door curtains ruffled in response and once, an eye looked out, took in the sight, and disappeared like Carter wasn't even standing there. But every twenty houses equaled one tramadol from the guy behind the Mobil station. So Carter kept an eye on the prize. The sun was out, and the homes in this part of Olde Towne were mansions, really, grand Victorian dames with widow's walks and solariums and retaining walls and carriage houses and other features with fancy names. Carter's grandmother had lived in one of them long ago. She remembered a pond in the backyard with fat orange koi, a framed-in patio with this ornate iron trellis that had a pattern like lilies. *Fleur des lis.* She had some family memories from that time that weren't total shit, so she was in a pretty good mood as she walked around and got into a rhythm.

She was almost up to four tramadols when she happened to look across the street: that floral trellis. It had been painted white, and the rest of the house looked newer somehow, but that was the place. She hadn't seen it in, what, thirty years? But there it was. She knocked on the door but didn't get an answer, so she nipped over an ivy-covered garden bed and into the backyard.

The pond she remembered had been replaced with a small, bean-shaped pool surrounded with plush chaise lounges, and as she squinted into the sunlight, she realized the pool was occupied: a woman, topless, floating on a raft.

Carter froze.

The woman's eyes were hidden behind huge sunglasses with white plastic frames. When she didn't react to Carter's presence, she assumed the woman's eyes were closed. She gingerly stepped back into the ivy, hoping to leave before the woman realized she was there. As she backed away, the woman, still without moving, said, "Who the hell are you?"

"Um, I'm, so sorry, ma'am, I'm just..." Carter waved her satchel of flyers. "Have you had your radon levels checked recently?"

The woman slid her sunglasses halfway down her nose. She had long, opalescent fingernails and was beautiful in an artificial way, but one that made you want to believe, like Vegas. "Radon?"

"It's an odorless, colorless gas found in Central Ohio soil," Carter recited from memory. "And it's the second leading cause of lung cancer—"

"Why are you in my backyard?"

Carter couldn't tell how old she was. Maybe a rough thirty-five or a well-preserved fifty. Nothing surprised her anymore. But the woman's eyes were bright blue and looked at her with something like curiosity, so she told her the truth. "I was walking by, delivering flyers. And I saw this house. My grandmother used to live here."

Now she smiled. "Really."

"Years ago. There was a pond. With fish. I just wanted to

see if it was still here."

"My husband took it out," the woman said. "He said the fish were disgusting. Which they were, honestly."

"What happened to them?"

She took her sunglasses off. Her hair was dark and wavy, snaking in damp tendrils around her bare shoulders. "You know, I'm not sure. The construction people handled the demolition."

"Maybe they set them free. In the wild."

"What, like *Free Willy?*"

She still hadn't moved to cover up her chest. Carter liked that about her, that she didn't give a fuck about much. She could relate. As such, she made a point of not ogling the woman's breasts. "Or rehomed somewhere. Taken in by a backyard goldfish rescue organization."

She laughed, and then she looked surprised, like she had forgotten the sound of her own laugh. "Come over here and keep me company."

She took a few steps into the backyard. Once she crossed into a stripe of shade, she could make out fine lines around the woman's eyes.

She said, "That shirt can probably be seen from the international space station."

Carter sat down cross-legged on the smooth, cool concrete. "I know. It's bad."

The woman looked her over, those bright eyes lingering at the crook of her left arm, the ropy mess of pink and white scar tissue that, apparently, might never go away. She said, "What's that like?"

There were a lot of ways to answer a question like that. She could tell her that a heroin high was like floating on your back in Horseshoe Bay and masturbating while all your exes say they forgive you. Or she could say that addiction was like being chained to a radiator in a building that you set on fire yourself, or that it's damn expensive for something so desperate and ugly and small, that if you keep it up, you die, and if you stop, you die anyway. That the last time she got arrested, dopesick and shoplifting from the CVS on High Street by the Ohio Theatre, she got tramadol in the infirmary to stave off withdrawal symptoms, which almost kind of half worked, so there she was, the poor man's rehab. Instead, she said, "I don't really remember."

"Good for you." She snaked out a hand and grasped at a tumbler of something fruity on the edge of the pool. It became clear that she was quite drunk. "Take it off. Your shirt. It's hurting my eyes. I hate it."

"Not on the first date," Carter said, and the woman laughed and laughed and then started crying. Carter pulled herself into a crouch next to the pool. "Maybe you'd like to lay down in the shade for a little bit."

"Lie," she said thickly as Carter helped her off of the raft. "Lie down."

Once the woman was upright, she tottered past the chaises and into the carriage house at the back of the property. There was a small sofa against one exposed-brick wall, and the woman collapsed onto it. "Sorry," she mumbled. "About the fish."

She began to snore, softly. Carter found a blanket and draped it over her. She couldn't ever tell anyone this story. She had no idea what had just happened. She turned to leave, then paused to pull out a flyer, which she tucked into the doorjamb.

The following week, Carter stopped by the Radon King's office to pick up a new batch of flyers. "A lady called. Mrs. Deirdra Simons on Bryden Road," the Radon King said. "Scheduled an appointment to get an estimate, so good job. She said she was very impressed with your knowledge of local architecture."

"Excuse me?"

"Something about the prevalence of goldfish ponds. I don't know."

* * *

One benefit of being the Near East Side Restaurant King was that you always knew a guy who knew a guy. It was the nature of the business. Need to buy cocaine? Ask a waiter. Need to murder your wife for the life insurance money? Delicately inquire to the sketchy linen delivery guy if he knew anyone looking for work of the messy varietal. That was how Simons wound up in touch with Earl.

Their first and only meeting was in the produce department of the Main Street Kroger. As instructed by the sketchy linen delivery guy, Simons walked up to Earl with a shopping basket in the crook of his elbow and said, "Can you tell me if you have any blood oranges?" It sounded so stupid—*blood oranges*? What was he doing?—that Simons felt a deep rush of shame, not a guilty shame, but the embarrassed kind, and he started to retreat, but Earl's head snapped towards him in a vaguely reptilian way that indicated calling off the arrangement was not an option.

Earl said, "Blood oranges are expensive."

That was code for *give me the money*. Simons had an envelope of cash in his back pocket. Five grand, with another five upon completion. Simons took the packet and dropped it into his shopping basket, then covered it with a bunch of wet carrots. He set the basket on the floor and pretended to examine the radishes. "The address is in there," he said. "She's home most afternoons. Make it look like a robbery."

Earl deftly used a foot to slide the basket behind his stocking cart. Then suddenly the basket was empty. He'd had some practice at this. Clearly, the blood orange business was good. Earl cleared his throat and Simons realized he'd just been standing there, staring.

He said, "Um, is that it?"

Earl scowled deeply and pushed his cart towards the lettuces.

Simons swallowed a lump in his throat and went outside into the sharp sunlight. He felt a little sick. Was that really all it took? Shouldn't someone have tried to talk him out of it? He supposed he was that someone.

This was the only way out, he told himself on the drive home. Only one of them could prosper, and it was damn well going to be him. He'd already tried everything else, and if he let the project fail, or if he tried cutting his losses and walk away, there was no doubt that she'd tie him up in divorce proceedings for the rest of his natural life, or at least until he murdered her anyway, so really, he didn't *have* a choice, did he? The generous life insurance policy had been purchased years ago, shortly after they got married—one for each of them, his and hers—long before any money trouble or relationship trouble materialized. She had been a waitress in one of his restaurants when they met, a dark-haired spitfire who initiated a conversation with him out of the blue to tell him that the menu had a typo on it. *"Restauranteur,"* she said. "It's not actually a word."

His initial response was a spike of anger. "What are you talking about? Of course it is."

But Deirdra had been adamant. "That's a common misconception. The word is actually *restaurateur*. Technically. No. Look it up."

He ignored her and went about his day, but the idea needled at him—not that she might have been right, but that she had the guts to imply that he was wrong in the first place. When he eventually looked it up and realized she was correct, he found himself inexplicably aroused. Her nervy little mouth! He had to have her.

A brief seduction, a few trysts in the wine cellar, the jettisoning of his wicked first wife, and then Deirdra was his. The happiness this gave him was profoundly short-lived. She was beautiful and impossible, a perfectly-plated but prickly dish at the finest restaurant. After years of trying to get out of his first marriage, Simons felt a bit like the mad priest in *The Count of Monte Cristo*—all that time, he thought he was digging to freedom, but here he was, in another cell. Instead of being enthusiastic about Pilates and patronage of the arts like other housewives in their tax bracket, she was interested only in astrology, succulents, and in spending his money on impractical furniture. She was big into *textures*. Anything vinyl-slick, or hairy, or covered with tiny sharp beads. She rejected all wifely duties and spent her time correcting his grammar or complaining loudly about him on the phone or moving around the end tables. A footstool with black and white yak-like fur and a sickly tangled fringe had recently appeared in the living room. She left the price tag on it, like she was daring him to say something. Six hundred bucks! She was fully aware of the current cash-flow situation. He nearly had a stroke. He told her to return it, and she bought a second one instead.

This was what he was dealing with.

When he got home, Deirdra was on the sofa, flipping through a magazine, a sheer kaftan slipping off one shoulder in a way that made Simons feel almost tender towards her. Then she turned her head and said, "I made some appointments today. Radon remediation. And a landscaper, for the backyard. I miss the goldfish."

"Radon," Simons repeated. For the love of Christ, the woman's eyes were dollar signs.

"It's an odorless, colorless gas," she said. She pointed to a lime-green flyer on the coffee table. "It can cause lung cancer. And central Ohio buildings are rife with it."

Simons felt pinpoints of rage sweat along his brow. "I know what radon is! I've been dealing with buildings since before you were born, you miserable shrew. Why are you making *appointments*? *Remediation*, Jesus Christ."

Calmly, looking back down at her magazine, Deirdra said, "It means the act of remedying something, specifically of reversing damage."

Simons kicked over the yak stool. Oh, he had zero regrets.

Most days Carter enjoyed walking around Columbus with the horrible shirt and satchel of flyers. The work agreed with her, too—she was tan and strong for the first time in a while. But the job was also deeply boring. Her shitty cell phone would run out of charge if she used it to listen to music while she walked, and she only got paid if the Radon King's app was transmitting the entire time. So she thought about things. About her dead father, about basketball, about the limp trajectory of her life so far: high school point guard with decent college prospects, torn ACL, Vicodin during recovery, Vicodin recreationally, Vicodin cost-prohibitively, the switch to heroin because it was cheaper, at first, until her tolerance was sky high and getting enough to just maintain required some low-key thuggery, jail, rehab, eviction, homelessness, days—weeks—months she couldn't remember much of at all, shelter, jail, shelter, jail, freewheeling through the system finally, what appeared to be rock-bottom, the dope-sick trip to the county jail's infirmary and the nurse who told her, flat-out, "You'll be dead in less than six months if you keep going on this way. Probably less than three. Get high on something else."

And sometimes, she thought about the woman with the lovely, lonely eyes and the bean-shaped pool that had once been a goldfish pond. Deirdra. She imagined having a conversation in a restaurant with her, exchanging witticisms over glasses of jammy red wine and thick slices of bread slathered with miso butter. It seemed to her that butter flavored with something other than itself was the pinnacle of luxury. On the opposite end of the spectrum, you had the artifice of margarine, an oily nothing with a fake buttery flavor. That was where she had spent most of her time, letting herself be swindled by something that was almost good enough but never quite would be.

She wasn't sure if Deirdra's life was any different. She'd seemed just as unhappy despite having what appeared to be a nice life, or at least a comfortable one. On a hot Tuesday in August, breathing humid air that felt like the inside of a plastic bag, Carter let her thoughts linger on that slice of shade next to Deirdra's pool. She had a momentary vision of swimming in it, though it was hard to imagine what series of events would allow that to transpire. Maybe she could show up. Maybe she'd be happy to see her, even. Maybe she still wanted Carter to take off her lime green shirt, and maybe she was in the mood to do it. So after she was done with the flyers, she got off the bus at Wilson and walked over to Deirdra's section of Bryden Road.

She could tell something was wrong as soon as she turned up the narrow sidewalk. The sun reflected unevenly off the windows that flanked the front door; one of the panes had been punched out, a jagged, flat hole in its place. Carter peered through, her view suddenly occluded by the appearance of a silent figure inside the house. Then another sound—the hard metallic click of a handgun's safety flicking off. "Don't fucking move," Deirdra hissed. Then she stepped backwards, leaned down to look her in the face, sighed softly, almost contentedly. "It's you."

"What," Carter said, "the hell is going on? Are you all right?"

"I almost shot you just now," she said. With peculiar emphasis, on *you*. Not on *shot*. "You picked quite a day to finally come back here." She stepped aside, pointed behind her. There was a man on the floor, splayed across a smeary bloody ooze on the tile.

Carter started, "Is he—"

"Dead? Yeah. He is."

"No, I was going to say, is he your husband?"

Deirdra stared at her for a second, then began to laugh and laugh and not stop. It was like the crying from last time, except more disturbing, because there was now a gun and a murderous intent in the mix. Finally she got a hold on herself and opened the door and let Carter inside. "No," she said, "but my husband is next."

Earl had a system. He would call the restaurant and relay a message to Simons via code. If he asked if they served peach pie, it meant the job was done. If he asked about key lime, it meant there had been an issue and the deed had to be postponed. If he asked about blackberry, it meant there had been a serious issue and Simons needed to get his ass over to the produce department immediately.

But on the day that it was supposed to go down, Simons didn't get any calls. The phone didn't even ring once. It was actually bordering on suspicious, telephonically. Simons kept checking for a dial tone—always present, infuriatingly reliable—before he realized that this could interfere with Earl getting through.

By three o'clock, he was getting antsy. By four, he was downright panicked. What did no call mean? This hadn't been part of the code. He worried that it meant Earl had been caught in the act, arrested, had sung like a canary, and now there'd be cops on the street waiting for him when he went home. He considered the possible solution of not going home, but that required complete confidence that something had gone wrong. If Earl had simply flaked, or died of natural causes in the night, then Simons not coming home on time would be its own kind of suspicious and would alert Deirdra that something was up.

The late afternoon sun was hot through the windshield as he parked on Bryden Road in front of his house. He'd driven past once, looking for cops, seeing none, but he noticed a broken pane of glass in the front door. Make it look like a robbery, he'd instructed Earl. So maybe there had been something wrong with the phones all along. Maybe everything had gone off without a hitch. Simons realized he had spent more time reflecting on the pie-related code words instead of what he would actually do in any of the three cases—he was now wholly unprepared. Should he call the police and say that he thought an intruder might be in the house? Rush in, concerned for the safety of his darling wife? Probably that.

He tried to make up for lost time and quickly map out his next steps. How did a person normally get out of a car and walk into a house? He tried to picture it. Lock the doors with the clicker. Stride up the sidewalk, squinting in the sunlight, whistling—no, stop whistling, Steve Simons was not a whistler. It would be impossible to see the broken window on foot until he'd entered the patch of shade cast by the porch's overhang, at which point he would gasp. No, his jaw would harden. His grip on his keys would tighten. He would say, desperately, urgently, "Deirdra. Oh my God," in case anyone happened to be walking by at just that moment. Then he'd rush up the steps and open the door, shouting her name as he bustled into the house, looking handsome and distraught and brave. He'd grab the first weapon he could see—there was a golf umbrella in the stand just inside the front door, with a savage metal point on one end—and charge forth, ready to defend his wife's life or seek instant vengeance for her death.

Simons was in the process of enacting this plan, her beloved wife's name on his tongue as he threw open the door, shards of glass crunching beneath his shoes, when he noticed the gun on the polished tile floor of the entryway. A Ruger 380, black and silver, that looked an awful lot like his Ruger 380, the one he kept in his study at the back of the house. He froze. The visualization exercise had not accounted for this at all. He looked around the sitting room but nothing appeared out of the ordinary. The yak stool was on its side, but it had been that way for a month.

He picked up the gun, and that was when Deirdra stepped out of the kitchen and into the doorway.

"Steven, Steven," she said. She was wearing the slinky robe and holding a gun he'd never seen before. "A divorce would have been so much less painful for you."

"I don't know what you think—"

She shot him in the thigh, without a hint of hesitation. Simons was on the ground before he even realized the bullet had left her gun, before the pain exploded through his body. Blood spurted from his leg, hot and wild.

"I think you're an idiot for assuming you're the only one to know about Earl and his blood oranges," Deirdra said. She took a few steps closer, the big gun still trained on him. "Remember, I worked in the restaurant business too."

"Let's talk about this—"

"No," she said.

The Radon King was shaken by the news, which was everywhere for the next few months. He brought it up every time Carter came in, marveling in the near miss of it all. "Just think—I could've been caught in the middle of that. If I'd scheduled that appointment at her house a few weeks later, I could've walked right in on it all."

"Yeah, wow," Carter said. Again. People loved to co-opt a tragedy, as if the only way anything could be understood. Through the risk to one's own self. Her father the carpet salesman had once been inside a bank two days before it was robbed at gunpoint, and over the years his telling of the story had shifted so that it had been only one day, then a few hours, then a few minutes. By the time he died he practically had himself convinced that he'd been in the bank when it happened. Probably the Radon King would do the same thing, but Carter would not be in his employ when that happened. She handed over the green polo shirt and shook the Radon King's hand. "Thanks for the opportunity, sir."

"Sir!" The Radon King loved that. "You take care, kid."

Carter walked out of the cramped office and down the sidewalk. It was November now, the air cool and crisp through the sleeves of her jacket, which was leather, actual leather, as she headed up the block and over to the building that she now called home. A building with a buzzer and a name—The Fleur Des Lis—which was at least as fancy as miso butter. The building wasn't one-hundred-percent finished yet, but every unit was sold already.

She just happened to know the developer and got to move in early.

Deirdra was on the phone in her office on the first floor when she got there. "Dormant? What do you mean, dormant? Like, dead?" Her bright blue eyes flashed at Carter as she talked, leaning back in her chair, legs parted. "I don't want them to look dead. Let's just do it inside then. That solves the problem, right?"

Carter sat on the edge of the desk and watched her. Deirdra was terrifying, certainly. It would be a long time before she got over the calm clip to her words as Deirdra had requested her help in the house that day—move the dead guy outside, into the pool, like he staggered outside and fell there. Help her clean up the blood on the black-and-white tile. Then leave.

"It was self-defense, wasn't it?"

"Yes, of course."

"Then you could just call the police—tell the truth—"

"No, this isn't just some guy, some robber. I know exactly who this is and why he's here."

"Who is he?"

"I'll tell you someday."

Carter had done exactly what she asked her to do, buoyed by the idea of a someday. A few days later, she read about what had happened in a newspaper that someone left in the bus shelter at High and Long. *Local restaurateur and real estate developer killed in apparent home invasion*, the headline said. It appeared that Deirdra's husband had interrupted said invasion, shot the robber, who then fled out the back but succumbed to his injuries in the backyard. Ballistics confirmed it all—bullets from Steve Simons' gun had killed the robber, and bullets from the robber's gun had killed Steve Simons.

Funny, the way things worked out sometimes.

Now, Deirdra said on the phone, "I want a koi pond in this lobby, and I want it now. I don't care how much it costs. You know I can afford it."

She hung up and looked at Carter. "I told you I was going to do it."

"You said you thought the koi were gross."

Deirdra shrugged. "I hear the residents might like them."

They stared at each other. It was only eye contact but felt like a full-body collision. Carter said, "Are we ever going to talk about, you know, everything?"

"Yes," Deirdra said, "but not today."

THE LAKE

ANDREW WELSH-HUGGINS

Glenn looked out over the lake, wondering for the second or third time that night what he was doing here. Had the call even been real? To hear from her, after all this time. Ten years ago, he would have given just about anything to answer his phone and hear her voice and accept an invitation like this. Sure, they talked a few times, afterward. But those talks and calls dried up as the town hardened against her, and even he began to have his doubts, his suspicions, that she'd escape the finger-pointing and the whispering intact. Because, after all, there was good reason for it.

Nearly dusk now, coming earlier each evening this September. A hint of color in the leaves of the hardwoods climbing each side of Lima Lake—a reservoir for Rochester and so off limits to construction of any kind, not to mention boating and fishing, though the rangers tended to turn a blind eye if a motor wasn't involved. The gravel access road off the country road off Route 20A was marked as a true no-trespassing zone, reserved for the water department crews that puttered at the pumping station on the south end of the lake nestled in the Bristol hills. Which is why they—meaning any ambitious kid with a rod and reel and a car that didn't make a whole lot of noise—beelined for it on weekend summer nights, the chance of a string full of perch outweighing the risk of the sheriff rousting you. Glenn had done it many times himself. As had Paul, probably the most diehard angler of the gang; a six of beer, a pack of smokes and a cup of worms, and he was happy.

A crunch of gravel and then a tap on the door. Glenn jumped a little, his heart racing, surprised. And then his heart raced for another reason.

"Jesus. I didn't hear you." He twisted his head around. "Where's your car?"

Leslie laughed. "I parked it up there, in that little turnaround. You can't see in there from the lane. Old habits I guess." She raised her left arm and displayed a six of Genny. "Bar's open. Mind if I come in?"

He made to open his door but she waved him off and a moment later was inside in the passenger seat. He accepted a beer and cracked it open and they clinked the cans together and both took long pulls. He snuck a sideways glance at her as she drank. Her dark hair, once long, was cut much shorter now, stopping above her neck. He thought he saw a line or two around her eyes that hadn't been there before. But other than that, she hadn't changed that much.

"Lima's supposed to be the deepest Finger Lake, after Seneca," Leslie said, pointing through his windshield as she suppressed a burp. "What makes the fishing better. At least farther out. Did you know that?"

Glenn looked at her curiously. "I guess I didn't. That's interesting."

"Not really. It's just something I read."

An awkward silence descended, and both took another swig of their beer. He kept his eyes on the lake, watching the swallows skimming the surface, trying not to focus on how close she was, how easy it would be to reach out and touch her.

"So how was it?" Glenn said at last, not sure what else to say.

"How was what?"

"The reunion."

"Oh, that. About what you'd expect. Everybody's fatter, with less hair and less to talk about. But still pretty fun. You should have come. Ten years—that's a big one. People were asking about you."

"Well, you know. Bet people were happy to see you, though."

"You mean surprised?"

"I didn't—"

"It's okay. A few were happy. Most were surprised. I don't really care. It's my town too. Or used to be, anyway. Hell, my mom still lives here. What'd they expect?"

"How is she? Your mom?"

"Fine, I guess. Misses being in the village. At the shop. She's at the Walmart now. Better hours, but not as personal. Half the people she doesn't know anymore. They come in with all these prescriptions for Percocet and Oxys and she hasn't a clue if they're legit or pill poppers."

Glenn nodded. "She gave me a flu shot last year. So I see her around."

"That's nice. She says I should come back here. Says they've got an opening."

"Would you?" Glenn said too quickly, sneaking a glance at the lightweight cream cardigan she'd thrown over her blouse.

Leslie laughed again, and his heart leapt at the sound, loud and raucous, just short of a man's laugh and all the more inviting, and sexy, because of it. "I'm happy at the hospital, thank you very much. Plus, come back here? Yeah, right. A reunion's one thing. People had to be nice—as nice as they could. But you know as well as I do: half the town still thinks I did it."

Did it.

Even Glenn, after all these years, averted his eyes and turned away when people asked him what he thought. He knew everyone assumed that meant he believed the rumors about Leslie, that she was guilty. Why argue with them? It was impossible to tell them the deeper truth.

The few months he'd dated Leslie their junior and then beginning of senior year were among the best in his life. He couldn't get enough of her. And it wasn't just the sex either—well, not sex, exactly, but the hand jobs and blow jobs and dry humping, since she adamantly refused to let him inside her. "They don't take babies in college, sweetie," she'd say, slowly unzipping his jeans. "And that's where I'm going—and where you should to." College and pharmacy school, just like mom. She had it all planned out.

No, not just the sex. Her sense of humor. Her ideas about the future—the things she wanted to accomplish. The crazy true crime shows she made him watch—super interesting in hindsight—stuff he wouldn't have dreamed of looking at without her. But with her, it all made sense.

Then, sometime around Christmas, they just started drifting away. At first, he thought it was his fault. He'd tried to break the rules, up in his bedroom, his parents out for the night, his hands tugging her panties down to her knees. She'd gotten upset, really upset. He apologized up and down, but somehow it wasn't enough. And then she told him one day it—meaning *them*—just wasn't something she wanted to do anymore. For now. Maybe later. But later never came. Paul Newcomb did.

Paul was a transfer their sophomore year, but it didn't take long for him to fit right in. His dad an engineer at Cargill Salt, brought over from Cleveland to work on a new project. He'd grown up fishing on Lake Erie, so he knew what he was doing. If they snuck down to the lake to fish, he was always the one who took it the most seriously. Kept at it after the rest of them put their rods down and picked up another case of beer and lit another joint. And, though it didn't make any sense to Glenn at first, he realized later it was this steadfastness of purpose that attracted Leslie. The two of them just seem a bit more serious, a bit more centered, than the rest. They were an item by Valentine's Day and serious by Easter. Glenn would spy them in the library during study hall, bent over their laptops, whispering. He snuck a glance once and saw something about college courses.

It happened the summer they graduated. Paul never came home after a night's fishing at Lima Lake. They found his car the next day, hidden in the same turnaround where Leslie's was parked tonight. His rod still on the shore, a cooler full of dead lake trout beside it, the ice he'd packed to freeze them thawed into cloudy water. It took divers two days to retrieve his body. Leslie was right—the lake was deep. A steep drop-off from the shore, plunging dozens of feet. Speculation that he'd been drunk and stumbled in, or possibly thought swimming by himself in the dark on a cloudy night had been a good idea. Not that the why mattered. He was dead either way.

"What about you?"

Glenn shook his head, scattering his thoughts.

"Me what?"

"What've you been up to?"

"You know, same ol', same ol'."

"Peggy said you're still at the pasta place?"

"You saw Peggy?"

"Sure. She was at the reunion. Said she doesn't see you all that much."

"Guess I'm not that social." He felt a little bad, since Peggy had been a friend going way back. But there was only so much time in the day, he guessed.

"You like it?"

"Like what?"

"Making pasta?"

He shifted uncomfortably in his seat. He'd forgotten how direct Leslie could be. She was a person who wanted answers. She'd play-slap him if he dared utter "Dunno" back when they were together.

"I don't really make pasta. I run one of the machines that

makes the boxes that the pasta goes into." The plant on the outskirts of Avon one of the few decent places to work around here if you didn't want to commute up 390 to Rochester.

"So do you like making the boxes that the pasta goes into?"

"It's all right. It pays the bills—for now," he added quickly, hoping to forestall an inquiry about his own future.

But instead of responding Leslie took another drink of beer, finishing the can. She pulled another one free from the plastic ring, popped it and took a long swallow. Glenn looked on curiously. Leslie had never been that kind of one-after-the other drinker. At least, that he remembered.

"Yeah," she said. "That's what Peggy said."

"What do you mean?"

"She said you're just paying the bills."

"She said that?"

"Yeah. That, and some other stuff."

Now he was more than a little interested. Truth to tell, he wasn't sure he'd seen Peggy to talk to in two years.

"Like what?" he asked.

Leslie took another swig of beer. Even as the lengthening shadows dimmed the interior of the car, Glenn thought he saw her hand shaking.

"Stuff," she said.

The problem was, Leslie and Paul had fought two nights earlier. A big fight. The whole town knew it. And had known the cause of it, too.

There'd been this party out at the Jenkins farm. Almost everyone had gone. Everyone except Leslie, who wasn't feeling well and stayed home with her mom. The rumor was that Paul was half okay with that, because Leslie had been moody lately, and demanding, which appeared to have something to do with her approaching departure date for Cornell and the fact that Paul, with his own plans for college out of state, hadn't been as sympathetic as he might have been. And all that might have been okay if things hadn't gotten a little crazy at the party and somebody took a photo of Paul and this girl nobody knew from Canandaigua, the friend of a brother of a friend kind of a thing, and he had his arm around her waist and her face was flushed and two of the buttons on her tight blouse were unbuttoned. The photo shot around every cell phone in town like a bullet ricocheting through a tiny room. Leslie was furious and made it known. There'd been a very public shouting match at Mike's Pizza right downtown in the village. And then two nights later, Paul was gone.

In the dark days that followed, Glenn hung at the periphery of Leslie's mourning, not sure what to say, or how. But he also couldn't ignore what everyone else in town thought too, when they caught his eye bagging groceries at Wegman's or aimlessly shooting hoops at the school or worst of all, at the funeral. The question on his and everyone's minds: did this amount to Glenn's second chance? A tragedy about Paul, but what did you expect, messing around the lake by yourself like that? And there was Glenn, who'd had such a good thing with Leslie before their break-up. Maybe there was hope for them after all.

Except suddenly, it all went to hell. Instead of wrapping things up, the police kept asking questions. It turned out that Leslie wasn't home the night Paul died, but she wouldn't say where she was, either. Wouldn't even tell her mom, the story went. Detectives were at her house, more than once. That was right around the time Leslie and her mom hired a lawyer.

To his credit, Glenn tried to stick by her, despite more than one person telling him he was crazy, that he'd be next. He ventured to her house, sat in the backyard with her, listened to her cry. Even held her hand from time to time. She'd had to put off her fall semester to deal with everything, and she was convinced her life was over—her boyfriend dead, her college dreams up in smoke. He comforted her the best he could, and without being a jerk about it, tried to suggest that he was there for her if she needed. The way he'd been there when they were together. But it wasn't to be. He still remembered the night she kissed him on the cheek and told him no and that she needed to be alone for a while. Maybe a long while. And that was the end of that.

"Well, stuff like what?" Glenn said.

Leslie didn't say anything for a minute. She drank more of her beer and stared through the window at the lake. Despite the dark, the rippling water was still visible in the light of the rising moon. Stars began to brighten overhead, like tiny winking candles emerging from a gray fog.

"Lots of stuff. Her folks, for example."

"What about them?"

"They're not doing very well. Fighting a lot. Peggy thinks they're going to get divorced."

"I'm not surprised," he said, unable to help himself. Peggy's mom had never treated her dad with the respect he deserved, at least in his opinion.

"She also talked about Charlie. A lot, actually. She's still broken up by it, all these years."

"Yeah," he said. Peggy's boyfriend's suicide two weeks after Paul's death, though not related—they didn't know one another—had cemented that summer as the lowest point of Glenn's life. To date.

"She has all these regrets about it. About Charlie. Which I guess is natural. Like she wonders if she had done something, said something, it would have made a difference."

"That's natural, I guess. Right?" Glenn said, gingerly reaching for his own second beer from the dwindling six-pack balanced on Leslie's lap. Leslie, he noticed, was well into her third.

"I think it is. But they'd had a long talk right before it happened. Went for ice cream and then just walked around town. Talked about all kinds of things. She wonders if she missed something. She doesn't think she did, because he seemed fine, but you never know."

"I suppose not."

"The funny thing was, that was the night that Paul died. The night she and Charlie had that talk."

"Huh. That's a little weird."

"That's what I thought. In fact, I told her so."

"Really?" He supposed he wasn't surprised, given Leslie's reputation for forthrightness. For pursuing something—information, advice, love—regardless of the consequences.

"Yeah. I told her that was weird. Because, you know."

"What do you mean?"

"Because of what you said."

If Leslie ever came home after leaving for college, Glenn wasn't aware of it. He supposed she must have snuck in once or twice. But the fact of the matter was, too many people in town still harbored their suspicions. Everyone knew she could be a little controlling. Everyone knew she was smitten with Paul, and his lapse at judgment at Jenkins' farm had crushed her. As had the angry words they'd exchanged at Mike's Pizza, which appeared to include him breaking up with her. And then there was the plain fact of her whereabouts the night of Paul's death. She wasn't at home, but she wouldn't tell anyone where she was. The rumor was she'd broken down during an interview with detectives as they demanded to know what she wasn't telling them, but she wouldn't say. For lack of any hard evidence, they eventually closed the case and Paul's death was ruled accidental. But even Glenn found it difficult to persuade people they were wrong about what they thought Leslie had or hadn't done. Over time, he stopped talking about her at all.

But he never stopped thinking about her.

And then the call came earlier that day, the number unfamiliar to him. But on the other end, her voice.

* * *

"What do you mean? What I said?"

"Honestly, it's probably not important."

He turned to look at her. He hadn't wanted to admit it earlier, but the way she did her hair now only accentuated her beauty, drawing attention to her brown eyes and the slightest rose blush that always tinted the tops of her cheeks.

"Tell me."

"Can you roll the windows down? It's so stuffy."

He obliged. He would have done about anything for her just now.

She pulled a fourth beer from its plastic ring, but only held it between her hands.

"Just what you said about Charlie."

"What did I say?"

"That you were at Watkins Glen with him that night."

He paused, not certain he'd heard correctly. He took a breath, and then another, and focused on the trilling of the crickets rising around them.

"I said that?"

"Yes," she said, not looking at him but at the lake, the gentle cascade of riffs illuminated by the moon. "You said you were at Watkins Glen. For a race. But Charlie was here in town that night. Talking to Peggy. I'd never heard that until she told me."

"I think she's mistaken."

"I don't think so, Glenn," she said, and he felt an electric shock as he heard her say his name for the first time in a decade. She hadn't even used it when she called to ask him to meet her here. Just a "Hey, stranger" when he answered.

"She is. Mistaken. Really."

"She's not," she said softly. "I checked online. It's so amazing what's on there now. There weren't any races that night. None."

"That's not true—"

"So, where were you?"

* * *

There'd been other girls. Not a lot, but a few. A couple from the pasta factory, dating for a few months before things petered out. Some one-nighters with girls he met at the brew pub on the edge of town on a Friday or Saturday night, college kids from Geneseo looking for a taste of something a little wild. He'd even been engaged once for about a week before they both realized the whole thing was crazy. But truth to tell, he'd never really moved past Leslie, either the time they were together or the fragile few weeks when he thought they might have another shot.

"Listen, maybe we should get going. It's getting late."

"I'll tell you if you tell me."

"What?"

"I'll tell you where I was that night if you tell me where you were."

"I really don't think—"

"Please?"

And with that, before he knew what was happening, Leslie leaned over, took his chin in her hand, and kissed him. Her lips were warm and full, just as he remembered them. He hesitated a moment, but only a moment, before reaching for her hungrily. Closing his eyes, breathing in the scent of her shampoo—she'd never worn perfume—he wondered just for a moment if there were such a thing as third chances. It came to him a moment later. Of course. Third time's the—

"Ow."

He pulled back, reacting to the prick. He touched his throat. He stared at Leslie, who was staring at him, a syringe between the fingers of her right hand.

"What the hell?"

"I'm sorry if that stung. I tried to be gentle."

"What—"

"It's ketamine. The hospital has a lot of it. There's all these safeguards, but you can figure it out, if you're really serious."

"What are you talking about?"

"Don't be alarmed, okay? It's fast-acting, especially straight into a vein like that. You're going to feel it almost immediately."

"Feel what?" But already something was different. He felt sluggish and light-headed.

Leslie opened the fourth beer. She took one long gulp, then emptied the rest into the footwell of his car.

"Do you know where I was that night, Glenn? I was in Buffalo, spending the night before I got an abortion. I went a day early. I was too nervous to drive over first thing. I couldn't tell my mom. It would have killed her. Did you know she won't fill morning-after prescriptions? She almost got fired over it. She got saved by some court ruling, said she didn't have to."

Pregnant. Her and Paul.

They don't take babies in college, sweetie.

"Leslie," he said, forcing himself to say her name. He turned to look at her, but the gesture seemed to take forever as he struggled to move his head.

"Charlie didn't kill himself, did he?"

He couldn't speak.

"It's okay. I figured as much. He was the only one who might have screwed up your story, wasn't he?"

He tried to shake his head but nothing happened.

"Poor guy," she said. "Anyway, now you know where I was. That's what Paul and I were fighting about that night. Oh, the girl, sure, but I believed him when he said it was a drunken mistake. No, the thing is, he thought we should keep the baby. I told him no."

"Please…"

"So how about it? It's your turn."

Glenn tried and failed to swallow. He felt immensely tired but also oddly alert, as though observing himself from just outside his line of vision.

"Ask—"

"What's that?"

"Accident," he said.

"What was?"

"Didn't mean. Just wanted to talk. Knew...he'd be down here."

"To talk? About what?"

"Accident," he said again.

"There was nothing to talk about," Leslie said. "You and I were finished. We weren't getting back together. Paul was the boy for me. So why would you come after him? Because of the fight? That gave you no right."

"Had a fight. Slipped. Water. Accident."

Leslie sat back in the seat. "Everyone still thinks I did it. That I'm a killer. Maybe I am, depending on what you think about abortion. But I'll never get past it. No one will ever believe me. The jilted girlfriend. It's so stupid, you know."

"Suh-sorry."

"The thing is, I believe you. I really do. That you're sorry, I mean. I want you to know that."

He slowly nodded as a single tear slipped down his cheek.

"Did you know the only reason they found his body is it snagged on a tree stuck halfway down, wedged into a shale out-cropping? Because otherwise, it's like a couple hundred feet straight down. Deepest Finger Lake, after Seneca."

"Just wanted—"

"Just wanted what?"

"Second chance. With you. That's all."

"Oh, Glenn," Leslie said. He watched as she placed her left hand on his right knee and forced his foot onto the brake. As she did, she slipped the car into neutral. She opened the passenger door and slowly, almost stiffly, got out of the car.

"Don't you see?" she said.

Slowly, Glenn shook his head. Hardly able to move a muscle now.

"*I'm* the one who's due a second chance, Glenn. Not you. *Me.*"

She shut the passenger door softly and disappeared from sight. A moment later he felt the car begin to rock from the force of someone pushing from behind. A moment after that the car began to roll.

Three long, slow seconds after that, he met the lake.

THE OTHER ONE
KAREN DIONNE

I'm sitting on the sofa with my husband watching television. It's seven-thirty on a Sunday evening. *60 Minutes* is half over. Next up is the segment I've been waiting for: the first jailhouse interview with Jacob Holbrook in thirteen years.

Jacob Holbrook.

The Marsh King.

My husband reaches over and takes my hand. He thinks he knows how difficult it is for me to watch this. He doesn't know the half.

"Are you sure you're okay?" he asks.

"I'm fine," I lie.

The segment opens with a closeup of Holbrook's face. He looks nothing like I remember. The man who kidnapped my best friend twenty years ago wasn't young then, but at least he was clean shaven and respectable looking. Now the Marsh King looks like Charles Manson: crazed eyes, pitted skin, hollow cheeks, long gray hair, Rip Van Winkle beard. He sits in a concrete room at a steel table bolted to the floor. His hands are shackled to the table, his ankles bound to the chair. The cameraman has set up the shot to make it look as if the prisoner and the interviewer are alone in the room, though the presence of the camera belies that. A guard watches from the other side of a pane of reinforced glass in a heavy steel door.

The program begins with a voiceover reminding viewers of Holbrook's many crimes. The reporter focuses first on Megan's kidnapping. Everyone knows how the Marsh King kidnapped Megan Harju when she was a teen and kept her in a rundown cabin surrounded by swamp in Michigan's Upper Peninsula wilderness for fourteen years before she and the daughter she bore to him escaped. What no one knows is why.

"I wanted a wife." Holbrook answers matter-of-factly when the reporter asks about his motive, as if wife-snatching was as normal as taking an extra piece of pie.

"Did you know who she was? Had you been stalking her?"

"I'd never seen her before. She meant nothing to me."

Each time he answers I cringe. His voice hasn't changed since the day he lured Megan away. I close my eyes. Instantly, I'm back at the abandoned stationmaster's house next to the railroad tracks that Megan and I had been exploring. I hear Holbrook calling for his dog, thanking us when we offer to help him find it, telling us he doesn't want to put us to any trouble, but after we insist, conceding that if just one of us will help him look for his wife's little white cockapoo puppy, the search will go faster. Of course, separating us was what he intended all along.

The reporter keeps digging. She seems to think that she can coerce the Marsh King into admitting that he is sorry for his crimes. I could have told her that this will never happen. Jacob Holbrook is a narcissist, incapable of feeling anything remotely approaching remorse. This isn't my professional opinion only; psychiatrists for both the defense and the prosecution agreed on his diagnosis, though the defense argued mitigating factors such as the traumatic brain injury he suffered from being beaten as a child.

"Are you saying you don't have *any* regrets?" the reporter presses. "There's *nothing* you wish you'd done differently?"

Regrets? The Marsh King may not know the meaning of the word, but I have plenty for both of us. Since Megan was kidnapped, not a day has gone by in which I haven't wished I could undo the past. If I'd had any idea of what was about to happen, I'd have grabbed Megan by the hand and run away screaming. Maybe this man wasn't offering us candy or a ride in his car, but we were fourteen. We knew about stranger danger. We should have known better.

But that's not all. It gets worse. Because after the Marsh King said he needed only one of us to help look for his nonexistent puppy, I told Megan that she should go with him since she loved dogs more than I did. Everything that happened after that is on me. I was the leader, Megan the follower. She trusted me. If I had told her not to go with this man, she wouldn't have.

"Regrets?" Holbrook repeats, jolting me back to the present because of course, the question was for him. "Absolutely. I should have taken the other one."

His words knock me back. My stomach twists. It's all I can do to keep from throwing up.

The interviewer leans forward. "What other one?" she asks on behalf of the viewers who have forgotten that the Marsh King had two girls from which to choose.

Holbrook ignores her and looks directly into the camera. "I know who you are," he says, as if he can see me cowering on my sofa. *"I know what you did."*

"Well, that was—interesting," David says when the interview is over. "What do you make of that 'I know what you did' business?" David knows I was with Megan when she was kidnapped. He doesn't know that I am responsible for what happened to her.

"I have no idea," I say lightly, as if this man and the things that drive him mean nothing to me.

"I don't like him talking to you like that."

"It's just a bid for attention. The big, bad Marsh King is nothing but a pathetic old man. Pour us some wine, would you? I'll meet you on the deck in a minute."

While David busies himself in the kitchen, I go to my home office and collapse into my desk chair. I scrub my hands over my face. Those soulless eyes, that emotionless voice, the memory of that horrible day—if the Marsh King was hoping to rattle me, he succeeded. But I can't let him get to me. I'm a psychiatrist. I deal with personality disorders every day. I know this man better than he does himself. Holbrook agreed to this interview because he knew I'd be watching. He wants something from me. The question is, what?

There's a simple enough way to find out. I rummage through my desk for a blank piece of paper and an envelope. *Dear Mr. Holbrook,* I write in large, looping letters as if I were still a teen. *I saw your interview on TV. I know you were talking to me. What do you want? Sincerely, The Other One*

Psychiatrist versus narcissist. Let the game begin.

Two weeks pass, during which I do a deep dive into Holbrook's background. The better I understand the reasons for his narcissism, the better I can use his weaknesses against him. I realize that this goes contrary to everything I represent. Mental health professionals are supposed to help people, not harm them. But when the Universe gives you a second chance, you'd be a fool not to take it. It's too late for Megan—she returned so damaged from Holbrook's abuse that two years ago, she took her own life—but I can make this man suffer for what he did.

What I learn is disturbing, but not surprising. Although the exact causes of narcissistic personality disorder have yet to be determined, some researchers believe that overprotective or neglectful parenting styles have an impact. Holbrook, it seems, suffered both. He fetishized his mother, keeping intimate items that belonged to her in a shoebox that the police discovered in the closet of his childhood bedroom. His father beat him mercilessly as evidenced by the spanking stick they found in the woodshed with its handle worn smooth. He dropped out of school in the tenth grade, and after cutting pulpwood for a while, he joined the army, where he was kicked out after a year because he couldn't get along with his commanders and was always fighting.

But it's the things he did to Megan and her daughter that mark him as a *malignant* narcissist, the clinical term for a person whose narcissistic personality disorder is augmented by antisocial behavior, aggression, and sadism: chaining Megan to a post in a woodshed for the first fourteen months of her captivity, beating her and humiliating her until she lost the will to escape, putting his daughter in a deep hole in the ground for hours as a punishment when she was barely a toddler, nearly drowning Megan by shoving her head in a bucket of water after she had the audacity to borrow his canoe without his permission. Clearly, Jacob Holbrook is one bad dude.

Knowing all of this gives me the advantage. Exactly how I will take him down depends on his response to my question. Which is why today, when I check my post office box and find an envelope from the Marquette Branch Prison, I feel like cheering. I slide the envelope between two pieces of junk mail and hurry out to my car and slit it open. Inside, Holbrook has written his answer on a single sheet of paper in big block letters reminiscent of a ransom note: *YOU.*

It's impossible not to grin. By confessing his desire for me, he has given me all the power. I can string him along, make him think that I've fallen in love with him, and then, when I judge that our relationship has progressed to the point where telling him the truth will inflict the maximum damage on his fragile ego, I will break his evil little heart.

Dear Mr. Holbrook, I write once I'm back at my desk. *I'm flattered that you've been thinking about me. I'll confess there was a time when I found you attractive. But that time is long gone. I'm married. I love my husband. Please don't contact me again. Sincerely, You-Know-Who*

* * *

Of course, he writes back. How can he not? When I see his letter in my post office box the following week, I want to rip it open and read it on the spot. But the postmistress is watching. Newberry is a small town. Everyone wants to know everyone else's business.

"My brother," I say airily and wave the envelope in her direction as if daring her to comment on my wayward sibling and hurry outside to my car.

My dearest Rose, the letter begins. *Or should I call you Dr. Preston?*

I shiver. I was Rosemary Neimi when Megan was kidnapped. Prisoners don't have access to the internet. And yet somehow, the Marsh King knows both my profession and my married name.

May I remind you that you *wrote to* me, his letter continues. *Surely, as a psychiatrist you understand that you have no control over what I do. I will write to you as often or as infrequently as I wish. That said, your letter intrigues me. Are you saying you would have come with me willingly if I had taken you instead of her? Would you have cooked for me? Cleaned my house? Sewn my clothes? Borne my children as that one did?*

The corners of his letter are decorated with hand-drawn clusters of wild roses that are so lifelike, I can practically smell them. *Roses for my Rose,* the flowers are obviously meant to say. He's like a little boy presenting an apple to his favorite teacher. I suppose if he could have sent me real roses, he would have.

I compose my reply in my head as I drive back to my office. *Nice pictures,* I will write after I concede that I am powerless to stop him from writing to me and without letting on that I noticed the significance in his choice of flower. *I've always wished that I could draw. I'd love to see more of your work. Sincerely, Rose*

* * *

He writes back. I write to him. He writes again, as do I. *You are stupid; I don't know why I write to you; you're a terrible psychiatrist and a fraud* are themes he returns to over and over. Nothing he says bothers me. Belittling and demeaning others is classic narcissistic behavior. Each time I write back, I tighten the noose. My admiration for his artistic skills and for his ability to live in the marsh undetected gradually morphs into something more until finally, I write openly that I have fallen in love with him. *I wish I wasn't married. I wish that we could live together in the marsh.*

His reply drips with scorn. I'm a wicked woman for even thinking about leaving my husband. Have I no respect for the sanctity of marriage? No sense of right and wrong? He draws a picture of a woman wearing a hooded robe with a big red "A" on her chest so I'm sure to get the point.

You're right, I reply meekly. *I'm sorry, I shouldn't have said that. Thank you for correcting me.* Showing that he can't push me away no matter how cruelly he speaks because narcissists value loyalty above all else. He's so easy to manipulate, I almost feel sorry for him.

Almost.

His artwork becomes more elaborate. Lovely pen-and-ink wilderness scenes as idyllic as the Garden of Eden. Frogs and raccoons hanging whimsically from the top bar of a capital T or peeking out shyly from the middle of an O as if from a hollow tree. Apparently, my love has given him permission to drop his mountain man persona and reveal his tender side. I'm genuinely impressed by his talent. *Your drawings are amazing. You should be in the marsh painting from life, not locked up in prison with only your memories. I wish so much that you could be free...with me.*

I'm content to live in prison, he replies to my surprise. **I'm sorry for my crimes. Please don't speak of this again. Prison is where I belong.**

I tap his letter against my lips. The Marsh King is *not* repentant, and he certainly is *not* sorry for his crimes, of this, I am one-hundred-percent certain. So why does he write that he is?

Then it clicks. *I'm so glad to hear this. I agree that prison is where you belong,* I write back, bracketing my sentences with asterisks as he did his.

My dearest Rose, his next letter begins, *I knew you would understand.* *I was hoping that one day we could live together in the marsh, but we both know that this can never be.*

I grin. His code is so simple, a child could have broken it. Any sentence set apart with asterisks means the *opposite* of what is written. If I'd had any doubt, the picture he draws on the back confirms it: a cabin on a ridge surrounded by marsh beneath which he wrote, *The cabin I will never see again.*

The cabin he *will* see again. He's hoping we *will* live together in the marsh.

Understanding dawns. It's so obvious I wonder that I didn't see it from the beginning. Jacob Holbrook doesn't want my love or admiration. He wants me to help him break out of prison.

It's so perfect, it's almost too easy. All I have to do is devise an escape plan that has a reasonable chance of success, and after he's absolutely convinced that he's about to taste freedom and I have raised his hopes as high as they can go, I will shatter his dreams as he did Megan's.

I become his internet researcher, his boots on the ground. I dole out my findings in bits and pieces, in part so as not to alert the prison officials who are no doubt monitoring our correspondence, but mostly to torment him. *I checked out the prison,* I write without asterisks because this is true. *You should see the satellite view. That place is a fortress! Six level-five single-cell housing units surrounded by a twenty-foot-thick stone wall topped with a ten-foot wire fence with eight gun towers—it's unbelievable!!!*

You should see it from the inside, he writes back as if he too, is impressed. *There's no way anyone will ever break out of here.*

Of course, he means the opposite. As it happens, I've already come up with a viable escape plan, but over our next several letters, I let him think that I'm struggling. Not until I judge that his frustration level has gone through the roof do I send him a copy of an article I found online about two men who escaped during a prison transfer after they murdered the guards they had befriended. Jacob occasionally makes court appearances at the Luce County courthouse in Newberry, the town where he was arrested, a hundred miles east of the Marquette prison. He could easily do the same.

How stupid is this? I write across the top of the article.

World class idiots, he agrees, and so I drive the highway between Newberry and Marquette looking for the best place for him to make his move. I settle on the Driggs River that bisects the highway and leads into the Seney National Wildlife Refuge. Escaping here plays to Jacob's strengths. The wildlife refuge is made up of almost a hundred-thousand acres of wetland. Jacob can lay down a trail to make the police think he's heading into the marsh, then double back using the river as cover and swim through the culvert beneath the highway to where I'll be waiting on the other side. From there, we can drive across Michigan and Wisconsin and up through Minnesota and cross the border into Canada on one of several remote, unmonitored woods roads before the police even realize they've been duped.

I'm putting the finishing touches on a picture of us leaning against my car surrounded by pine trees and wearing matching plaid flannel shirts as if we were the lumberjack versions of Bonnie and Clyde when David stops outside my office doorway.

"What's so funny?" he asks.

I hadn't realized I was smiling. Quickly, I stash my drawing in my bottom desk drawer.

"It's nothing. I'm just writing to a—client. She said some-thing funny."

"You're treating a client by snail mail?"

"She's anthropophobic. Afraid of people. Since we can't talk in person or by video conferencing, this is the only way I can help her."

My story is utterly ridiculous, but my dear, sweet, trusting husband only shakes his head. He comes over and stands behind me with his hands on my shoulders and kisses the back of my neck.

"That's what I love about you, Rose. You're always so kind. You'll do anything to help."

We're so close to the finish, I can taste it. All I need is the date of Jacob's next court appointment. Jacob will think that this is going to be the day that he escapes. Instead, he will get a letter from me the day *before* his court appointment in which I tell him everything. Without asterisks.

His reply, however, is a puzzle. There's no mention of a court date, no reference to our plans, just a drawing of himself striding across the marsh like a Colossus with a rifle over his shoulder and a clutch of rabbits dangling from his hand. Above the picture in big block letters are two words: *I WIN*.

I don't get it. He wins what? His freedom? If so, then shouldn't he have written "we win?" Shouldn't I be in the picture with him? We planned his escape together. He can't make it to Canada without me. I'm missing something. Something in my letters must have tipped him off. Maybe I was too eager. Maybe my plan was too solid. Or perhaps he's known that I was manipulating him all along, and he's been using me as I've been using him.

Regardless, I have to send him my final letter. I started this game; I'm the one who'll say when it is finished. Jacob *has* to know that I deceived him, that he means nothing to me and never did, that there will be no happily ever after for the vaunted Marsh King. I don't expect him to understand that I did this as payback for what he did to Megan because in his eyes, he can do no wrong. But it doesn't matter. The Marsh King will know that there is no hope for him and there never was, while I have the satisfaction of knowing that he will spend the rest of his life in his six-by-nine jail cell where he will never hurt anyone again.

Weeks pass after I send my final letter. I feel oddly deflated at his lack of response. I can imagine Jacob's reaction—screaming and cursing, shredding my letter and throwing the pieces in the air, pounding his cell walls until his hands bleed, spending days, maybe even weeks in solitary for his out-of-control behavior. But imagination is only that. Without knowing how he reacted, our business remains unfinished. I feel like I've failed Megan all over again. I realize now that I should have gone to the prison and confronted him face-to-face. Doing so by letter was an act of cowardice. The interviewer wasn't afraid to sit down with this man. Why was I?

"Penny for your thoughts," David says as the *PBS Newshour* program we're watching cuts to a commercial and he mutes the set.

"I was just thinking about that client. The one I'm treating by snail mail. She hasn't written in a long time."

"Write to her again. Tell her that you've been thinking about her, and you hope she's all right."

I smile at the absurdity of renewing my correspondence with the Marsh King and cuddle closer. David might not know why I'm distracted, but I love that he cares enough to want to help.

The program resumes. As David unmutes the set, a breaking news alert scrolls across the bottom of the screen. The program cuts to a local reporter behind her desk.

"This just in," she says. "State Police report that a prisoner serving life without parole for child abduction, rape, and murder has escaped from the maximum-security prison in Marquette, Michigan. The prisoner is believed to have killed two guards during a prison transfer and escaped into the Seney National Wildlife Refuge south of M-28. Listeners should consider the prisoner armed and dangerous. If you see anything suspicious, call law enforcement immediately. Do *not*, repeat, *do not* approach. The prisoner, Jacob Holbrook, was convicted of kidnapping a young girl and keeping her captive for a dozen years in a notorious case that received nationwide attention—"

I can't see. Can't breathe. Can't hear anything over the blood rushing in my ears. *Jacob set me up.* He killed two guards and disappeared into the wildlife refuge exactly as I told him to do. I think about our correspondence in my bottom desk drawer, my internet search history which will point to me as his accomplice. He won, just as he said he did. *What do you want?* I asked in my first letter.

YOU, he replied.

Now the Marsh King is out, and he's coming for me.

PROVIDENCE
CLARK BOYD

I pick up the ringing phone. There are no such things as pleas-antries at this hour.

"Just listen, wiseass."

One Shot Valenti's voice is rusty metal dragged through gravel. And it gets right to the point. The Boss has it in for some dimple-chinned prick. Again.

As Valenti talks at me, I sip chamomile tea and glance down at my nine fingers. Best to do what he says and keep my thoughts on this matter, and all others, parenthetical. Luddington (Yep, prick). Federal prosecutor. Hates the Family. (Shocker). Laptop. Evidence. USB. (Mumbo meet jumbo). Tonight. In his study. (With the knife?). Meet us. (Us?) This kid. "The Vape." Genius. (Sure). Six p.m. Warehouse. East Providence.

"You won't need your blade," says Valenti. (The lead pipe, then).

"Sure thing, Boss."

I cradle the phone between my chin and shoulder, waiting for his signature line, the one that's earned him his nickname and a nasty rep.

"Remember, X., you got one shot at this."

And then he hangs up and I'm not a mid-level wiseguy, but just another insomniac watching replays of classic Red Sox

71

games in the dark (darkest) hours before dawn. I leave the sound off because of the neighbors, sure, but also because I don't like the banter. Or the Sox, really. What I enjoy is watching human beings use bats for more constructive purposes. Plus, when there's a conference on the mound, I amuse myself by pretending, aloud, that they're discussing existentialist philosophy.

"Coach, I can get this guy. Take a leap of faith."

"But Pedro, did the great Dane not also say, 'The specific character of despair is precisely this: it is unaware of being despair?' Now hand me the goddamn ball."

That's how it should have happened. But it didn't.

I know the insomnia and flowery tea and wishful thinking are not a good look for an enforcer with a reputation for having his shit together. For twenty-five years of a brutal sort of competence, if not outright excellence. They're symptoms of something, perhaps a deep and abiding malaise, but more than that I can't say. The point is that my work's been suffering of late, and my employers know it. Valenti, for one, wasn't surprised when I answered the phone on the first ring at four a.m.

I look down at my left hand. At the spot where my pinky finger used to be.

To dispel the creeping dread, I reach for my laptop. I usually start the day by reading the obituaries in the Journal, looking for the dark undercurrents running beneath the too-rosy recaps of people's lives. But instead, I type "how to disappear" into the search engine again. It's become an obsession since I realized that while I'm good at vanishing others, I'm less confident about erasing myself. Should the situation require it, I mean.

My alarm rings and I jump. Thank Christ, I made it through the night.

It's time for my Portuguese lesson and a cigarette.

Flakes of snow are falling as I leave my apartment.

I watch them tumble in the half-light of the antique gas

lamps they installed in this part of town last year. I say half-light, because most of the bulbs are burnt out and the Family has the supply contract. No historic atmosphere, no safety for citizens or tourists, until City Hall pays up, probably at twice the original price. I can hear Valenti in Hizzoner's office, lamenting the ongoing disruptions in the global lightbulb supply chain.

"You've got one shot to lock in a new price before they go higher, Mr. Mayor."

"I'll see what I can do, Vito."

Assholes, both of them.

The snow devolves into sleet as I drive to East Providence. The heater's just starting to pump warm air when I pull up in front of Beatriz's place. I sit and wait for the clock to hit five-thirty a.m. That's when the day's first *pasteis de nata* come out of the oven and the cafe opens. Hüsker Dü's *Candy Apple Grey* spills angrily out of the car's CD player. Bob Mould tells me he's hardly getting over it, and I can't disagree with the sentiment. This album accompanied me as I drove from Wisconsin to Rhode Island for undergrad all those years ago. I'd never left the county before, let alone the state, and my parents were convinced I'd meet a bad end among the Catholics and immigrants.

"It's called Providence. What could go wrong?" I asked my dad.

"You'll see," he said.

Beatriz unlocks cafe door, and I hurry inside. Unlike my car, her place is warm and welcoming. It smells of cinnamon and coffee, not confusion and regret. And the *fado* is an excellent counterpoint to Midwest post-punk.

"*Xavier. Bom dia!*" Beatriz beams.

I give it my best shot. "*Olá, Beatriz. Tudo bem?*"

She switches to English. "Your accent's...slightly better."

"*Obrigado.* The usual, please."

The usual is coffee with a splash of brandy and two custard tarts. On the saucer, next to the cup, are two sugar cubes and a single cigarette. I lied to her once that "one a day keeps the wolves at bay," and she's quietly enabled my habit ever since. She always makes sure it's my favorite—a Gauloise bleu.

It's her way of thanking me for getting her son out of a tricky situation a few years back. João—"a good boy, really"— had tried to boost a high-end ride in a neighborhood that's considered Valenti territory. This drew the attention of One Shot's nephew, Giovanni, a mustachioed little douchebag who fancied himself the Family's one-man car procurement division. Gino took the car from João at knifepoint, then told the kid he had two weeks to pay an inconvenience fee of five thousand dollars. In cash. Or else. Beatriz told me Giovanni used One Shot's catchphrase when he made the threat.

I told her not to worry. I told her some other things, too.

Then I tried to talk Giovanni down using nothing but my imposing presence and the .38 I keep strapped under my armpit.

"I'll tell my uncle," Giovanni screamed. "You're a dead man."

"Go ahead," I said. "He hates you anyway."

It's true, he does. Or did, rather.

Not long after Giovanni ratted me out, he got T-boned by an Amtrak train. The brat's car—the one he took from João— happened to get stuck on the tracks. Wrong place, wrong time, I guess. An acquaintance of mine in the Providence PD, a cop named Stevens, called and told me they found Lil' Gino, or what was left of him, wrapped up like a mummy in the back seat. Duct tape. Five or six rolls. Then he leaned on me, as usual.

"You been to Home Depot lately? Should I check your credit card receipts?"

"Duct tape is handy, Detective, but you know I always pay in cash."

Stevens chuckled. "Never steal another man's catchphrase, right?"

The upshot is that I now get a free breakfast whenever I visit East Providence. And today, I also get something extra. Something I've been waiting for. Beatriz comes over to my table and hands me a book. On the cover, it's all sun, sand, and deep blue sea.

"What you asked for," she says. "The guidebook, I mean."

"*Muito obrigado.*" I rub my temple, trying to massage away a sudden headache.

"I hope you get to Portugal soon."

"You never know, do you, Beatriz?" I smile at her. "Give my best to João."

"*Sim.* And thanks again, X. My dinner offer still stands, you know. Anytime."

As she moves off to the kitchen, I look up at the picture of her late husband on the wall behind the register. Then I quickly finish my coffee and stuff the guidebook in my coat pocket. On the way out, I slip ten C-notes into the tip jar.

No, Beatriz, thank you. But I'll have to take another rain check on dinner.

The cigarette is already in my mouth as I open the door.

Outside, I fumble for the matches and then cup my hands around the cancer stick. The tip glows red in the murk. Five long drags are all it takes. The headache relents and the back of my neck tingles. I take a moment to savor the buzz.

Back in the car, I crank the ignition. While I wait for some heat, I open the book. Inside the hollowed-out pages, there's a Portuguese passport and identity card, both flawless. João's skills have improved since I introduced him to some people I know a few months ago. His new employers, I understand, are quite happy with his progress.

The face beaming back at me from the documents is my own.

Hello, Inácio Nóbrega. You look happy and healthy this morning.

Clearly, the picture was taken a while ago.

Despite his intake of caffeine, sugar, and nicotine, the newly minted Senhor Nóbrega almost falls asleep at the wheel twice on his drive home. Then, after he crawls into bed, he lies awake for three hours. When he does finally drift off to sleep, a vivid dream keeps waking him over and over. In it, a close friend is repeatedly diagnosed with brain cancer.

Obrigado, Providence. You piece of shit.

I've been losing hours recently. Whole days sometimes.

Fugue state. That's what the neurologist calls it.

I finally had it checked out two weeks ago, after I woke up on a Persian rug next to a dead guy. I couldn't remember who he was. Or who I was. Or why I had a boning knife in my hand. Then Valenti's ugly face sprang into my mind, and I remembered it was just an ordinary Tuesday morning. The dead mope was helping Valenti move drugs. But he skimmed too much off the top, which earned him a visit from me.

I laid my head back down and slept for another hour.

"It's probably stress," said the doctor. "But we'll do an MRI just in case."

Lo and behold, they found a glioblastoma. Advanced. Terminal.

"You have insurance?" asked the doctor.

"Single-payer," I said. "Although I'm not sure he'll cover this."

"I meant life insurance."

I'm standing with my eyes closed, thinking about that soft Persian rug, when One Shot arrives at the warehouse for our meeting. He doesn't know about the tumor. Nobody I work with does.

"Asleep on your feet, X.?"

"Just visualizing a means of escape, Boss."

Valenti snorts. We both know every inch of this building, a clapped-out fire hazard by the docks where he enjoys giving me marching orders. He probably thinks that no matter how unpalatable the task, it can't be worse than spending one more minute in this rat-infested hellhole. And he's right.

A wave of nausea hits me.

"You don't look so good lately, Xavier. Ghosts haunting you?"

"Only the ones that didn't have it coming. But we know they all did, so..."

"Speaking of which, the mark's name is Luddington. Like I said on the phone. Gerald Luddington III. Fancy lad. Harvard Law. Ronnie says he's got a laptop filled with compromising information on the Family. Enough for a RICO prosecution."

"Or five?" I mutter a bit too loudly. Stupid tumor.

"Probably. But I didn't ask you, did I?"

Two decades of loyal service doesn't earn as much goodwill as you might think.

"Ronnie says he keeps it in his study. And Ronnie would know, right?"

Valenti loves to brag about his plant in the DA's office. Anyone who's met Ronnie knows he's the thickest brick in the wall. A complete dupe. But his last name's Valenti, so...

"You're going to break into his house tonight and copy the hard drive."

"Why not take the laptop? Smash it. Chuck it in the river?"

"Because I want to know what he has on me, but I don't want him to know that I know. Maybe it will help me figure out who's been grassing on us."

Valenti's convinced there's a mole in his organization. He loves devising overly complicated ways of trying to expose him. His ideas are right out of *Get Smart*.

"And I want some leverage on this bastard. I want to blackmail him. Get him working for us, maybe. So while you're removing our shit circus from his machine, you'll be uploading a different kind of carnival. Very unsavory."

"Boss, I don't know much about computers."

A door slams behind me and One Shot's eyes brighten.

"That's where my boy here comes in."

A ropey kid in a black T-shirt and a backwards Sox cap lopes up and stands next to Valenti. He's got a Jansport backpack with reflective trim slung over one shoulder. Twenty-five years old and eager. I can see it in his eyes. It's the same look I saw in the mirror a couple of decades ago. The Boss has probably told him he's going places in the organization. It's the kind of thing that gets you dead, or at least three consecutive life sentences, if you start to believe it. I look down at my pinkyless hand. No, the only way up this slime-coated ladder, the only way to survive, is obstinate reluctance. That, and luck.

"This is The Vape," says Valenti.

"Just Vape."

"The Vape's a digital genius. He's going to help us stay relevant. And wealthy."

The royal we, obviously.

"Got a soft spot for him?" I ask the Boss, knowing he's got a hard spot for him too.

"Your mouth's moving too much, X. Look to that, okay?"

The kid extends his hand and breaks the tension. "Billy Hammond."

I point to his backpack, and redirect the venom.

"Mommy pack your lunch too, 'Just Vape?'"

He doesn't miss a beat. "Sandwich. Mortadella with spicy mustard."

"Great. Maybe after we can go beat up a sissy on the playground?"

"Sure. I've got brass knuckles in there too."

Then he holds up a tiny plastic banana. I raise an eyebrow.

"It's a USB drive, Gramps. Find the laptop, plug it in, and let the magic fruit do all the work. Sucks up everything on the machine, then spits out porn and fake chat room threads with the mark's digital fingerprints all over it."

I take the drive and watch Billy suck on his e-cig. Nice touch. He nods at Valenti, smirks at me, and then turns to leave. Through the bubble gum reek of the vape smoke, I watch One Shot's eyes follow the kid out the door.

"He's going places."

"I was too, Boss. Remember?"

"Still are, X." He hands me a US passport and a Vermont

driver's license. Twice in one day. The universe really wants me out of Providence.

"Take a long break when you're done with this job, okay? There's an open-ended business class ticket for you at the airport. To somewhere far away. A land of sunshine and gelato. You've earned it."

"'Earn' is a funny word in this business, Val."

"Shut your hole, Morgan."

I look down at the license. Christ.

"Morgan Church? What, I manage hedge funds? I work in public radio?"

"It'll throw them off the scent if there's trouble."

"Should I dye my hair blond? Buy a yacht and a Prius? Really sell it?"

He hands me a slip of paper.

"Here's the address, smartass. He's always in his study on Sunday evenings."

As usual, I read it twice. Then I wad it up, chuck it in my mouth, and start chewing while Valenti watches me. When I've swallowed, he says, "You know the drill, X."

I hold up my left hand. "Understood."

As I walk back to my car, I scan what's left of my memory. When has Valenti ever given someone a vacation, other than a permanent one? The answer is never. It's a good bet some distant cousin in Palermo will be waiting for Morgan Church at the airport or ferry terminal. Even the thickest of them couldn't miss a name as ludicrous as that.

There's now a bullseye on my back.

I get out the burner phone I keep hidden in the car and make a few calls.

Each conversation starts with a single word: Providence.

Luddington's faux Tudor is in the swankier part of town. New build. Totally out of place with the houses around it. Slam the basement door and the walls of the upstairs shitter will probably rattle. I'm guessing a construction company owned by a friend of Valenti slapped it together. I wonder what the laundry room looks like?

Inside jokes are the only things keeping me loose at this point.

Christ knows how many bugs Ronnie has put in this house. Ears everywhere. Plus, there's the grey Chevy sedan that's been tailing me since I left my place. Probably Valenti's brother. Gino's father. He'd be motivated to play enforcer's enforcer, considering my role in his son's tragic demise. Which reminds me: I forgot to expense the duct tape. Too late now.

Focus, Morgan.

I drive past the house and park two blocks away. Then I walk back, keeping out of the streetlights as much as possible. I can feel my holster digging into my armpit. A trail of cold sweat runs down my torso.

Time to go to work.

Melanie, Luddy's wife of twenty years, has left the back door unlocked for me, but I pretend to pick it anyway. Someone's always watching. I step inside and head for the study. As I pass the living room, I see Mel on the couch. She's watching *The Real Housewives of New York* with the volume turned up. She sees me, winks, and raises her eyes toward the fire alarm above the sofa. Bug.

I blow her a kiss, and then continue down the hallway.

Gerald Luddington III is sitting at his big oak desk. Behind him are bookshelves filled with those familiar blue and red volumes, federal and state penal codes. Luddy's leaning back in his chair with his feet up, reading *The Economist* and sipping a single malt. It reminds me of our days in law school together, before he went one way and I went the other and yet we managed, somehow, to stay on the same side. On the desk are a laptop and a stack of cash.

I pull out my gun and step toward him.

"Good evening, Luddington. My name's Morgan Church."

He feigns surprise and spills his drink. When he protests at this outrageous violation of his privacy, I tell him to keep his voice down. Or else he gets it, the wife gets it. The kids, maybe even the dog. I've got a little message for him from Vito Valenti. The usual spiel.

When he threatens to call the police, I almost start laughing.

But I hold it together and pull the banana out of my pocket.

"Christ, you are such amateurs," Luddy says.

"Shut up, you dimple-chinned prick. We probably don't even need to put animal porn on that thing. I bet it's full of your furry little friends already."

He shrugs. "I do like hedgehogs."

I hope Detective Stevens is enjoying this banter. I'm sure Luddy's wired.

"Smartass," I say, ramming the USB drive into the laptop.

The banana does its job quickly. Billy Hammond is a pro. The kid not only seduced a notoriously unsentimental mob boss, but managed to gain access to what looks like every computer file, every festering digital trail, ever created by the Family. Illegal wire transfers, bogus contracts, logs of Valenti's drugs, weapons, and human smuggling operations. It's all there, moving steadily from the drive to Luddington's laptop. I'm sure this trove also contains proof of the crimes I've committed, however reluctantly, in my years spent deep undercover.

"Hope you're proud of yourself," my old friend and colleague says.

"Most of them had it coming."

"And what do you have coming?"

"A vacation. Fun and sun. Ice cream."

"I suppose you think you've earned it."

"'Earn' is a funny word in this business, Luddington, but yeah."

"Rot in hell, pal."

"You'll be hearing from us. Not from me, you understand, but from my employer."

I shoot Luddy a wink, grab the cash, and slink out of the house.

The Feds nab Morgan Church while he's taking a pre-flight dump at T.F. Green.

Following the script to perfection, they frogmarch me out to an unmarked van in full view of a gaggle of reporters. I make a show of hiding my face from the cameras. There's a press conference, lots of men in windbreakers using words like "decimated," "significant," and "finally." Luddington's there in a suit and tie, promising to put Vito Valenti away for a long time. He plays up how this Church idiot in the van got sloppy and led an undercover cop, codenamed Providence, to a USB drive filled with damning evidence against the Family.

He holds the banana up for all to see.

Just as Luddington finishes talking, Billy Hammond leaves the Boss asleep in bed and opens the door for Detective Stevens, who is waiting outside with a crew of uniformed officers and another array of cameras and reporters. The phrase, "Why, Vape, why?" gets fifteen seconds of fame, courtesy of a half-naked Valenti screaming it through crocodile tears as he's led away in cuffs.

I watch the scene unfold on a giant flat-screen television in a four-star hotel room near the airport. The best moment is when Stevens gets right up in One Shot's face.

"Hey, Valenti. How many shots do you think we'll give you to stay out of prison?"

"Screw you, pig."

"Oh, Vito, one more thing. X. sends his best."

The look of shock on Valenti's face brings me immeasurable joy.

A week of tied-up loose ends later—after that shitheel Ronnie's caught trying to steal the banana from Luddy's desk and Billy Hammond's received public commendations (but not a raise, I'm sure)—a grey Chevy sedan drops off Inácio Nóbrega, a Portuguese national, at Logan Airport in Boston. He's booked on the overnight flight to Ponta Delgada in the Azores, and then on to Faro. He spends the entire trip practicing his new native tongue.

After I land, I take a cab to a bungalow by the water. It's my new home, although I made sure the boys put the deed in João's name. There's a new fishing rod on the kitchen table, along with five cartons of Gauloises and a note that reads: "Rot in hell, pal." Luddy and Mel. A parting gift, because they know they'll never see me again. Although not necessarily for the reasons they might think.

When I go to the ATM that afternoon, I confirm that the money I asked for is there. Then I find a cafe with *pasteis* and Wi-Fi, and transfer almost all of it to Beatriz.

Only then does the despair relent and I finally feel free.

I've been waiting for this a long time. To be done with Valenti and his band of idiots. To leave behind the murders and lies. The crosses and double crosses. All the beatings, both given and received. To be free of the curses of the boning knife and the .38, not to mention the baseball bat and the goddamn Red Sox. To try to forget Providence and every other alias I've used. To give it...Christ, why not?...one more shot.

But the tumor has other plans.

Inácio Nóbrega is as good a name as any for a short obituary, I guess.

That night, I sleep peacefully. A full twelve hours. No dreams. In the morning, I stroll down to the waterfront with my fishing rod in one hand and a bottle of ten-year-old tawny in the other. As I chain smoke Gauloises, I see a fishing boat for sale. It's a gleaming fifteen-footer with blue lettering on the side: *Beatriz*. Providence, indeed.

Over a glass of port, I strike a deal with the seller. He compliments me on my Portuguese and hands me the keys. I thank him and give him the rest of the tawny.

Then I sail out into the Atlantic, and never look back.

TURNING HEART
DAVID HESKA WANBLI WEIDEN

I parked my truck in the lot at Turtle Creek, the Rosebud Reservation's supermarket, and looked around for dogs. A pack of them had attacked a woman on the street last month and nearly killed her. They'd gone blood crazy, biting her repeatedly and ripping the skin off her face and arms. We had an animal control officer, but he couldn't keep up with all the escaped and abandoned canines. People in the border towns outside of the rez dumped their mutts here if they wanted to get rid of them. Some of the dogs were picked up immediately but others adapted quickly, turning feral and joining packs. Those were the ones you had to watch for.

I didn't see any, so I walked inside. I headed to the freezer cases at the back of the store, underneath the hanging sign that said WOYUTE TASAGYAPI. I'd pick up some pizza rolls, a couple of frozen macaroni and cheese dinners, a six-pack of Shasta Cola, and maybe a few Tanka bars for later. I was reaching for the frozen food when my cell phone started vibrating. A number I didn't recognize flashed on the screen.

"Is this Virgil?" A woman's voice.

"Yeah, who's this?"

"Janeen. Remember me? Rob's sister."

Janeen Turning Heart. My buddy's little sis. Rob and I had

been tight back in high school—classmates, best friends, comrades. We'd taken the same classes, hung out after school together, and cruised up and down Main Street endlessly on the weekends, hoping that someone would notice us. When my mom died, the first place I went was to Rob's house, where they gave me food, burned some sage, and helped me through the roughest days. In our last year of high school, we'd talked about getting some money and opening up an auto body shop on the rez. But I'd started drinking and listening to heavy metal music. Rob joined the Army instead, got shipped out to fight in the war, and came home in a body bag. I'd always felt guilty over his death, thought it was my fault, somehow. I hadn't gone to the funeral. Instead, I'd hopped on my motorcycle and rode flat out to the Black Hills, pushing the bike to its limit, the road just a blur beneath me, riding until I couldn't see anything, stopping only when I ran out of gas.

"Hey, Janeen, been a long time," I said. "How's it going?"

"Not so good, actually. Wondering if I can talk to you?"

"Sure. What's up?"

"Well, are you still, you know, helping people out? If they have a problem?"

Damn, she wanted me to kick the shit out of someone. I was the reservation's enforcer, the guy you hired when the police wouldn't take action. The person who'd make sure justice was served when the feds released a child molester or rapist. No set fee—I got paid according to the number of bones I broke, teeth I knocked out, and black eyes I gave. Now my dead friend's sister needed my help. How could I let her know that I was trying to quit beating people up?

"What's going on?" I asked.

"Kind of complicated. Rather tell you in person. If that's cool."

I put the pizza rolls back in the freezer. "Yeah, no worries. Where you at now?"

"Living out by Parmelee. Just past the elementary school."

Twenty miles away. "You going to be in Mission any time soon?"

"No, that's sort of the problem. Any way you could come out here?"

Images of Rob Turning Heart flashed in my head. The goofy way he'd smiled, the ratty ball cap he always wore. The last time I'd seen him before he shipped out, both of us too embarrassed to say anything meaningful, instead just giving each other an exploding fist bump.

"Yeah, I'll head over now."

Half an hour later, I pulled up in front of a little trailer off Highway 18. The yard was neat, the little patch of grass mowed and free of weeds. I tried to remember the last time I'd seen Janeen. I vaguely recalled speaking to her a few years ago—maybe at the Rosebud Wacipi, but I wasn't sure. I rang the doorbell and waited.

"Virgil!" She smiled as she opened the door. "Come in."

I stepped inside the tiny living room. A small couch, an old television, and, off in the corner, a crib. She noticed me looking at it.

"Six months old," she said. "He's asleep, for now. Go ahead and sit down. You want some pop?"

"Yeah, sure." I hadn't heard about Janeen being pregnant, but that was no surprise. I'd quit drinking and didn't go to the bars anymore, so I didn't hear a lot of the rez gossip. I had no idea what her situation was now.

"Cherry cola or grape?" she said from the kitchen.

"Grape sounds good." While she was pouring the sodas, I took a look at her. Long dark hair, tall, blue jeans and a red T-shirt. I could see some of the little kid I'd known back in the day, but she was her own person now.

"Thanks for coming over." She handed me an old jelly jar filled with purple liquid and sat down.

"Yeah, good to see you." I noticed there was a framed photo of Rob in his Army gear hanging on the wall. I didn't see any other pictures.

"You, too." She looked me over, up and down. "Dang, you're even bigger than before. You lifting weights?"

"Naw, just working, gettin' by." I drank some of the soda. "So, how you been? Don't know the last time I saw you."

She looked at me with a strange expression on her face. "You don't remember? We ran into each other at the Depot a while back. We stayed there a long time, talked about Rob. You started crying."

I didn't remember, which wasn't surprising. If we'd talked at the Depot, then it was back in my heavy drinking days. I'd put all that behind me, although it was hard to avoid the ghosts of old conversations and past incidents.

"I'd probably had a few. Sorry."

"Yeah, you were pretty smashed, but whatever. It was all good. We were just missing Rob. Drowning our sorrows, I guess. You told me some stories about him I never heard before, had me laughing."

Yeah, I missed him. He was another one of my ghosts—more than just a friend, he had been like a brother. I still heard him in my head sometimes, cracking jokes or telling me to get off my ass and do some work.

"Seems like only yesterday he was here," I said.

She got up and threw the empty soda can in the trash. "Yeah, it does. I named the baby after him, you know. That's little Robbie."

"That's...really great." I turned away and pretended to take a drink so she couldn't see my face. I took a few seconds, then walked over to the baby. He was starting to wake up, blinking his eyes and looking around.

"Hi, Robbie, how you doing, little guy?" He grinned, his tiny face lighting up. "Hey, he smiled at me!"

"He might be pooping," Janeen said. "He makes a weird face when he goes."

She came over and picked the baby up, then smelled his bottom.

"No, he's okay." She put the baby back down in the crib. I could hear him making little noises. It sounded like a forest after a rainstorm, crows and jays returning to the nests, talking among themselves.

"Listen, I appreciate you coming out here," she said. "It's hard for me to get around now. That's what I wanted to talk to you about. You know, with a baby, I got to be able to buy formula, diapers, all that stuff."

I nodded, not sure where she was going with this.

She went on. "Here's the thing. Last month, I wake up, Robbie's screaming his head off. I don't got enough formula for the whole day, so I need to run to the store. I feed him, get him dressed, and we head out. Except my car's gone. Missing."

She looked at me like I knew who'd done it. "Well, it's not a car, I guess. It's a minivan. A crappy old Dodge Caravan, but it runs. I'm like, shit, somebody stole my ride."

"You sure it was stolen?" I said. "It wasn't repo'd?"

"No, it was paid off. Bought it in cash. Someone took it."

"Okay. Anyone else have the keys?"

"Yeah. My shitty ex-boyfriend. Robbie's dad. He's gotta be the one who did it." She went to the kitchen and put some water on the stove. "Hold on, I need to get some formula ready."

I watched her scoop some powder into a baby bottle. "Who's this guy?" I asked. "The ex-boyfriend."

"Just some asshole I met at the bar. You know, we hooked up, I let him stay here, then I got pregnant. My fault, but I'm not sorry. Only thing I'm sorry about is being with that jerk. Turns out he was messing around with some skank. I told him to pack up his shit and get out."

"Why do you think he took your minivan?"

She scowled. "Because he's a lazy dick! And he's got my spare set of keys. Who else could it be?"

"It's not that hard to steal a car, you know, especially the older models. You don't need keys, just a slim jim and some wire cutters. Could have been anyone."

"Who's going to come all the way out here to steal a '95 Caravan?"

This was compelling logic. "Okay, so what do you want me to do?"

"Well, I just need my ride. Can you go see him and get it back? Hey, you gotta rough him up, that's cool with me."

I hadn't laid down a beating on anyone for a while. I'd decided to change my ways, do things the right way. Wolakota, the Lakota path. Restorative justice and all that, not leaving some guy by the side of the road with a broken arm and a bloody face. But I looked at Janeen. She had Rob's eyes, his mouth. Rob, the friend I'd let down. The guy who'd always stood by me. Some debts can't be forgiven so easily. This was my second chance to do right by Rob.

"I'll help you out, okay? See what I can do."

"Oh jeez, thank you so much!" she said. She came over and hugged me, which I wasn't expecting. "You don't know how hard it's been without a car. Look, I don't got much money, but there's sixty dollars—"

I held my hand up. "Don't want your money. Save it, buy some baby food. Just give me the key to the van, in case I find it. And what color is it?"

She smiled. "Silver. Used to be anyway. Kinda rusted out now. Oh, there's a sticker on the back window—you can't miss it. It's that Calvin cartoon kid taking a pee. The asshole stuck that on."

I finished the last swallow of grape soda and put the glass down. "Hey, you haven't told me who this guy is, where he lives."

"Oh, right," she said. "His name's Gil. He's out in Norris, last I heard."

"Gil? What's his last name?"

"Uh, White Eyes. Gil White Eyes. But most people call him Chunky."

Chunky White Eyes. My cousin.

90

* * *

As I drove home, I tried to remember when I'd last seen Chunky. He was my second or third or tenth cousin—tough to say on the rez, given that we were all related. He was about five years younger than me and had been a goofy, gangly kid who always smelled like dog food. We used to play together when we were little; I remembered one day when we were climbing on wrecked cars at the junkyard. We'd been having a fine time until he pushed me off an old Duster and I hurt my arm. He'd laughed like a hyena until I hit him in the neck. Then he ran home and told his mother.

He moved away to the Pine Ridge reservation with his mom when he was a teenager, so we lost touch. I'd heard that he dropped out of high school and was a wannabe gang member, but that was all I knew. We'd simply drifted apart—the fifty miles separating the Rosebud and Pine Ridge reservations might as well have been an ocean.

And now he was back, and living in Norris, of all places. A small, isolated community on the rez, people who lived in Norris didn't take kindly to outsiders. Most of the people there only spoke Lakota, and they lived in the old Sioux 400 and transitional houses. Cheap, shoddy homes built in the 1970s, with split floors and cracked foundations. Some of the houses had been used as meth labs and were permanently boarded up.

I decided to head out to Norris right away. If I found the minivan, I'd drive it back and leave my truck there and hope no one messed with it. But the bigger issue was Chunky. If he had the minivan, would he hand it over or would I have to take it? I had no idea if he was still affiliated with a gang. It was hard to imagine Chunky as a hard guy, but maybe he was a different person now.

As I drove, I thought about him. Was he the same person, sometimes annoying and sometimes funny, or had he changed over the years? I wondered if it was possible for a person to alter their basic nature, or if some part remained fixed and absolute. I'd been filled with anger for so long, but I'd tried to let that go and become calmer, peaceful. Part of that meant giving up vigilante jobs, but people still came to me with their problems. Problems that could only be resolved with violence, which I was trying to quit. And now I was right back in it.

I slowed down and made the turn on Route 63 into town. There were only a few hundred people living in Norris, so I'd be able to find the place pretty easily. I drove around slowly for a while, keeping my eyes open for a silver Caravan.

A kid rode by on a yellow bicycle. I motioned to him.

"Hey, you seen Gil around?"

"Who?"

"Chunky."

"No, not today." He started moving his front wheel from side to side, so he didn't fall over.

"You know where he lives?"

"Uh, over there." He pointed off to the north. "About two blocks down. Big dog in front."

The place wasn't hard to find. A huge mutt was tied up in the front yard with a metal chain. It looked like a Rottweiler or Pit bull or maybe something else. Heinz 57. When I got closer, the dog noticed me and started barking ferociously. I kept my distance and looked around the place. Weeds and trash in the yard. No minivan, but a beat-up Toyota Tercel parked in front, one window gone and replaced with a piece of plastic sheeting.

"Hey, anyone here?" I shouted. The dog barked even more loudly, growling and straining at its chain.

I saw some movement through the window. After a minute, the front door opened, and a man stepped out on the small front porch. He was tall and skinny, had long black hair, and was wearing sweatpants and an old T-shirt that said RED CLOUD WARRIORS. He didn't look like the Chunky I remembered.

He grabbed the dog's chain and pulled it back. "Diesel, shut up."

When I heard the voice, I knew it was him.

"Chunky?" I said.

"Yeah?" He stared but didn't recognize me.

"Hey, it's Virgil. Your cousin. Virgil Wounded Horse."

He looked at me closely, top to bottom, and his face slowly changed.

"Shit, Virgil? That really you? Damn, you look different. Bigger. It's been, like, I don't know, maybe twenty years since I saw you."

I kept my eye on the dog, who was quiet now, but still watching me. "I know. Long time."

He stayed on the porch and didn't ask me inside. "So, uh, what are you doing here? I mean, how'd you know where I lived?"

"Don't mean to bother you," I said. "Thing is, I was talking to Janeen Turning Heart today."

His face darkened. "That bitch."

I felt my anger start to rise up like a red wave. "Hey, I know you two had a thing. Not my business. But she tells me that you got her minivan. That true?"

He looked down the block, both directions. "She here?"

"No," I said. "It's just me."

"Huh. So, where is she?"

I moved closer to the house. "That's not important. I just want to get her ride back."

He took a step back. "It's my goddamn car. I bought and paid for it. Don't know what horseshit she told you, but it's mine."

I figured he'd say something like this. "I don't want to get involved in any beef between you two. She tells me it's hers and I got to believe her. How about I just take the minivan back and you guys can work it out on your own?"

He bent down and unhooked the dog's chain, then looped it around his hand. "Yo, that skooch did nothing but whine and complain for three months. I figure she owes me about a grand for the shit I put up with. You talk to her, tell her she can kiss my ass. How 'bout that?"

So it was going to be like this. "Chunky, where's the minivan? Tell me now or we're gonna have a problem. I get the Caravan back, it's all good. Best offer I can give you."

"Here's my offer," he said, smirking. "Get the fuck out of here or I'll sic Diesel on you. You don't want to mess with this guy. Tear you up."

He yanked the dog's chain, tapped it in the face, and pointed at me. The dog was at full attention now, staring and growling. Its short tail was rigid and sticking straight up. I could see that the dog's face was scarred and its ears were mangled. Diesel was a fighting dog.

Chunky must be one of the shitbags who entered their dogs in these matches. I'd never been to one, but I'd heard about them. The fact that Diesel was still alive meant that he'd won in his fights, because they'd shoot the loser, if it managed to survive. This crap sickened me. In the past, the Lakota people valued the sunka, using them to serve as guards against intruders and even assist in ceremonies. Now, assholes like Chunky used dogs for sport.

I didn't want to harm the animal, but I knew it could hurt me badly, even kill me. I looked at the dog, still growling. The animal wasn't snarling or showing its teeth—it was in fighting mode.

"What's it gonna be?" Chunky said.

Stupidly, I'd come unarmed. Given that I wasn't beating people up anymore, I didn't feel the need to carry. I had a baseball bat in my truck, but it was parked two blocks down.

The only play I had was to walk away.

"All right, you win," I said, and took off my jean jacket. "Just let me grab a smoke."

"That's what I thought." He sneered at me. "Take off, homes."

I fumbled in the pockets of my jacket, looking for my cigarettes. "You got a light?"

"Eat shit," he said, and turned away.

"One more thing."

He turned back and looked at me. "What?"

"Fuck you and your goddamn dog." I opened my jacket, leaned over, and quickly wrapped it around the dog's head so he couldn't see, and then I lifted its hind legs in the air so it couldn't move. He started squirming and I fell on him, using all of my two hundred seventy-five pounds on the dog's torso to break its ribs. It started whimpering and yelping, and I moved away quickly in case he got up, but the dog stayed on its side.

"What the fuck, man! What'd you do to him?" Chunky started moving over to the dog, but I got behind him and pushed him face down. I grabbed his right arm and twisted it, then put my knee on his back.

"Get off!" he shouted.

I increased the pressure until he stopped moving.

"All right, dude," I said. "You gonna give me any shit if I let you up?"

He grunted and mumbled something.

"I'll ask you again. You gonna be cool?" I ground my knee into his shoulder blade.

"Yes!" he shouted.

I let go of his arm, slowly stood up and moved back a step. I glanced over at Diesel. The dog watched me but was no longer in attack mode—it was lying on its side and trembling. Chunky sat up and stretched his arms and his neck.

"You'll be all right," I said. "But you better take that dog to the vet—the one in Valentine. That Toyota yours?"

He nodded.

"Take him today. If I find out you put that dog down, I'll kick your ass for real. You hear me?"

He stayed quiet then nodded again.

"Okay, let's get back to it. You got Janeen's minivan?"

He glared at me. "Yeah, but I paid for half of it. She gonna give me my paper back?"

"I told you, you guys work that out. I don't give a damn who paid what—she needs that ride for baby stuff."

He turned his head to the side. "Wait, what?"

"I said, she needs her car for baby stuff—you know, diapers, formula, all that."

His mouth dropped open in surprise. "Baby?"

No, it couldn't be. He didn't know about little Robbie?

"Uh, have you been out to Janeen's place in a while?"

He shook his head. "Not since early last year. I mean, I went out there to take the Dodge, but I didn't go inside, you know?"

I stood still for a minute, trying to figure out what to do. This dipshit had stolen Janeen's car, then threatened me with his dog. I didn't owe him anything, right?

But then a memory flashed into my head. When I was just eight years old, Rob Turning Heart was already my best friend, and he got sick. Really sick. He was coughing up blood and unable to get out of bed for over a month. I'd talked to him on the phone, and he'd asked me to come over to his house because he was lonely. But I didn't go. I was scared. Scared that I'd get sick, too, and scared that I wouldn't know what to say or how to act around him. I never did go to visit him when he was ill. He got better, slowly, and finally came back to school. When he first returned, I was embarrassed and tried to pretend like nothing had happened. But after school, Rob walked home with me and told me it was okay I hadn't come over. He said he understood. And I started crying then. Crying for my cowardice and for Rob's compassion. And I was happy I hadn't lost my friend, my blood brother.

I looked over at Chunky White Eyes. He looked scared, like he'd entered some new, unfamiliar territory, a land where he didn't speak the language or know the customs.

I sighed. "Come on. Let's take a ride out to Janeen's place. You can put the dog in the back of my truck—we'll go to the vet afterwards."

THE RIVER OF MY RETURN
ELIZABETH ELWOOD

A fortuneteller once told me that I would redeem my self-esteem when I stepped across the Mississippi. Of course, I didn't believe her. At the time she made the prediction, my self-esteem seemed perfectly adequate, nothing necessary to redeem. I had completed my nursing qualifications, I was a week away from a glitzy Saint Patrick's Day wedding to the most gorgeous guy I had ever seen, and life looked promising. I could not foresee the gradual attrition that would come after giving up my career to be a stay-at-home mother, not to mention the snare I had placed myself in by pandering to my Irish charmer—who turned out to be more Orangeman than lyrical romantic dreamer—and two children who grew up emulating their domineering, bad-tempered father.

After forty-five years of marriage to Duncan and mothering the twins, my self-esteem was irredeemable and I was far too tired even to consider it. It was easier to keep quiet, say *yes* when necessary and avoid any kind of confrontation. Besides, as a downtrodden Canadian housewife—yes, that antiquated title still applied to me, in spite of my daughter's fury at both my lack of political correctness and my inability to stand up for myself—what chance did I have of ever seeing the Mississippi, let alone crossing it. We were moderately well off, but Duncan would never have considered shelling out for a family vacation.

His golfing weekends were all the holiday he deemed necessary. No, I would continue on, crushed as regularly as a vat of grapes in wine-making season, cooking Duncan's meals, keeping his home spotless, running his errands, looking after his dog, and believing his mantra that I never managed to get anything right. Crossing the Mississippi was as much a dream as crossing the Rubicon.

The one thing I suppose one could say in Duncan's favor was that he was faithful. No philanderer, he. In spite of his girl-magnet looks, he didn't stray. "Why spend money on a lady-friend when you have a perfectly adequate female at home?" he used to say to his buddies. Then, after being diagnosed with coronary artery disease in his sixties, he was noticeably lax in the bedroom department anyway. As long as he had his three rounds a week at the golf club, he was content to be a miserly and despotic homebody, king of his own castle with a resident serf to grant his every wish.

Therefore, you can imagine my amazement when, five years into retirement, Duncan announced that he had bought a motorhome and intended to make a trip around North America. I also noticed that he had become uncharacteristically cheerful when issuing his daily decrees.

It did not take me long to figure out what had caused the dramatic change. Two months previously, our next-door neighbors, George and Debbie Graham—an affable couple our own age who got along well with Duncan by virtue of never disagreeing with him—offered their vacant in-law suite to Debbie's widowed sister who had sold her home and was looking to downsize nearby. Lucy Brock was ten years younger than Debbie, and the difference definitely showed. A merrier widow one could not find anywhere, nor one better preserved from all the services the best hairdressers, cosmeticians and couturiers could provide, not to mention some work that one was tactfully not supposed to comment on. Lucy, we were told, in addition to the huge influx of cash from the sale of an upscale West Vancouver

THE RIVER OF MY RETURN

mansion, had so many portfolios that her financial advisors fell over themselves salaaming when she entered their precincts. She was also an avid golfer, and I soon realized that her rounds on the course were coinciding with Duncan's.

Therefore, when the announcement about the motorhome trip came, I naively thought that Duncan, stimulated by the glamour of our new neighbor, had decided that a second honeymoon might prove to liven up our marriage. But I was soon disillusioned. It appeared that the Grahams, who were keen motorhome travelers themselves, were planning to take their Winnebago on a North American trip, and had invited Lucy to come along in the luxury campervan that her late husband had purchased shortly before his demise. Duncan was buying a motorhome so that we could join the convoy. One jolly group doing the grand tour together. I could visualize what lay ahead: cooking campsite meals for five, daily cleaning to keep the motorhome up to Duncan's draconian standards, pet-sitting both family's dogs while the rest of the gang went sightseeing, and clearing up at the end of each day while listening to Duncan chat up Lucy around the campfire. The prospect was dismal and demoralizing.

The next few weeks were a marathon of preparations. Duncan, of course, did not overexert himself. His main contribution, other than writing lists of things for me to do, was making test runs in his precious new toy, even using it to run back and forth to the golf club. When the golf-club visits became more protracted, I began to suspect that it wasn't just the irons and woods that were swinging. I noticed that Duncan had become particularly careful about having his nitro spray with him—in the past, I had always had to remind him to take it along—and I naturally speculated about the increased activity that was causing him to be so conscientious. I had resigned myself to the fact that the upcoming trip had nothing to do with a sudden enthusiasm for motorhome travel, but I had never anticipated anything more serious than a mild flirtation with the wealthy widow. Now, I had to accept the possibility that my husband's late-middle-age crisis had erupted into a full-scale affair.

Two days before we were due to leave, Duncan made a comment that chilled my blood. He and George were sitting in our living room, drinking coffee and flipping through a copy of *Next Exit* (Neither one had graduated to the computer age). They had charted our route down the west coast, across the Border States, and back up the east coast, but had stalled as they reached the highway that ran below the Canadian-U.S. border. Somehow, they had deviated from the subject of the itinerary and were discussing the marriage breakup of one of George's former work colleagues. I had not taken much notice of the conversation, but I pricked up my ears when I heard my husband laugh. I had heard that gleeful chortle before. Duncan was contemplating doing something to his advantage, which meant someone else was going to be seriously disadvantaged.

"*I'd* consider it worth the hassle of divorce, too," he was saying, "if I had a prospective Number Two who was loaded."

I could read Duncan's mind. After all my years of caring for his needs and submitting to his every whim, I was scheduled for the discard pile. As I came into the living room to take their empty mugs, my teeth were clenched. Duncan avoided my eyes, something he never did, which proved that my instincts were right. As I picked up the mugs, my eyes lit on the map spread out on the coffee table, and beside it, the campsite guide, flipped open to a page listing places to stay in Louisiana. A site in the French Quarter of New Orleans had been circled.

Moving like a sleepwalker, I took the mugs out to the kitchen and placed them in the dishwasher. My mind was on another plane. I was back at the fairground with my fortuneteller from so many years ago. Her prediction flashed across my mind in neon lights. Duncan and I were going to New Orleans. We would see the Mississippi. If I stepped across it, I would redeem my self-esteem.

I had no idea how I was going to do it, but I had made up my mind. I was going to kill Duncan.

* * *

The following day, as I packed clothes and supplies, I mused over the possibilities. An accident or a heart attack? The latter seemed most promising. Duncan had never been one to pay attention to things medical. His was a you-don't-keep-a-dog-and-bark-yourself attitude, so, having married a nurse, he expected me to look after his prescriptions. I certainly knew a lot about drugs, but I also knew how easily they could be detected. And now that Duncan was being meticulous about having his nitro at hand, it would be impossible to engineer a heart attack that became fatal because he'd forgotten his spray.

But in the afternoon, while Duncan was ensconced in front of the sports channel, I found my solution. It was waiting for me in his precious motorhome. I was loading supplies and I noticed that he had already placed his personal travelling kit into the cabinet that hung on the wall of the bathroom. Curiously, I pulled it down and unzipped it. And there was the evidence to prove my suspicions. In the side pocket was a bottle of Viagra, clearly ordered off the Internet, for there was no doctor's label encircling the vial. Duncan was trying to improve his performance, and I wasn't the beneficiary.

I put everything back as I had found it and returned to the house. Duncan was still glued to the television. Just as well, because I needed him to stay blissfully unaware that I knew about his geriatric high jinks. I smiled. His adultery and his ignorance of things medical were going to provide *his* Next Exit. It would not have occurred to him that Viagra in conjunction with nitro could have deadly consequences. He had handed me his death on a platter.

Other than his recent lapses with the widow, Duncan was careful about avoiding physical strain, but controlling his temper was more of a challenge and I knew exactly how to provoke him into a rage. His golf-club membership renewal had arrived in the mail and, instead of paying it as I usually did, I slipped the envelope into my purse. The club was an exclusive one and waiting lists for memberships were lengthy. Rules were also rigid. Failure to renew on time meant cancellation and a humiliating process of negotiation and contrition to get back on the waiting list. I could guarantee what would happen when I "discovered" the unpaid bill and cried: "Oh, no, how could I have forgotten!" Duncan would be apoplectic. A seizure would be guaranteed. Mind you, I would have to find the right time and place. It had to be somewhere where there was no help at hand.

The day before we were due to set off, I found what I needed. I was scrolling the internet—yes, we did own a computer, but since the role of secretary was another of my duties, I was the only one who used it—and as I viewed the tourist attractions, I came upon a picture of the gleaming white paddle wheeler that offered day trips on the Mississippi: The Natchez, operating out of New Orleans. The perfect location. On board a ship, with no ambulance at hand. It was perfect timing, too, for having already booked our campsites, I knew we would be in New Orleans for Saint Patrick's Day. I could end my marriage on the day it had begun. What's more, as my fortuneteller had predicted, I would be on the river that was to redeem my self-esteem. It seemed fate was taking a hand.

Once we set off, the trip followed a predictable pattern. I cooked, cleaned, dealt with reservations, pet-sat while the others went sightseeing, and ignored Duncan's evening "dog walks" once everyone had supposedly turned in. His surreptitiously purchased keep-it-uppers had definitely invigorated him. Maybe I wouldn't need to resort to artifice to finish him off. At this rate, he might manage it all on his own.

Still, he continued to be fit as the proverbial fiddle as we proceeded down the west coast and made our way across the Border States, sightseeing all the way. Unlike the legendary heroes who fell at the Alamo, Duncan survived his stay in San Antonio. He seemed indestructible as we forged on through the eastern part of Texas, and because he was in such good humor, I enjoyed the trip more than I had expected. I was being treated with unusual courtesy, even, dare I say, affection, and I suddenly realized why. Empowered through my knowledge of what was to come, my usual martyred air had been missing. Duncan had happy wife, happy life, and a mistress thrown in for good measure. He was grateful for my compliance, and I was content to comply. Knowing that his come-uppance was imminent, I could cheerfully put up with my role of dog's body.

But as gator signs started to appear at the side of the highway and we drove on stilted roads where twisted pines rose ghost-like from the surrounding water, my nerves began to fail me. We had reached bayou country, and by the time we crossed the Sabine River into Louisiana, my confidence was at an all-time low. How could I pull it off? How could I bear the torrent of vitriol that would be hurled at me when I produced the unpaid membership bill? How could I break the mold that had been set over forty-five years of marriage? I trembled at the thought.

I passed the next day in a daze. Oblivious to the charm of the plantations on the Great River Road, I was dimly aware that in reaching New Orleans, I had already crossed the Mississippi and was still as much of a wimp as ever. Feeling miserable, I stayed at our campsite in the French Quarter, organizing dinner with George and Debbie, while Duncan took Lucy for a jaunt into town. However, by the time they had been gone for five hours, I had stopped feeling miserable and was just plain annoyed. When they finally returned, having toured the fourteen spectacular dining rooms at Antoine's and dined on Oysters Rockefeller, deep-fried crab, and meringues with chocolate sauce, my nerve was back. And once I saw the glittering leprechaun jewelry that Duncan had bought for Lucy at a tourist trap on Bourbon Street, my resolve had hardened. The die was cast.

Come morning, I made Duncan a tasty cheese omelet, generously spiced with Emeril Bam and ground-up Viagra extracted from the vial in his kit. After breakfast, we set off from our site in the French Quarter and walked to the Café du Monde for coffee. Then we headed for the river to buy tickets for our tour. In honor of St. Patrick's Day, the Natchez was playing Irish melodies on its steam organ, so we boarded to "I'm Looking Over a Four-leafed Clover" and tapped our toes to "The Irish Washerwoman" as we stood on the top deck and watched the boat gliding away from shore. The deck was swarming with day-trippers while the tour guide delivered her spiel, but once she had finished, the crowds thinned. It was getting cold and Lucy was already making noises about warming up in the saloon where the jazz pianist was performing, so I couldn't wait too long. Then, suddenly my opportunity came. Debbie and Lucy announced their intention of finding a washroom. George, Duncan and I were left alone on the deck.

I steeled myself to open my handbag and "discover" the re-newal letter, but as I reached for the clasp and slowly released it, I looked up. The steam organ was playing an Irish lullaby and a blissful smile had enveloped Duncan's face. He put his arm around my shoulders and looked down indulgently.

"Are you having a good time, dear?" he asked.

And I couldn't go through with it. The purse snapped shut. The moment had passed.

When we set off from New Orleans the next morning, I was suffering from mingled emotions: depression over my inability to act and hope that Duncan's tender gesture meant that his affair with Lucy was only a temporary fling. My ambivalence must have showed, because Duncan lapsed into irritability again, and it was under an uneasy truce that we continued the trip. Once again, we crossed the river—one more strike against my for-tuneteller—and traversed the State of Mississippi in a day. Next, was a lightning hop through Alabama, into Florida and on to Key West. The next month passed quickly, as we took in the historic and cultural sights of the east coast before heading into Canada to visit George and Debbie's relatives in Toronto. By the time we reached Sarnia and came back across the bridge into Michigan, we were all tired. Duncan's temper became shorter, and my regret for my failure on the Natchez grew stronger.

The next day we crossed the Mackinac Bridge, seemingly floating across a mass of deep turquoise blue, with Lake Huron on our right and Lake Michigan on our left. Soon afterwards, we turned onto Highway 2 for the final trek home. As we proceeded through Wisconsin and into Minnesota, the state signs started to become a blur. We were either travelling or camping, and my life had returned to a routine of drudgery: cooking, cleaning and laundry, whatever it took to keep the wagon train going. Duncan continued to snap and my spirits continued to decline.

The next morning, Duncan decided we should visit a tourist site only slightly off our route. It was a murky wet morning. We set off early, and after a dreary forty-minute drive, we reached a vast wooded area with lots of trails. The information booth was closed, but surrounded by plaques and a map of trails to the lake at the park's center. Duncan meticulously studied these while the rest of us stood about, freezing in the damp air. Having absorbed his fill, Duncan herded us down a nearby path until we reached the lake. Adjacent to the edge was a row of rocks, over which flowed a little brook that streamed off through the trees. A log was placed over it for those who wished to cross. I was lost in gloom, and failed to see why the others were taking such delight in fording the baby river, so I lingered behind as they went across.

Duncan and Lucy set off on the path on the other side of the water, but George and Debbie came back to wait with me. They were being kind, but I felt nettled by their sympathetic glances—after all, it was their relative who was turning my marriage upside down—and my irritation grew as our wait by the brook became more and more protracted. Finally, after what seemed an eternity, we heard voices. The others were returning. Duncan's rumbling bass did not project quite as clearly as Lucy's clipped soprano, but there was no mistaking the tenor of the conversation.

Duncan obviously had not realized we were still waiting by the brook and overhearing every word.

"Don't worry," he said, "I've hired a cutthroat lawyer, but we have to maintain a low profile so that I can demonstrate that the trip was a last-ditch attempt to work things out. Mary's a pushover, anyway. With any luck, I can shunt her off onto our daughter in Kelowna and not sell the house at all."

It was the last straw. All the resentment of forty-five years of oppression surged to the fore, and I snapped. As they emerged from the bushes, I stepped carefully across the log, which was slippery from the rain, and then stormed up to Duncan on the other side of the stream.

"How dare you!" I cried. "After all the years I've pandered to your every whim, raised your children, looked after your home, toiled through your accounts, and made your life such a cushy cakewalk that you've never had to lift a finger to do anything you didn't want to do! You may think you have a cutthroat lawyer. Well, I'm going to find one that has razors growing out of her fingernails, toenails, kneecaps and eyebrows, and between us, we're going to slice you and your assets into so many little pieces your brain will look like a jigsaw puzzle."

I finished by delivering a stinging slap to his face; then, ignoring his bellow of rage, I turned and stalked back to the stream. I stepped towards the log; then I froze as I heard a choking noise behind me. I turned back. Duncan's eyes were bulging and his face was a bizarre shade of purple. He was struggling with the pocket of the sleeveless vest inside his jacket. Finally, he succeeded in pulling out his nitro spray.

And in that moment, I had an epiphany.

I had been trained as a nurse, taught to heal, not to destroy. It wasn't in my nature to cause harm. Duncan didn't need to die in order for me to gain my self-respect.

"No, wait!" I cried, rushing forward and seizing the spray.

Lucy's eyes blazed.

"What are you doing?" she shrieked. She snatched the spray from my hand, shoved me away, and turning to Duncan, blasted the nitro into his open mouth.

Duncan's bulging eyes glazed and rolled upward. Then he crumpled into an ungainly heap at Lucy's feet.

Once the paramedics had come and gone, and the police had assessed the situation, I was treated with a great deal of sympathy: the betrayed but forgiving wife who, finding out belatedly about her husband's illicit medication, had tried to save him, but failed. Lucy seemed stunned for the remainder of the trip. George and Debbie were mortified, and were falling over themselves trying to make up for the trials I had suffered.

I, on the other hand, was feeling better by the minute. I was free to move on. The husband who had paralyzed my will was no longer there. I could mourn the loss of what had been good—minimal, in retrospect, now that my head was clearing—and be glad to be free of what was not. And as for my self-esteem, it had been restored the moment I told Duncan what I thought of him. It had nothing to do with fate and fortuneteller's predictions. I had simply found the courage to stand up for myself.

On the remaining trip along Highway 2, I joined George and Debbie on their sightseeing excursions. Lucy had gone on ahead, and it rather looked as if her plans of settling near her sister had changed. But my good-natured neighbors were kind and supportive, and as we strolled around Rugby, the pretty little town at the geographic center of North America, George suddenly smiled and turned to me.

"You know, there was a moment in New Orleans that I thought you had figured out what was going on," he said. "It was on the Natchez. There was a look on your face that I'd never seen before. But then, Duncan put his arm around you and it faded away. Funny that it occurred again when we were in Itasca Park."

I blinked. I didn't understand what he was getting at. Seeing my puzzled frown, George continued.

"It was when you marched across that log and laid into Duncan. It was such a strange coincidence, seeing that expression again in that particular spot."

"Why?" I asked. "What's so special about Itasca Park?"

"You didn't read the signs by the information booth?"

"No. What about them?"

"We were at the headwaters of the same river we were on in New Orleans."

It was my turn for my eyes to bulge.

"Headwaters?" I was flabbergasted. "That tiny little stream?"

George nodded.

"Yes," he said, "fascinating, wasn't it? That's why we wanted to stop there. It's the one spot in North America where you can step across the Mississippi."

FAT MOTHER

DAMYANTI BISWAS

Having reached her new workplace, Fei Ma throws up as discreetly as possible, not far from the tabby cat curled up at the car park. She hurls out bile and water. She has not eaten breakfast, yet her stomach won't let her get to the washroom. The morning breeze from Singapore's east coast carries away her grunts, her coughs, the acrid smell.

She reaches into her old black van to grab tissue, but at the sight of the pushed-back passenger seat, returns to her hacking again. Her dumpy, rolling frame, dry-heaves. That tabby she's been feeding leftover chicken pieces for the last week remains asleep.

Once her breathing calms, she rinses her mouth using her plastic water bottle, pops in a few breath mints and combs her thinning salt-and-pepper hair. Her first appointment won't start for another hour, but she must look neat even as she lays out the towels, straightens the massage beds, and restocks the changing gowns.

She slams the van door shut, using more force than necessary. The van has been an albatross, but she couldn't do without it. At any rate, she needn't set eyes on it again till the end of the day, and that is something. End of the day. That's when she will think about her errands, her shopping list for the evening, last night's events. *Not before*, she whispers to herself. Nothing before, because that would be out of the ordinary.

Relax Oasis, the shop sign says in large, arty letters—very different from the signs of twenty years ago when Fei Ma joined the original branch at Raffles Avenue as a masseuse. Her stomach now cramps, but this is not nerves. Her body has been invaded too far for her to be able to send the enemy back across the border now. Ignoring the discomfort, she smooths her hands over her T-shirt and heads over to the changing room, picking up her crisp, lilac cotton uniform on the way.

The receptionist gives Fei Ma a practised porcelain-doll smile, and the wide-eyed Maneki-neko beckons an additional welcome with its swinging plastic paw. The owners have spent thousands of dollars decorating the place in sleek lines, chrome and beige, reflected through concealed lighting. Only the garish-yellow Maneki-neko and the old Chinese music playing like birdsong over the tiny speakers in each room before the clients come in, betray the salon's working-class roots. Fei Ma enjoys this one hour of music meant for the therapists—that's what the masseuses are called. The pianos start their wailing afterward, and she hates that. Today though, the familiar strains of pipa take her back to the music she plays in her van. She gulps air. She mustn't think of the van.

She has to get through this one day. A day of nine one-hour massages—more than her usual, because some of her regular clients from the last branch where she worked have followed her here. No one has fingers as strong, or hands as soft as Fei Ma, they say. She's worth the extra drive.

"You late, ah," Fei Ma's birdlike supervisor says, her dyed hair and lipstick the same shade of purple, her stringy-veined hands at her hips.

Fei Ma is not late, but she does not argue because she can do without added scrutiny, today of all days. Her new colleagues have gathered in the changing area. Other than two middle-aged women she has worked with in other branches of the outlet before, they're all strangers to her. She nods to everyone, answers their good-natured queries about breakfast with an unwavering, and what she hopes looks like a genuine smile. They're like pink and purple magpies, these women in their ironed, body-fitted, Chinese collared uniforms, nodding and preening, exchanging stories of staying awake with a child who had the flu, what they packed in the school tiffin, the plans for tuition ferrying for the evening. She does not need stories. Not those particular stories. Must avoid them at all cost. Drawing a curtain about her, she changes into her uniform and practises her smile. Her first client for the day is a white woman, one Fei Ma calls the American.

The American always books an aromatherapy massage. Fei Ma knows enough English to be able to list the names of massages and their benefits, even some of the names she finds difficult to say, like aromatherapy. To pronounce it, she pretends she's chewing on large pork knuckles.

The American walks in, her blonde hair stuck in a ratty hair-band and her face blotchy without make-up. Fei Ma smiles at the giant of a woman, wishes her a bright good morning and hands her a robe to change into. She's glad she worked on her smile, because the American seems to expect it from absolutely everyone, and definitely from her masseuse.

"How's your day," the American says upon her return to the common area in her robe. Her booming voice matches her size, and Fei Ma knows this is not a question, merely an invitation to ask about things the American wants to speak about.

"How's work?" Fei Ma fills one of the salon's fake stone plastic basins with warm water. Work is a reliable topic that keeps the American talking.

"Not bad." The American places her well-manicured claws on Fei Ma's shoulders before dipping her toes in the basin. She gingerly puts in her entire foot, and finally lowers herself into the chair. "But you know what they say. A woman's work is never done."

Kneeling, Fei Ma adds shampoo to the water, rubs the American's foot with a light brush, and places a towel on her hip so the American can present her feet to be dried. She wipes the American's feet, who has been booming away in the meanwhile, telling Fei Ma, and everyone within hearing distance, about her boss, who doesn't allow her enough hours of work-from-home. Fei Ma nods, makes a sympathetic face, and lets the American slip her feet into fluffy slippers. It is exhausting to be nice, today of all days.

The American follows her into the massage room and shrugs off her robe without waiting for Fei Ma to leave the way some of the other clients do. The American is unconcerned about who sees her body, and lies prone on the massage bed, butt pointing in air, barely covered by a flimsy, ridiculous pair of pink disposable panties. Fei Ma lays a large towel along the length of the American's large, toned body, and responds with *yes*, and *sure* to every line spoken by the American, her voice muffled by the way her head is positioned over the bed's face cradle.

The woman's shoulders are muscular from years of Pilates, and as soon as Fei Ma starts kneading, circling, stroking with her oiled palms, she moans, "Oh that's so good!"

Bodies do not lie. In their animal honesty they tell you more about a person than he or she might want you to know. The American's shoulders are stiff as a backrest and even without her constant chatter, Fei Ma recognizes that the American is stressed to breaking—her body needs soothing, its kinks straightened out or they might cause her to splinter. For all her muscles, the American's body is not at its best. Fei Ma knows all about muscles— hers have been trained with years of lifting an almost full-grown body from bed to wheelchair, and wheelchair to car seat.

"Mark is away on one of his business trips again, and I have to look after the boys alone. Soccer, taekwondo, piano, and to top it all my helper isn't here. These boys have almost as much to do as a corporate manager, and they eat like an entire football team."

Fei Ma's body stiffens at the direction the monologue has

taken. She doesn't want to hear about sons, not about how sons need to be fed. Spoons and feeding tubes come to mind, when she fought to keep an inert body alive. The triumph she felt when she managed to feed one meal without mishap or at the suck of lips, at her nipples for the first months, then her fingers over the years, but it is too early in the massage to ask the American to please be quiet, relax, just enjoy the massage. Prone as she is, the American feels entitled to her space and comfort, which she is paying for, and for her twangy whining, which she is not.

"Jax has a taekwondo class at six in the morning, then soccer practice at seven-thirty, and the drive between both is a good twenty minutes. Then school and his endless projects. When he returns from school, he goes for his violin lessons. He's fourteen and can take a cab alone, but his dad won't hear of it. At this rate we'll need a driver just for him, Fei Ma."

The American pronounces her name as *Feema*, but Fei Ma doesn't correct her. She got her name decades ago when she fell pregnant and remained thin as a stick other than her middle. Her colleagues took to calling her Fei Ma, to encourage her entire body to put on weight, so she'd become Fei Ma in truth, a Fat Mother. No one even knows her original name now. Fei Ma tries to tune out the American's voice, the antics of her off-spring, and focus completely on her knuckles and forearms as they knead the muscles on the American's shoulders, draws a stroke along the spine, keeping the pressure even. She doesn't have to worry about pressing too hard, so she punishes the woman for bringing up her sons. The American sighs in pleasure, and Fei Ma restrains herself from pouring all of her devastation into her hands.

The scented oil makes the journey smooth, not too slippery, and Fei Ma breathes in long and deep, taking in the scents layered over days: bodies, perfumes, cleaning fluid. She catches a putrid note beneath it all, and braces herself, returning to the loud singsong as the American addresses the massage room floor.

"And they fight so much. Jax and Yosh are forever snatching

and growling. Soon they will be bigger than me. God help me then."

Fei Ma can't help picturing Yosh and Jax, like grinning apes gambolling about, filled with obscene health. They'll never have been near a wheelchair, nor needed feeding tubes, worn their diapers only till they were toilet-trained. Thighs, legs and feet done, Fei Ma asks the American to turn over, and covers her again with the towel, removing it only from the areas she plans to work on first: the clavicle and the shoulders. She places a heated, lavender scented pad over the American's eyes. It is filled with flaxseed. The seeds slide as she adjusts it.

"We need to be quiet for this to work," she says, because behind her indulgent smile she's filled with an almost irrepressible urge to lean with her forearm on the woman's throat, and her hand on the woman's nose. She's done it before, with all the steel and softness in her heart. Pictures of her hand holding a pillow rush to her, and she closes her eyes against them for a second. They persist. They live on the inside of her eyes now. She did what she had to do, because without her, he would suffer. For years, perhaps. She does not hear the other, gagging sounds, the rattle of a frail, painfully familiar body struggling to breathe, because in the now where she stands, there are these other noises her client makes: sighing, exclaiming, "So good," as Fei Ma kneads the area knotted with tension, above the towel-covered breasts.

Fei Ma puts a drop of oil on her palm and starts on the arms next when the door softly opens and her supervisor beckons her out into the corridor.

"Your phone squealing for last ten minutes so I must open your locker. Why you never put it on silent, ah?"

Fei Ma wants to go check her phone. Maybe it has already begun. Someone reported her. How did they find out? She says sorry and scurries back to the American, who has fallen asleep. Soft, purring snores fill the room. Her mouth hangs open, drool at her lips.

When the massage is done, Fei Ma lets the American doze while she gathers the oils and the towels. She wakes her groggy client gently, helps her sit up and hands her a warm, sweet ginger drink. Doles out the usual advice to drink lots of warm water. She suffers through a clammy hug, and sees off the American. She has fifteen minutes until her next appointment. On other days, she gets herself a drink of water and visits the toilet during the break, but today she heads straight to her locker.

For a moment, she stares at her phone lying among her folded clothes and her bags, as if expecting it to sting like a scorpion hidden in the dark. She doesn't want to, but she must check who called. She needs to make plans, or not. Maybe they will come and pick her up. Singaporean law is famous, with good reason.

She switches it on, and checks the number. Her oncologist's office. What fresh hell do they want to talk to her about? She considers not calling them back, but recalls her instruction to herself: do nothing out of the ordinary. Not responding to them would only make them contact her again and again. She can't call them from inside the salon, though, so she steps out.

At the parking lot, she dials the number, and waits. Not far from her, a family disembarks from a grey van the same model as hers. From the boot, the father pulls out a wheelchair, unfolds it, and takes it to the passenger seat. Fei Ma turns away. The call goes unanswered, so she is about to head back towards the salon when it rings again. Her hello is answered by a harried, breathless woman's voice.

"Ms. Ng, is that you? I've been trying to call you!"

"Yes." Fei Ma tries to keep her voice even because the tabby has decided to brush itself around her bare legs. Its fur tickles, sending shivers through her, but she does not move away.

"We're very sorry, Ms. Ng, there was a mix-up."

"Mix-up?" Fei Ma half-listens as she watches the tabby, which now sits leaning against her leg, cleaning its paws carefully.

"I would like to tell you in person, but it is better I also tell you beforehand on the phone."

"Yes?" Fei Ma doesn't want to say too many words, because the last time she'd spoken to this hospital, things hadn't gone well.

"The reports got mixed up. One of the new interns printed the wrong results with your details."

Fei Ma stands between the wall and a dustbin on the other side from the salon, to make sure none of her colleagues will spot her. From here, she can't see the van, nor the sea, nor the line of trees in the distance. Just the wall, herself, the words on the phone that don't make any sense. And the tabby, which has followed and decided to sprawl down right next to her feet.

"Are you there?" The female voice sounds scared now.

"Yes."

"You have stomach ulcers, Mrs. Ng. Nothing serious. You don't have to worry about your son any longer. If you stop by, we can fill up a prescription for you. Really very sorry about the confusion. The hospital would like to apologize to you in person."

She tries to reply, but there were no words.

"Are you there, Ms. Ng?"

She makes an incoherent sound, and clears her throat.

"We're really sorry, Ms Ng. I know you must have been under a lot of stress lately. Please think of this as a chance, a beautiful second chance at life."

Fei Ma sinks to her knees, and when her thighs give up, she lets her uniformed butt touch the pavement. The cat nuzzles her, but she pushes it away, unseeing. She leans on the dustbin, and tries to calm her breath. Nausea hits her for the second time that morning. Is she still a mother? She stopped being a wife so long ago—one day she was a wife, and then she was not. Did she stop being a mother exactly the same way?

She startles at a touch on her shoulders. The supervisor has found her.

"What are you doing here? Your client is here early."

"I'm sorry." The words come out before Fei Ma can stop them. Of course she is sorry, but not about where she is sitting.

"You look like death, and your dress is stained. Go change

into a fresh uniform. I've asked the receptionist to take care of your client till you are ready. Use the back door."

Fei Ma nods and escapes. If only all escapes were this easy.

In the toilet, she changes into a clean uniform, forcing her arms through its starched sleeves. She tries to pull the dress down and gets it stuck over her head, turning her world dark, smothering her for a moment. She holds herself like that till she can't breathe, but can't stop herself tearing through the top of her uniform in a desperate bid for air. It rips right under her armpit, and she swallows in a loud, shaky breath. The body does not lie. Hers wants to live despite what she has done. When she was diagnosed, she'd not been afraid for herself, or so she'd thought. Maybe she'd refused to see it—that she cared more about living than the one she was supposedly living for.

She won't think about the van, or the wheelchair or the boy who sat on it. Her boy. Flesh of her flesh. Torn from her body seventeen years ago, a body separate from hers that would not talk, nor walk, but whose eyes and grunts and moans followed her everywhere. She understood when a moan meant she had to readjust him on the wheelchair, when a sigh told her he was hungry, or his cries informed her he needed changing.

She closes her eyes, but now there are sounds besides the images. His voice. His smile, twisted a little to one side, his protruding forehead, his ears sticking out like on a baby monkey. The boy she chose over everyone is right in front of her. She sinks to the toilet floor, and lets the wracking sobs take her body, defuse the explosion building within. The tile is cool beneath her hands.

Outside the toilet, her supervisor calls to her, voice rising by the minute, but she doesn't respond. She's alone now, no enemy to eat her up from the inside—or at least not swallow her up completely—and no one to sigh or wail for her attention. She is alone. There are no chances now, and she wants none. She takes a deep breath, only to smell the detergent, the air freshener, and faint, far beneath it all, the lingering traces of the fumes meant to be removed.

Now that she won't be joining him any time soon, there is no need to keep it to herself. The police will give her son a far better funeral than she ever could with all the money she has set aside for this.

She grips the phone and dials 999 to turn herself in. When a gruff voice answers, she makes a report in a calm, unwavering voice, and gives them her home address and tells them her present location, so they can pick her up. She never wants to sit in that van again.

THE HONOR THIEF
MARTHA REED

The tires screeched and I turned to see a pimped-out Crown Vic sweeping up to the curb. So it was happening. Two gorillas I had never seen before clambered out of the illegally tinted car. The bigger thug grabbed me around the waist. He tossed me into the back seat, pointed his stubby finger and said: "Sit." Neither one of them said another word until we reached Manny's park-like estate in Jamaica Plain.

Now I sat perched on a surprisingly uncomfortable mahogany Chippendale chair in Manny "Big Toad" Toducci's private office. The room smelled like fine Cuban cigars and lemon oil polish, the scent of power. The antique chair's central supporting rail kept cutting sharply into the back of my thighs. Ignoring the discomfort, I focused on re-buttoning my blouse.

"She's clean," Thing One said. He tossed me my bag.

Manny nodded curtly. The big goon crossed his arms and went to stand by the door. Manny sat back, drumming the tooled leather blotter with his fingers.

"We got a problem. Your brother Stefan died owing me big money."

I settled the bag between my feet. That's why Manny's goons had snatched me off Boylston Street. Manny Toducci was Boston's most ruthless and untouchable crime boss. He managed Combat

Zone prostitution rings, ran numbers rackets and kept high-dollar book. He owned an empire of backroom pawnshops and usurious drive-through check cashing kiosks that took criminal advantage of desperately struggling people. I was a part-time art school student, and I knew Manny by reputation only. Maybe my brother Stefan was dead; but with Manny and money, next-of-kin meant next in line. I had to press my knees to keep them from knocking together. Taking a deep breath, I decided to try for bold.

"Guess that means you won't get paid."

"Ha!" Manny barked a laugh. "Figures. Smart-ass, just like your brother." He waggled his hand. "I'll get paid. Stefan had sticky fingers. Pretty good at working the five-finger discount, but craps was not his game." He moistened his lips. "Your brother died owing me ninety-seven thousand dollars, plus change. Congratulations, girlie. You just inherited his debt."

Oh, Stefan. Black dots pulsed before my eyes when I heard the actual number. I laid both hands on Manny's desk. "Listen. We'll never be able to pay you back that kind of money. Never. I'm supporting my mother and my two sisters. We live in a crappy basement apartment near Fenway Park, ankle deep in backsplash half the time. I'm working three jobs now as it is."

Manny stared unblinking as he toyed with a Napoleonic bronze eagle paperweight. "Not my problem."

I considered bolting for the door. Thing One guessed my intent. Opening his jacket, he flashed his holstered 9mm Glock. Even if I sprinted past him, I'd never make it through Manny's Black Ops home security system. He had his McMansion, his two-acre landscaped lawn and his gated driveway wired up like a maximum-security Federal prison, which in my humble opinion was exactly where the Big Toad really belonged.

Manny picked up a tablet, swiping his fingers over the screen. "Zita Zeechee? What the hell kinda name is that?"

And this was coming from a man named Toad.

"Central European, probably Czech." I shrugged. "The

borders got confused a couple of times between the wars."

"Z-t-s-c-h-e-s-c-h-e?" He glanced up. "Is that really how you spell it? Fuck. Bet Immigration had some fun with that. Did they say *gesundheit*?"

"Funny guy." I folded my hands in my lap. "We didn't care how they spelled it as long as they let us in."

"Funny girl." He sat back. "You should try stand-up comedy. Earn me back my money that way."

"Is that an option?"

"No."

He kept scrolling through that damn tablet. I didn't know what Manny was reading there, but Stefan had warned me that if I was ever in this situation to ignore him, that it was a bluff, that Manny did it on purpose to rattle people. I ran my eyes over his opulent office instead.

No wonder the Toad's security system was so impossibly tight. His rumored art collection was mythic, but members of the general public were never allowed in to see it. I was only in Manny's inner sanctum because of my brother's outstanding debt. Stefan had mentioned seeing some important looking paintings on the walls, but I hadn't believed him. Now I noted a Vermeer, one of only thirty-four Vermeers in existence, next to Rembrandt's only known seascape hanging in a gilded frame behind Manny's desk. Mellow afternoon sunlight filtered through a jeweled Louis Comfort Tiffany stained-glass panel featuring boughs of lavender wisteria draped over opalescent water lilies floating in an emerald pool. A golden imperial Faberge egg glittered on a marble pedestal under a single canister light. Botticelli's *David*, cast in solid sterling silver, shone from a scallop-shaped alcove.

"Did you kill my brother?" I asked. I already knew the answer was no, because I'd found Stefan's note. Stefan wrote that he owed Manny a lot of money, that he felt like a failure, that suicide was the only way out. I was still furious with Stefan for even thinking that way after all we'd been through. Stefan was wrong. Suicide is never an option. Case in point. It only makes things worse.

"Me?" Manny looked up. "Nah. Stefan wasn't no good to me dead. Your brother wasn't pushed; he jumped. Even the cops are saying it. He took the coward's way out." His chair cracked as he rested his weight on his elbows. "What we really need to discuss is how you're going to pay me back. Luckily, your family's good-looking enough to work the street." He pursed his lips. "That's a bonus I didn't expect."

"I'm not dancing in one of your clubs if that's what you're thinking." I choked on the words. "Shoot me now. I refuse. I won't do it."

He seemed to consider my suggestion.

"Wouldn't work. You're tall enough, but too flat-chested. We'd have to invest in a bigger cup size. Besides, I wasn't talking about you." Manny sat back. His shirt gaped open to reveal wiry hair growing in a straight line up his pale potbelly. "I was thinking more about your two sisters. We've never had twin strippers in the club before. That's something fresh, something different." Opening the humidor, he selected a cigar. "My clients will like it."

I slapped Manny's desk so hard it stung my hand. Thing One flinched.

"Stasia and Iris," I hissed, "are only fourteen years old."

"That's okay." Manny shrugged. "It's a private club." He snipped the end off the cigar. "The more I think about the idea the more I like it."

"You can't do that." I scrambled to find another option. "Give me time to come up with another way, with something else."

"Sure." He chuckled. "Like you've suddenly got a hundred grand you're sitting on, tucked away, hidden. Must be driving a lot of Uber in that piece of shit Hyundai you own."

Fingers of raw fear clutched my belly, like the sick feeling you get when you wake up in February with a cold nose and you know that the furnace has crapped out again and you'll need to find the money to make the repair. Now I really felt frightened, because Manny seemed to know way more about me than I'd figured.

"Stefan mentioned you were working on a degree." Flicking a gold lighter, Manny lit the cigar. "Art history, right?"

"That's right." I inhaled a slow deep breath as butterflies battered my stomach. Sometimes my darling brother talked too much.

"Why waste your time?" Manny stretched out his arms. "What'll it get you? Look at me. Got some of the best art in the world right here. Didn't need to study art to appreciate it or to own it, neither." He jabbed the cigar for emphasis. "Earn the money and buy the art you like. That's the smart way to go about it."

Leaning forward, I rested my elbows on my knees. "You're saying that you bought all of the artwork in here?"

"No, I'm saying that I own all of it." His cheeks hollowed as he puffed. "Not exactly the same thing, but close enough."

"Funny thing, because unless my art history prof is wrong, that Tiffany window was stolen from the Griffin family crypt in Cleveland's Lake View Cemetery in 1983." Turning sideways, I pointed. "*The Concert* by Vermeer and Rembrandt's *The Storm on the Sea of Galilee* were snatched during the Isabella Gardner Museum heist in 1990. That Botticelli statue is Nazi loot stolen from the Basilica of San Frediano in Lucca, Italy, in 1944." Straightening to face him, I felt no need to mention the Cherub with Chariot Faberge egg swiped from the George M. Hensley Museum during Hurricane Katrina in 2005. That egg alone was worth fifteen million dollars. "Not to be too critical, Big Toad, but I'd say that technically none of this artwork really belongs to you."

"Smart girl." Manny tipped the silken gray ash off his cigar. "You've been paying attention in class. You get a gold star. I may need to find another use for you."

There was a sudden hubbub from the hallway and a drumming on the door. Thing One reached for his Glock.

"Don't be stupid." Lowering the cigar, Manny swiveled his

chair to face the door before carefully placing both hands in plain sight. "Until we see who it is."

The heavy oak door swung open, followed rapidly by Thing Two, who was tripping over his heels as he backed into the room.

"Couldn't stop 'em, boss. They got a warrant."

FBI Special Agent Cesar Mayas and three beefy associates I didn't know filled the doorway. I felt the tension ease from between my shoulder blades and it surprised me, because I'd never been happy to see that solid hunk of G-man before. Cesar's brown eyes glittered with triumph and righteous amusement. He extended the folded bench warrant in his outstretched left hand.

"Manny Toducci, wish I could say it's good to see you again. Brought you a little something extra this time. Been a long time coming."

Snatching my bag, I scrambled behind the carved marble pedestal, moving out of the direct line of fire because I didn't know exactly how stupid Manny really was. The two men kept their eyes locked on each other as Cesar cocked his thumb at the paintings lining the walls.

"Emmanuel Lorenzo Toducci, you're under arrest. I'm charging you with receiving stolen property under federal statute 18 USCA, Section 662."

I jumped as Manny pointed at me.

"You little snitch!" He spat. "I'll make sure they skin you alive before you die!"

Cesar calmly snicked his tongue against his teeth. "And thank you for that. USCA Section 1512, witness intimidation. Keep it coming, Manny. I'd love to add more to this list." He slid the warrant across Manny's blotter with his fingertips. "And just so you know, anything happens to this woman or her family, whether you're involved in it or not, we'll be coming for you. And that means you'll get life without parole. You're already looking at five-to-ten in the Sumterville pen. Hope you like

Florida weather. It can get humid."

Taking one hesitant step toward the door, I swung my bag to my shoulder, my mouth suddenly bone dry. "I loved my brother." My voice quavered and cracked. "You pushed him to suicide." I clenched both fists. "You threatened my family. You needed to be stopped."

"Easy, Zita," Cesar said. "Take a breath." Draping his heavy arm across my shoulders, he guided me outside as his fibbie associates cuffed the three goons. "Let's get some air."

I had forgotten that it was a normal spring day, well, as normal as a day can be with four black Suburbans and three Boston blue squad cars parked at the front door.

"You did good with this one, kid," Cesar said. "The Bureau appreciates your assistance, and your expertise. Like we told you, we knew they'd come for you eventually, and they did. And that in there took real guts." His brown eyes warmed. "I knew you could do it. We've been trying to get inside Big Toad's office to ID his artwork for years."

Slipping my fingers into the frayed lining of my bag, I placed the bug in the center of my palm. "That big goon didn't look hard enough. Got distracted studying my bra. Did you want this back?"

"I do, actually. Inventory will ask for it. Thanks." Wrapping the wire in his royal blue silk pocket square, he tucked it away. "Manny's going down hard for this one, Zita. We had to be careful, walk the line on probable cause. Couldn't give him any chance to wiggle out of it in court. He hires top-notch lawyers." Cesar looked up, and his face split into a wide smile. "Never thought we'd crack it. And there's a silver lining. You're going to be rich. The Gardner Museum is still offering a reward for the return of those paintings."

Hope flared in my heart like the sound of a distant and welcome train whistle. "Don't tease, Agent Mayas. It hurts too much. I heard the museum cancelled that reward."

"You heard wrong." He tugged his ear. "They extended it. And they raised it to ten million dollars, if the paintings are returned in good condition. I'm no expert, but they looked to be in pretty good condition to me."

Cesar grabbed my arm to steady me as I missed a step. Swinging my bag over my other shoulder for balance, I clutched the iron railing with both hands. "Ten million dollars? And the money is mine?"

"It's all yours." He laughed easily. "See? Crime does pay." He studied me carefully for a moment. "I didn't want to mention it before in case you got flustered. Someone from the Bureau will be in touch to make sure you get it. I'm sure you'll be hearing from the tax guy, too." He glanced reflexively up and down the shaded street. "Need a lift back to town?"

"No, I'm good." I tapped my iPhone. "I've Uber'd a ride. Two-minute warning. He's on his way."

"Alright then." Cesar's forehead puckered. "You be careful out there, Zita. And don't worry about what Manny threatened. He's blowing smoke. They'll close his book and leave your family alone. They've got bigger fish to fry." He scratched his chin. "You've got my number, though, right? Promise you'll call me if you need to, okay?"

"I will." I felt genuine and humble gratitude welling up from my soul. "Thank you, Agent Mayas, for all that you've done for me, and my family. This means a lot to us, to get this cleared up. To clear my brother's name. To clear his memory."

"It wasn't for revenge though, right? It's done. We don't want to make any more trouble."

"No." I gave it some thought. "It's done. It was more like... justice."

"Good. I can live with justice. Here comes your ride."

A dinged-up, rusted-out beater Sonata puttered through the security gate, rolling up the driveway and navigating around the obstacle parked cars. Just like any gentleman would, Cesar opened the rear door and I slid in. He shut the door firmly and I waved the nice FBI special agent goodbye. "221 Buswell Street,

Kenmore Square."

"Like I don't know that." A pair of hazel eyes studied me in the rearview mirror, identical to mine. His new spiky blonde haircut still shocked me. "So, Double Z? How'd it go?"

"You're a free man, Stefan. They bought it. They all think you're dead."

Spinning the steering wheel with the heel of his right hand, we returned to the street. "You're the best, Zee. Truly. I owe you big."

"True. But you were right." I dug through my bag to check on things. "Manny had that house wired tight. Infrared cameras, heat-sensors, pressure pads under the oriental rugs, invisible key laser ports. It was a good plan, using your debt to get me in there. I never would've made it into his office, otherwise."

"But *you* contacted the FBI and suggested they use you to take Manny out." Stefan happily tapped the wheel with his fingertips. "Brilliant! And the reward money from the museum we talked about? What's up with that?"

"It's still ten million dollars. I pretended I didn't know about it." Tipping my head back against the seat, I closed my eyes for a beat. My blood sugar level was somewhere down below my knees. "Agent Mayas said the fibbies will help me claim it."

"Excellent." Stefan paused. "And you'll take care of Mom and the twins, right? When I'm...gone?"

"Of course, I will. I always do." Making my final decision, I reached back into my bag, feeling very sorry for my poor, desperate, and terminally unlucky brother. Stefan was so bright, so engaging, but he was always chasing after the easy money the wrong way and placing his trust in the wrong people. "I have something else. A surprise for you."

"Really, Zee?" He smiled his goofy crooked smile, the smile I remembered from our childhood, that dumb innocent smile etched forever in my heart "What is it?"

We cleared the overhanging canopy of leafed-out maples. Sunlight streamed into the car, fracturing against the slim lines of the colorless D class baguette diamonds set into the peerless layers of guilloche enamel I held in my hands. Hundreds of miniature rainbows danced across the Sonata's ceiling like the reflections from a spinning mirrored disco ball. Peter Karl Faberge had truly been an artist of staggering and monumental genius.

"What is it, you ask?" Reaching over the front seat, I dropped the imperial Easter egg into Stefan's lap. "It's your second chance."

MARRIED SEEKING MARRIED
LUCY BURDETTE

I was startled awake by a text. Even my tiger cat Evinrude, who is always up first, was still sleeping. I grabbed my phone from the nightstand and squinted at the screen. The message was from my ex's secretary, Deena Smith, and it was five-thirty.

Must talk asap. Any chance of coffee this morning?

Puzzling, because we were friendly, but not ICE-friendly—In case of emergency. Deena and I had recovered from our initial awkwardness after Chad dumped me. Her boss—aka Chad Lutz the putz—had the busiest divorce practice on the island of Key West. After my whole dumping drama had played out, Deena told me his new girlfriend had paraded in and out of the office for weeks *before* Chad kicked me and my cat and my stuff out of his apartment to the curb. Putz. Now I lived with my darling detective husband on Houseboat Row and couldn't be happier.

My friendship with Deena was the one of three good things that came from my spontaneous but ill-considered move to Chad's place in Key West. One, once I realized that I'd dodged a bullet rather than taking one, I could stay friends with Deena while avoiding her employer. Two was that I'd fallen in love with the island even after Chad showed himself to be the biggest loser. Three years had gone by, and my life had gotten happier.

That was the third thing. Much happier.

She wasn't one for hysterics, so I agreed to the coffee, dressed quickly in gym clothes, and fed the pets, musing over what could be bothering her. From time to time, one or the other of us would call to check in or make a date for lunch or coffee. But she certainly wouldn't call at five-thirty in the morning to schedule a routine coffee and gossip date. And we'd caught up on the normal stuff last week when we'd had lunch.

Chad Lutz. He took all the nastiest and most expensive cases—no thoughtful mediation for this crowd—and he couldn't have managed without Deena's calm presence in the front office. And organization. And writing skills. I zipped across town on my scooter and parked in front of Ana's Cuban Café. I had enough time for a quick coffee with Deena before my appointment at the gym. She had to be pretty worried about something. Plus, I was curious.

"Oh, Hayley. Thanks for meeting on short notice." Deena looked harried and a bit pale, sitting at one of the picnic tables on the porch with two cups in from of her. She slid one across the table to me. "I didn't know who else to reach out to."

"Are you okay?"

"Yeah, I guess. But listen." She ran her fingers through her dark curls and took a sip of coffee. "Of course, I can't name names," she said, "but one of our clients is angry to the point that I'm worried about what he might do."

"Whoa. Like what?" I asked, blowing on the top of my café con leche. The rich fragrance woke me right up. Key West prided itself on good coffee, and Ana's was darned good.

"Before I say another word, understand that it's too early to go to the police. Even Nathan." Her large brown eyes were pleading. "Promise?"

"Promise," I said, though I kept two fingers crossed behind my back. Nathan was a detective in the Key West Police Department and my new husband. Like I said, much, much happier. He was not a fan of me getting involved in solving mysteries. Even if they appeared to be innocuous domestic matters.

She gave a quick nod. "Thanks for understanding. You know that I'm used to handling angry people. It comes with the territory. Chad calls me vice president in charge of difficult people." She gave a chuckle that sounded raspy and forced. "It's not that unusual for our clients to threaten their spouses and anyone else they think is responsible for the divorce proceedings. But they're red hot angry in that moment, and I understand that perfectly." She narrowed her eyes at me. "You've been through a bad break up so you know what I mean. But this feels different."

She paused, nibbling on her bottom lip. I waited her out. I learned that technique from my psychologist friend Eric—if you don't rush in to fill the quiet spaces in a conversation with your own blathering, you learn a lot more about what's in the other guy's mind.

"Can you say a little more?"

"In some ways, it's the same old story. His wife cheated on him and he was shocked to find this out and even more shocked when she moved out. That hit him right in his tender ego. And now this guy—let's call him Harry—wants revenge. He's got a decent settlement pending, giving him most of their money and half of both houses, and he only has to pay a pittance of alimony for a short time span. But every outgoing penny sticks in his craw. And he's generalized it so that each time he's in the office he rants at me about how all women are cheating bitches. He hates women, end of story. I don't know if he even realizes I *am* one!"

So far, this sounded super unpleasant, but I couldn't figure why she wanted me involved.

"And so?" My coffee was finally cool enough to take a welcome slug.

"He came in yesterday to sign a stack of papers, and when I was straightening up after, I found this. It must have fallen out of his briefcase." She handed over a small white card that read: *Married Seeking Married. Attractive, safe man (and with hon-*

orable reasons!) looking for companion for friendship and intimacy. Someday your prince might come, but I'm here all week. Visit my website and we'll take it from there!

I squinted and read it again. *Married seeking married.* What possible honorable reasons could there be? *Looking for companion for friendship and intimacy.* Wasn't that the point of marrying someone in the first place?

"Yikes. Disgusting. But—besides the gross factor—why are you worried?"

"I have a very bad feeling," Deena said. "He's angry enough to lash out. He's actually said threatening things about his wife, and we had to talk him down. I was hoping you could check out this website and let me know if I should do something, like tell Chad or alert the cops or something. Chad is a demon about protecting our clients' privacy, so he'd kill me if he thought I was snooping. Please?"

My phone alarm beeped telling me I was late for the gym. "He's only married in the technical sense right now," I said, gathering my stuff. "So I suppose he can do whatever he wants. But I'll take a look. It's probably nothing to worry about, just one more kinky Key West kook. Don't worry, okay? And you're such a good person."

She nodded, looking glum and unconvinced. "Thanks. Let me know, okay?"

I snagged my favorite treadmill to warm up before the weight work started, waving at Leigh who was working with a slim woman who could hold a plank for what seemed like hours. This gym was tiny, and you had to hire a trainer to come. Once it was my turn to lift and squat and burn under Leigh's direction, I listened with half an ear as the conversation between other trainers and clients eddied around me. And I mulled over the card and Deena's strong reaction. First of all, Deena didn't rattle easily. She'd seen a lot of nasty exchanges between angry people, and from my perspective, she'd always been able to shrug that stuff off. I trusted her intuition.

Then I thought about my own reaction to the card. It wasn't like I hadn't seen weird stuff from weird people before. Especially during this week's Key West Fantasy Fest celebration, they flaunted themselves naked on Duval Street, well, naked except for body paint and colored beads and maybe a tiny sling on the private-est of privates. Last year, "Adam and Eve" joined our local costume parade, Eve dressed in absolutely nothing but a fig leaf. She sashayed right up Fleming Street and posed for photos as if she didn't realize she was stark bare naked, as my grandmother used to say. Fantasy Fest, which was kind of a New Orleans-style Mardi Gras on steroids, brought out all of these crazies and more. This year the theme was fairy tales, and Duval Street was already teeming with demented, scantily clothed Cinderellas and Maleficents.

Maybe I hadn't been married long enough to feel jaded and bored—and honestly I couldn't picture getting to that stage. So the card's message kind of shocked me. I struggled up from my final wall squat to head home.

"See you next time!" I hollered to Leigh. I trotted out of the gym, and drove my scooter several blocks across First Street, to Houseboat Row. I let Evinrude the gray tiger cat and Ziggy the min-pin out of the cabin and sat on the deck with my computer and a big glass of water. I could not resist looking up the website printed on the card.

The page was slow to load, and simple to the point of amateurish—pink with a daisy border. Inside the border were these words in fancy script: "Hello! Maybe you're as lonely in your marriage as I've been in mine. I'm not looking to break up a happy couple or steal you from your husband, but I'm missing that important spark. And tenderness. Maybe you are too? Let's write a second act together! Would love to meet for drinks, conversation, maybe more, no strings attached. Bring a sense of humor but leave the drama home. You can be my Sleeping Beauty and I will be your prince. Come in costume and we'll see what's behind the closet door. You'll know me by my azure blue eyes and handsome beard, which I must admit women find compelling. Men instantly realize they have met their equal." He signed his invitation "Your prince is waiting."

Kind of sick, really. He sure didn't lack self-esteem. What kind of person would post an ad like that? And who in the world would respond? It wasn't even well written. I should know; I had become the go-to expert in copyediting at *Key Zest* magazine, where I worked as the food critic. Everyone ran their copy by my eagle eye before it went live—with a tweak here and there, I seemed to have a knack for making even a dog of a story sound desirable. I made a copy of *Married Seeking Married's* page and began to slash at it with a virtual red pen.

Focus on the strengths of the opening, I always told my colleagues. *Prince* was all over the place. What did he really want? Tenderness? No strings? A good laugh? Sex of course.

My dear octogenarian friend and former housemate Miss Gloria trotted down the length of our dock from the parking lot, holding up a white paper sack. "Join me for a cup of tea and a cookie?" she asked. "Key West Cakes has a special this week on fairytale character sugar cookies. I put dibs on the Seven Dwarfs."

"I'll be right over," I said. *Dwarves,* I wondered? Always the editor.

Once we had our tea and cookies in front of us with a dog biscuit for Ziggy and dried salmon bits for the cats, I showed her the card. "What do you think?"

"Oh pull-ease," she said, tweaking her short white hair so it stood up in little peaks. "I would love to give this asshat a piece of my mind. I know I've told you this a hundred times, Hayley Snow: Marriage isn't like a sparkler—light it once and watch the sparks whirl and arc for the duration. You have to make your own excitement as the years stretch on. It takes effort. And dedication. Sometimes if you act tender, the real feelings follow." Her eyes narrowed. "Why are you looking at this card?"

Hmm. How to describe this without breaking confidentiality.

Just tell the bare facts—she wouldn't press me. I explained that a friend was worried about how an enraged client might act out. "I don't get the whole concept. Either you're married or you're not, or that's what I thought."

"That approach definitely makes life simpler," said Miss Gloria.

She tapped the edge of the computer we were studying. "I suppose you looked this dude up?"

I nodded and smiled—she knew me well. I read the prince's invitation aloud. "He wants to meet potential dates at the Time-Out bar near the waterfront. He said he'd be at the bar between five and seven wearing tall boots and a hat with a feather."

"I wonder if we oughtn't to go over there and keep a lookout for unsuspecting Sleeping Beauties tonight?"

At quarter to five, we settled at a table for two that had a good view of the length of the bar and ordered glasses of the white swill advertised as the house chardonnay. As the waitress delivered our drinks, a man dressed a bit like Puss in Boots, only hairier, took the seat at the far end of the bar. He wore an embroidered coat that swung to his knees, above knee-high socks and boots, all topped by a wide-brimmed hat with a long white feather flowing off the back. I understood now his comment about facial hair—his beard was bushy—the kind that made me wonder how many crumbs were stored there—and dyed a deep blue. He appeared to be telling the bartender that the seat beside him would soon be taken.

"He's not dressed like any prince I've ever seen. I think he fancies himself a modern-day Bluebeard," I said.

Miss Gloria's eyebrows peaked in alarm. "The dude who killed multiple wives before somebody finally got on to him? What in the world do you think he has in mind?"

"My question exactly," I said.

I typed "Bluebeard" into the Google search icon on my

phone and clicked on a link that surfaced at the top of the page. I read the first paragraph to Miss Gloria. "Bluebeard was renowned for his unattractive facial hair, and yet he managed to snag several wives. No one seemed to wonder why they all disappeared, until the newest wife discovered the corpses of the earlier spouses in a blood-spattered room."

"Oh, dear," she said. "Not very subtle."

"And kinda scary, right?" Maybe Deena's instincts were correct.

We watched as a woman approached and took the stool next to Bluebeard. She wore a full yellow skirt topped by a tight blue bodice with a white collar, and a red bow in her blonde hair that matched her red slippers. She settled an apple with one bite missing on the bar next to her drink and smiled dreamily at the man.

"I'm getting this sinking feeling that he looks very familiar," I said. "I could swear this same man who—well, let's see."

I'd almost blown my promise of confidentiality. But I really thought this was the guy who'd come hurtling out the door ahead of Deena when I'd met her outside her office for lunch last Wednesday. The beard hadn't been blue, but it had the same bushy shape. And the expression on the face above the beard had been furious.

"I was thinking the same thing about Snow White," she said. "It's hard to tell in the costume and the make-up, but the hair and body shape look like Serena's."

Serena was the daughter of one of Miss G's substitute mahjong players, and she was embroiled in nasty divorce proceedings following her husband's infidelity. I knew this because Miss Gloria had heard the blow by blow every week for the last few months and reported all the details to me. Serena was apparently in the ugly stage where she couldn't see outside her own rage. Where no punishment would be severe enough to hurt her husband the way he'd hurt her and her family.

"Is *that* Serena's husband?" I asked.

"No," said Miss Gloria.

"Married seeking married," I muttered. "A second act..."

We watched in silence for fifteen or twenty minutes, sipping our wine and trying not to look obvious.

"Oh my word!" my friend said, at the same time I said: "You've got to be kidding me!"

"I swear he dropped something in her drink," Miss Gloria whispered.

"Yes, I saw it too! But—I could swear I saw *her* put something in *his*!" We stared at each other, and then back at the couple. They'd roofied *each other*? Only in Key West. But this was serious.

"I'm calling nine-one-one." I grabbed my phone and dialed. "And then I'm calling Nathan." We rushed over to the couple at the bar.

"Excuse me?" I began. What if Miss Gloria and I were wrong?

But then Snow White wobbled on her stool, and tumbled to the floor. Bluebeard stood up as if to leave, but staggered into the wall.

"I don't feel so good," said the woman in a slurred voice. "This good-for-nothing, two-timing bastard must have slipped me a roofie."

"She had that coming because she's a cheating bitch," said the Bluebeard, "exactly like my ex." And then he collapsed in a limp heap beside her, clunking his head on the metal foot rail as he went down.

Soon the bar was bustling with Key West's finest EMT Fire Department personnel. I explained what we suspected to be a double poisoning, or drugging anyway. As the costumed characters were carried off on gurneys, the long white feather fell off Bluebeard's hat and drifted down to the pavement. I was about to go pick it up when my husband, Detective Nathan Bransford, appeared in the doorway—every inch of his six-foot-two muscular self-tensed with worry. He relaxed a bit when he saw Miss

Gloria and me, alive and well.

He sat down at our table with a combination of mostly horror and the tiniest bit of amusement on his face. "This has got to be a doozy," he said. "Start from the beginning and tell me everything."

I explained about the coffee date with Deena and pulled the *Married Seeking Married* card out of my pocket to hand over to him. It wasn't breaking my promise to Deena—since he was my husband, I could tell him anything. And he was a cop, so he had other ways to investigate.

Nathan's eyes widened as he took the card and studied its contents. "And, honey? You were drawn to this because...? At least you didn't dress up and try to investigate on your own."

I'd thought about it, I admit, but I'd never tell my dear husband that.

"Honest to goodness, it felt so wrong," I said. "So creepy, and cheesy. And ugly. Deena asked me to check it out, and then I figured Miss Gloria could explain it." Which sounded completely lame even if it was true.

"Hayley somehow has the idea that I'm the expert on married people." Miss Gloria grinned. "And I guess I am. Frank and I had half a century of mostly good times before I lost him. But when we saw that guy with that ugly blue beard, and her with that make-believe poisoned apple—well, that was about as Brothers Grimm as you can get. And I do mean grim."

"He's gonna need more than a divorce lawyer now," I said, and tried to look sincerely dismayed. "Poor Chad. He hates to lose clients to the competition."

As I heard the sound of the ambulance sirens fading away, my cheap wine somehow tasted better, Not that I needed revenge on Lutz the Putz, but even in fairy tales, the bad guys get their comeuppance.

I couldn't wait to tell Deena. And couldn't wait to hear her boss's reaction.

Miss Gloria's stomach rumbled and she hooked her arm

through mine. "Ready to roll? I'm famished."

I leaned over to kiss my husband's cheek. "I've got a seafood gumbo in the crockpot for when you get home." I turned back to him and winked on the way out. "Don't worry, Detective, the only married man I'm seeking is you. And I cannot wait for tonight's happy ending."

TO CATCH A THIEF OR TWO
SHARON BADER

Saturday, April 19
2:25:09 a.m.

Claudio Ruggio, the night security guard at the Dell'Arte Museo in Florence, Italy, stepped back to admire the painting that he had just hung in the Art Nouveau gallery. The painting was his best work yet, a reproduction—a fake, he knew some would crudely say—of Gustav Albaugh's *Lady in Love.* He savored the moment, then touched the tips of his gathered fingers to his lips and blew a kiss toward the portrait. A dark-haired beauty with a provocative smile and gowned in blue velvet. He picked up the original Albaugh, newly released from its ornate frame, and ignoring his creeping arthritis and growing shortness of breath—*it was nothing*—he hurried down the dingy hallway to his cramped, but private, office in a repurposed section of an old kitchen.

2:30:00 a.m.

Claudio placed the *Lady* inside a padded black portfolio that sat on a shelf in the dumbwaiter at the back of his office, then sent it creaking upstairs to the apartment where he lived, the museum's traditional perk for an art lover willing enough to take the job as night guard. Claudio, a retired patrol officer, seemed perfect for the job. Sitting at his computer, he accessed the tape recording of his activity in the gallery for the previous hour. Deleted it. And inserted the carefully-timed sixty-minute clip of an empty night-time gallery in its place. He sat back in his chair and analyzed his artistry. In a click, nothing had happened in the Art Nouveau gallery. The split-screen images on the monitor for the past hour now showed no movement in any of the four Museo galleries. Exactly as they normally would.

The switch of the Albaugh was not all he'd erased. Over the last hour, Claudio had removed all of the stiff metal clips that held the stretcher frames of the targeted artwork to their ornate frames. All in preparation for *il furto*, the heist, scheduled for tomorrow. Because of Claudio's advance planning, il furto would now take no more than twenty minutes. He'd pass along news of the change later in the morning.

A twenty-minute tape switch would start shortly at 2:40:00 a.m., a test run to make sure it worked seamlessly tomorrow. Simultaneously, any gallery movement would record to a flash drive. No matter what happened in the gallery, the tape would look like the place had been empty. And video of the theft would record to a flash drive. Tomorrow had to be successful.

2:40:00 a.m.

Perfect! The tape switched over exactly on time and the blinking light on the flash drive showed it was recording. Claudio relaxed in his swivel chair, the monitor showing no one anywhere in the Museo. An unexpected sound from inside the Modern Art gallery startled him. He switched the monitor view to the real-life recording on the back-up flash drive. Claudio could clearly see a figure. Shadowy, stealthy, keeping to the edges. Claudio's heart raced. He grabbed his flashlight. Touched the taser on his wide black belt. *No one should be here. Not now. Not now.*

Claudio moved soundlessly. He braced himself against the wall at the end of hallway. Heart pounding, he peered into the gallery. Someone—*what?*—dressed and masked in black held a flashlight between chin and shoulder while balancing an ornate frame upright on the floor. An unzipped portfolio laid open near the thief's feet. A second black-clad thief knelt on the floor working the Albaugh reproduction out of the frame.

"What are you doing?" Claudio's indignation erupted in hoarse gasps, then a coughing fit.

The thieves paused in their work, then laughed. "What are you going to do, old man? Pummel us with your fists?" The words came from the standing thief, a woman all in black. He recognized the voice of the Museo Director, Annamaria Fannucci. Even in the dim lights of the gallery, he recognized the mane of dark hair, her sharp shoulders, her authoritative stance as she held the heavy frame. As she spoke, her partner popped the painting from its ornate frame and set it with care between layers of foam in the portfolio.

2:57:19 a.m.

The black void inside Claudio's head was thicker than the darkness in the gallery where his body lay crumpled on the marble floor. He felt stiff and immobile, but his head spun wildly, dancing its own tarantella. Alarm sparked in his gut and his head bobbed up. Pain throbbed behind his right ear, but he forced wobbly legs into a crouch, then struggled to stand.

Claudio lurched toward the fire alarm on the wall nearest him and pulled down its lever. He felt less dizzy now. And more furious. Inside the Museo, alarm bells wailed. Red and yellow lights flashed garishly over the walls and reflected wildly off the polished marble floors.

"Stop!" Claudio demanded, hearing the fear in his own voice. This was real, and it could not be happening. "What are you doing! This is not what—"

The man in black froze where he knelt in front of the Mucha exhibit. "Go!" he growled to Annamaria, as he grabbed the portfolio's plastic handles.

Annamaria, hair flying, ran to the heavy exit door on the far side of the gallery and pulled it wide open. Moonlight illuminated vertical metal rods that barred the exit, spaced at narrow intervals within the door frame. A wire mesh screen, fitted flat against the bars on the outside, was sliced open raggedly between the middle rods. She slipped easily between the bars and through the ruptured mesh, then reached a black-clad arm back into the gallery. "Hand me the case, Armando."

"Oh, no, you don't, mia dolce. The case stays with me."

"You don't trust me?" She paused, as the alarms clanged. Polizia sirens, high-pitched and urgent, wailed in the distance.

"Hurry!" Annamaria's voice pitched higher. She turned to Claudio. "And you keep quiet. Or we'll kill you, old man."

Claudio, feeling helpless, stood with his jaw hanging open as he watched Armando suck in a deep breath and squeeze his angular frame between the vertical bars. The oversized portfolio dangled from his gloved left hand.

Claudio needed to stop them. Needed to do something. But he couldn't think what—

He heard Armando's grunt of rage, as the man's black-suited torso melded into the darkness of the night. He pulled the portfolio behind him, but it twisted and flattened against the bars. As he yanked the portfolio to the outside, his glove snagged on a ragged edge of the mesh screen.

The sirens screamed closer.

Hurry, Claudio thought. But what would he tell the officers? They'd ask for the video.

And none of this would be on it.

Armando swore, tearing at the wire mesh screen. He yanked

furiously at his glove and the portfolio. The handle on the case snapped, and three stolen masterpieces tumbled onto the polished gallery floor. Armando's bare hand reached through the mesh at floor level, scrabbled to the nearest painting, an early Mucha, and eased it outside. His fingers then tugged at the Wyspianski portrait, flipped it right-side-up and pulled it toward the door.

The third painting, his Albaugh, had skittered across the marble floor and stopped near Claudio, still huddled in terror.

The Polizia would be through the front door at any moment. With the toe of his shoe, he slid his reproduction back toward Armando.

Two thieves and three paintings melted into the night.

Claudio hurried to his office, befuddled and terrified. The real Albaugh masterpiece was safe until he could sneak it away, but the sirens—and the authorities—would arrive in a heartbeat. Claudio closed the video editing program, then ejected the flash drive and tucked it into a waistline pocket in his trousers. He returned to the hallway and collapsed against the wall beneath the fire alarm, head in hands, grateful for the chance to sit and slow his breathing.

"Claudio?" He looked up to see Maggiore Luigi Fontina, Claudio's colleague in the Carabinieri Art Squad. "This secret assignment after your heart attack may not have been as safe as we thought it would be."

8:30 a.m. Sunday, the next morning

The next morning Claudio dangled his legs over the side of the hospital bed, then rubbed the back of his head. He slid his tray of uneaten breakfast aside when two burly men, dressed in neat gray suits, entered the cramped room.

"The doctor says you are out of danger and we can talk to you now," the bigger one said. "Do you feel ready to answer a few questions?"

Claudio winced, nodding his head.

"I'm Capitano Georgio Patregnani of the Carabinieri TPC. The Art Squad." Keeping his gaze on Claudio, he tipped his balding head in the direction of the man standing next to him. "And this gentleman is Maggiore Luigi Fontina."

Claudio barely lifted his eyelids to acknowledge Fontina, who took a seat at the foot of the bed, then nodded to Patregnani.

Patregnani pulled out a small notepad and a stubby pencil. "They hit you pretty hard, Claudio. I'm amazed you made your way to the fire alarm."

"I'm amazed myself. But when I saw the two of them pulling artwork out of their frames…"

"Two of them? Are you sure there were two thieves?"

Claudio's face opened in surprise and he moaned with the movement. "Didn't you look at the security tape?"

"There's nothing on the tape that shows any activity until just after the Polizia arrived. Had you come into the gallery during the theft?"

"I'm not sure. The taping—it is always broken. The gallery knows this. And maybe I—was there a flash drive?"

Patregiani shook his head.

Claudio took a deep breath. Winced. "The last thing I remember is sitting at my desk. My office is just off the Art Nouveau gallery, but…" He searched for the words. "Sorry. My head."

"Take your time, Mr. Ruggio." Patregnani eased his bulk onto a chair opposite Claudio, then scrawled on his notepad. "We know the security system has its problems, but it does show you making your way into the gallery minutes before the Polizia arrive."

"Yes, I awoke after that knock on my head and heard voices. I was still groggy. That's when I saw them. Removing a Mucha from its frame and setting it in an artist's portfolio."

"Any other details you can give me about the thieves, Mr. Ruggio? Height? Body build? Facial features?"

"They were dressed completely in black. Masks on their faces.

But one had a mustache."

"You saw a mustache through a mask?"

"Half masks—that left their mouths uncovered." Claudio shrugged. His hands turned palms-side up and moved out from his chest.

"Anything else you remember?"

"That mustache guy was tall, more muscular than the other fella." Claudio focused on Patregnani while he thought back to his last view of the crime scene before the Emergency Team put him on a gurney and whisked him to the hospital: three gilded frames and an unzipped artist's portfolio scattered on the floor and one large black glove snagged on the ragged-edged security mesh. "That's all I remember."

Patregnani scribbled some more, then stood and stuffed his notepad into an inside pocket of his gray jacket. It pulled taut across his shoulders. He should lose fifty pounds, Claudio thought. Why did il nostro Colonnello, our Colonel, allow this officious man to be on duty?

"Thank you, Mr. Ruggio. I'm sure we'll be talking with you again."

The door to Claudio's room opened partway and Annamaria poked her head through. "Oh, Carabinieri! I don't mean to interrupt. I'm here to pick up Claudio."

"Not to worry, Director Fannucci," Patregnani said. "We are just leaving, but I would like a quick word with you."

Annamaria stepped back into the hallway and Patregnani nodded to Claudio, then eased out the open door.

Fontina, whose only contributions to the questioning had been the frequent bubbles he blew from the wad of gum in his mouth, extended an open hand to Claudio. "Thanks for your help, Mr. Ruggio. Let us know if you remember anything more." Under his breath and with a head tilt toward Patregnani, he added, "A new transfer. Trying to prove himself."

Claudio shook the carabiniere's hand. And pressed the flash drive into it. "My pleasure, Luigi."

Annamaria passed Fontina in the doorway as he left. She hurried into the room, leaned toward Claudio and whispered. "We've got to talk. I need to know what you've told them."

Claudio's throat tightened. "Not here. Not now."

"In the car then. I'll take you home."

9:30 a.m.

Within half an hour, Annamaria had pulled her Audi to the curb in front of Claudio's hospital wheelchair. Claudio let his anger spike as he climbed, gingerly, into the front seat.

"Let's get one thing straight. I did not agree to getting a concussion from your 'mere tap on the head.' That's what you said and then I was supposed to lie on the floor until you left. And it was supposed to be *tomorrow*." Claudio snapped the seat belt closed and turned toward Annamaria, a scowl slashing a thin line across his pale face.

"Get a grip, Claudio. You'll have another heart attack if you don't calm down. Besides, I didn't hit you on the head. Armando did."

"And who is *Armando*? This was supposed to be a two-person job. You getting the artwork out of the building. Me editing the security video. *Tomorrow.*"

Annamaria turned on the ignition but sat gripping and ungripping the steering wheel, her knuckles alternately pulsing pink and white. "Yes, I am...sorry. I let information about the job slip while we were making love. He threatened to go to the Carabinieri if I didn't cut him in. And do it tonight instead."

"That was stupid of you!"

"I know. I know. But I thought his size and his strength could help if we ran into a problem."

"Didn't you take his brain into consideration?" Claudio wanted his frustration to billow, to overflow with exasperation, but fatigue settled in and his voice dropped to a mellow baritone.

"You were supposed to keep it simple. Fooling the Carabinieri should be easy. The idiots can't tell a Matisse from an Andy Warhol."

Annamaria shrugged. "Well, it's done now. We'll make the best of the situation. I've already contacted the fence you suggested in Milan."

"Alright. Get me home, would you? My head is pounding. And while you're driving, tell me what you told the Carabinieri."

Claudio listened, riveted, eyes closed. She told him about the call from the Polizia that had jangled her cell phone as she drove home after the theft. She'd arrived at the Museo, looking frumpy and tousled as if newly awakened, after dumping the black catsuit at her apartment. She met the Emergency Medical Team near the front entrance of the Museo as they wheeled Claudio out and she identified him as the nighttime security guard.

"Then what happened?" So far, so good.

Annamaria continued with the details. Claudio analyzed each moment, each word. Looking for holes. Carabinieri and Polizia in Claudio's office viewing the security video; evidence hanging from the mesh screen, photographed in place and removed. Questions about the outdated security system. Identification of the stolen artwork. The Mucha. The Wyspianski. The Albaugh.

Priceless. Irreplaceable.

Gone.

Eleven months later

Dusk settled like an indigo veil over the city of Florence. Pink, orange and lavender fingers of cloud floated low on the horizon and Claudio, sitting in an upholstered chair by the window in his fourth-floor hospital room, looked out over the city. He picked out the dome of the Santa Maria del Fiore cathedral, and was inspired again with the perfect symmetry of Giotto's bell tower. He spotted the Ponte Vecchio bridge over the Arno River.

Dr. Renato Feretti swept into the room and closed the door with a light kick, shutting out the voices of medical personnel and visitors in the hallway. He stood behind Claudio's chair at the window. "Beautiful, isn't it?" he said. In those few quiet moments, Claudio suspected that the doctor's news would be a somber reminder that the precipice between life and death may be nearer than he hoped.

Feretti turned away from the window, a smile dimpling his face. "I've looked at your X-rays and CT scan, Claudio. Your lungs look clear and clean. There is a bit of damage—scar tissue—in the upper left lobe from the chemo. I want to see you again in three months—or sooner if that cough returns."

"Renato, I came here expecting to hear the worst but..." Claudio stood and threw an exuberant hug around the doctor. "I'd much rather see you later than sooner, but I will keep up with my scheduled appointments."

"Good man." Dr. Feretti rapped his knuckles twice on the windowsill. "Is that leave of absence you took from the Carabinieri Art Squad over the past six months going to be permanent, then?"

"I'm thinking seriously of that. I've put many good years into investigating stolen art, but I want to use the time that is left to me for some serious painting."

"Excellent! I'm impatient for that copy of *Salomé* you promised me." Feretti clasped Claudio's outstretched hand within both of his. "Ciao, my good friend."

Relieved by the doctor's good news and humming tango music, Claudio grabbed the Rome newspaper, la Repubblica, from the bottom of the bed. He read the lead story for the third time, then slapped the folded paper against his knee, bare below the bottom edge of his hospital gown. "Ha! Grazi a Dio."

The story pleased him. Armando Caruso, a known art thief, had been arrested for last year's theft of three masterpieces from the Dell'Arte Museo. In return for Caruso's freedom, two of the paintings were returned to the Museo and rehung with great ceremony in the Art Nouveau gallery. Caruso had disappeared. As had the third painting, a rare Albaugh.

The newspaper report concluded with a brief paragraph about Capitano Georgio Patregnani, a carabiniere specializing in modern art recovery. Patregnani had located the two paintings, but had demanded a cut of the proceeds, millions of lira, from the man fingered as the fence. That unnamed fence was actually a Carabinieri informant, who would soon testify in closed court against Patregnani.

All will be well, Claudio thought.

Two years later

Claudio leaned back in his cafe chair, then forward, squeezing his shoulder blades together. As he stretched, he scanned the classic colonnades and gardens of the Dell'Arte Museo across the street. The late afternoon sun, reflecting off the light-colored minerals in the sandstone walls, cast a pinkish aura around the building. This was the most ethereal time of day for Claudio, but his attention focused now on several gardeners removing the celebrated ivy cascading from the west wall of the Museo. In its summer fullness, it covered the wall in lush green. As it faded, gardeners had to remove the barren stems. It was almost a ritual. Ivy Day, they called it, a changing of the seasons.

Young women strolled by the open patio that fronted the cafe, dance bags in hand, slouchy cut-off sweats over black leotards and white tights, chattering and laughing as they walked to a nearby bus stop.

As he eased back into the discomfort of the metal chair and clasped his hands against his belly, Claudio caught snatches of a conversation beside him. Two young men with Neapolitan accents proclaiming their compliments to the young dancers.

Claudio paid them no mind. Indeed, his mind was on a woman, a forever-in-his-heart woman whom he had loved since his middle age when she first enchanted him with her cloud of dark hair and beautiful face. His beloved wife Sophia, so like the woman in Albaugh's *Lady in Love*. That portrait waited now at the Museo across the street. He traced on the tabletop the remembered graceful line of her neck as she peered over her shoulder at him—as in the painting—sensuous but innocent, arousing and beguiling. Her eyes, soft with love, so blue above the high cheekbones.

The sudden clatter of cafe chairs banging against each other shattered Claudio's reverie and a broad shadow darkened his tabletop. Bubble gum snapped.

Claudio looked up. Saw a familiar face. "Still trying to give up smoking, Maggiore Fontina?"

The young men beside Claudio, hearing Fontina's title and seeing his uniform, swept up their phones and sweatshirts and scurried from the patio.

"Still copying masterpieces, Claudio?"

"As often as I can."

Luigi Fontina laughed, softly, and pulled up a metal chair. He clasped Claudio's outstretched hand with both of his. "It's been a long time since you retired from the Art Squad. We miss you. No one loves the art as you do. How are you, my friend?"

Claudio smiled and returned his gaze to the four gardeners across the street. "Doctor Feretti gives me a month, perhaps less." Both men sat in silence for a while, observing the activity across the street. One of the gardeners, smaller than the others, wheeled a large garden cart close to the front end of the Museo wall and piled ivy debris into it.

"I got your email, Claudio," Fontina said. "You're expecting the Albaugh portrait that was stolen three years ago to turn up this afternoon at the Museo? Is this true?"

"As well as the second thief."

"Ah. But, Claudio, you know that *Lady in Love* was identified about two years ago in New York. Found in a private collection and returned to the Museo after Caruso's testimony."

Claudio grunted.

"Actually," Fontina continued, "and between us. The authentication process at the Dell'Arte proved that painting was a reproduction. A fake, but an excellent fake. Nevertheless, it was hung in the Museo with a lot of to-do and celebration. As if it was the original. And no mention about the failed authentication. No one wished to alarm the public, or disturb the fragile world of collectors."

"I understand," said Claudio. "There are reputations involved."

Silence fell between them. As if neither wanted to be the first to speak.

Luigi blew a large pink bubble, then sucked it in. Wrapped the gum in a tissue, put it in his pocket. "I examined the returned painting before they reframed it, you know. I saw your mark, that faint white squiggle, on the bottom left."

Claudio shook his head and a slow smile erased the fatigue in his face. "It's a long lean capital C, Luigi. Not a squiggle."

"Noted—for the future. So tell me what I don't know."

Claudio settled into the hard chair. "Sometimes I laugh about it. I know our goal was to catch Annamaria. And the Squad would make her confess to the other thefts she'd managed. But—then I had my idea. And that, I fear, was not part of our sting. I'd swapped out my reproduction of Albaugh's original painting just minutes earlier that Saturday morning, and then hid the original. Annamaria had no idea.

"Then, part two of my plan: I set up a practice run of il furto with the security video, swapping in a clip of a normally empty gallery while I recorded actual footage on a flash drive. I needed the video swap for il furto to be perfectly coded and timed. After the twenty-minute segment, real security footage would resume and the recording to the flash drive would end. That way, the only evidence of the crime would be on the flash drive. The next thing I know, I'm waking up on the gallery floor. Annamaria—and poor Armando—showed up twenty-four hours early!"

"Why would they do that?"

"Greed. I'd told Annamaria that I planned a practice run to make sure the video swap ran smoothly. This Armando apparently convinced her to take advantage of that, so she advanced her plan by one day. Without bothering to tell me." He shrugged. "Thieves."

"About the flash drive you gave me after il furto." Fontina raised a shaggy eyebrow. "I looked at that clip again the other day. Used our newer tech stuff. Seems it's about a couple minutes shy of your twenty minutes."

"Ah. I was afraid you'd catch that edit someday. Yes. The missing video shows the third painting, my reproduction, slide across the floor—and me sliding it back to Armando." Claudio rested his hand on Luigi's coat sleeve and smiled. "My plan demanded that not only the thieves but also the Carabinieri—including you, my friend—thought the real Albaugh had been stolen."

"I see," Fontina said softly. "And you have it?"

Claudio sat forward in his chair. Hands outstretched, entreating. "I wanted the *Lady* for myself, you see. She reminded me of my Sophia. So beautiful. So...perfect. My poor reproduction never filled me with as much longing as the original painting."

Fontina sighed. "So. Now. You have emailed me. That it was urgent. That I meet you now, just before sunset in my uniform—not my usual everyday clothes."

"Ah. Of course. The email. A few months ago I came across a newspaper picture of Annamaria. At a small gallery opening in New York. And of course, she was not trying to hide, but her name, in the caption—it was an alias. So I contacted her to say that I'd come to regret stealing the original Albaugh—and I do regret it—and that I planned to return the painting to the Museo, where it belongs. Seems she hadn't yet realized that she'd stolen a fake."

"Ah, the world of art." Fontina took a square of gum from his pocket. Left it wrapped. "So much more than paintings are fakes. Go on."

"When she asked about my plan, I told her I planned to leave the Albaugh in a niche in the western wall of the Museo on Ivy Day. Just before sunset, I told her. It was sure to be found by the gardeners, and returned to its rightful place. And now—"

"That's today," Fontina said, looking at his watch, and then the sky. "Now."

Claudio nodded, tears welling in his eyes. He pointed toward the gardeners, his hand shaking. "See? That one pushing the cart toward the wall. The short one. That's Annamaria. She's about to retrieve the package from the niche where I left it."

Fontina had pulled out his phone and spoken rapidly into it while Claudio spoke. In seconds, he hung up. "Relax, Claudio. Two of those gardeners are my men," he said.

Claudio sat back in his chair with a deep exhale. "You'll find the real Albaugh in a padded portfolio wrapped in a green garbage bag that is tightly taped. It's time for *Lady in Love* to go home, dear colleague. And, I fear, time for me to leave this world as well. It's Ivy Day. The seasons are changing."

Fontina put the wrapped gum back into his pocket. "Claudio, my friend, it's been my privilege."

Standing, Fontina placed a hand on Claudio's shoulder.

Then Claudio, thinking of his Sophia, watched his colleague hurry across the busy street to save the *Lady in Love*.

LOVE'S LABOR
ALEXIA GORDON

*"If you ever get a second chance in life for something,
you've got to go all the way."*
—Lance Armstrong

Voicemail:
"My name is Eileen Almy, from Newport, Rhode Island. I'm looking for my lost love, Ned Clarke. I want a second chance."

Case submission form:
Your name: Eileen Almy
Lost Love's name: Ned Clarke
Relationship: First love
When/Where did you last meet? Twenty years ago/Newport, Rhode Island

Love's Labor's Found, Episode 178:
"Hello, sweeties, and welcome to another episode of *Love's Labor's Found*, the podcast about reuniting people with lost loved ones. I'm Rona Washington, your host. If this is your first

time tuning in, a special welcome to you, tender heart. Here's how things work: each case spans three episodes of the podcast. In part one, I interview the searcher; in part two, I update you on my progress toward finding the missing loved one; and in part three, you get to hear the happy reunion, broadcast live. We're close to our two hundredth episode; can you believe it? That's more than sixty reunions and sixty chances to start again.

"Today, I'm in Rhode Island to help Eileen, a woman who's been searching for her lost love for more than two decades. She desperately wants a second chance. Hello, Eileen."

"Hello, Rona. Thank you for taking my case."

"I'm a big believer in second chances, Eileen. We can't live our best lives if old wounds remain unhealed and old questions remain unanswered. Let's start with some background. Tell us about Ned and your relationship."

"I grew up with Ned, here in Newport. He's a year older than me. We started dating my freshman year of high school."

"You fell in love with the boy next door."

"Straight out of a romance novel, huh?"

"Take us ahead to the last day you saw Ned. What happened? How did it end?"

"It ended the way it began, in the water. There were seven of us: Bethany Tabor, my best friend; and her boyfriend, John Redwood; Patty Lyndon; and Isaac DeBlois, a boy she'd met at the start of summer; Ned and me; and…"

"Take your time, Eileen."

"And my kid brother, Stevie."

"The seven of you spent the day together?"

"Yeah. It was the last weekend before Ned went off to college. He was headed to Chicago, so we were having kind of a send-off celebration. Isaac—he only summered in Newport, so he wasn't part of our core group. We didn't know him until Patty brought him around. His parents owned a yacht, and they took us out sailing all morning. When we got back, we headed to

Van Zandt to swim off the pier there. We stayed until George Bruton and his buddies showed up. George and John hated each other. George and Bethany had gone out a few times, but he turned out to be a jerk and she dumped him. We didn't want to ruin Ned's last weekend with a fight, so we moved to the Elm Street pier. We swam until sunset, a quarter 'til eight, eight o'clock, maybe."

"This is difficult, Eileen. Would you like to stop?"

"No, thank you, Rona. I'm, um, I'm sorry. I'm okay. I want to tell the rest. We stayed at the Elm Street pier until sunset, then we went to the bridge."

"That big one, what's it called, the Pell Claiborne? You're laughing."

"I don't mean to. It's the Claiborne Pell. The Newport Bridge. No, not that one. We went to the Goat Island Connector."

"*Goat* Island?"

"A little island in the harbor. Locals used to graze their goats there, ages ago. Now, a luxury hotel and condos take up most of the space. But we didn't cross over to the island. We stopped at the opposite end of the bridge, where it passes the shipyard, next to the walkway down to the marina. John jumped first."

"Jumped? From the bridge?"

"Into the harbor. All the kids did it. Well, lots of us did it. Kind of a summer rite of passage, a test of courage. I jumped dozens of times, over the years, usually at Ned's insistence. He'd tease me, call me chicken, jump himself to show me how easy it was, that kind of thing. But I'd never done it at night. Until then, all my jumps had been during the day. But, that day, Ned's last weekend in town, we didn't want the fun to end. Ned thought of it first, dared us to jump in the dark...we were young and invincible, so we jumped. John, then Bethany, then Patty, then Isaac. Ned and I jumped together. Then—"

"Then?"

"Then Stevie. We all jumped."

159

* * *

Love's Labor's Found, Episode 179: Case Update:
"Hello, sweeties, welcome back to *Love's Labor's Found*, the podcast that reunites lost loves. This is part two of Eileen's search for Ned, her first love, who she last saw twenty years ago on a warm summer day in Newport, Rhode Island. If you're new to the show, a special welcome, tender heart. I'm glad you tuned in, but I recommend you pause this episode and go back and listen to part one, episode one-seventy-eight, first.

"If you're all caught up and eager for an update, I've got good news. It's much ado about something. I followed up on the information Eileen shared and, with help from my sweetheart sources, whose details I'll list in the episode's show notes, I found Ned. He lives in the Kansas City, Missouri area, where he works in the insurance industry. I spoke with him by phone and he agreed to let me air the recording.

"Greetings, Ned. I'm delighted to speak with you."

"Hello, Rona."

"We chatted by email and phone several times before recording this conversation, so you know who's been searching for you and why."

"Eileen Almy, my childhood sweetheart. Ha."

"What?"

"I'm surprised she remembered me, let alone wanted to see me again."

"What do you remember about Eileen?"

"Hmm. Her hair. I remember her gorgeous dark hair. And her eyes, a deep, chocolate brown you could lose yourself in for days."

"Beautiful memories, Ned. And how about the last time you saw her? Do you remember that day? Ned?"

"I don't like to remember the last day I *saw* her. I spent years actively trying to forget it, but…"

"But?"

"Hard to forget a kid's funeral, y'know. I prefer to remember the last day we spent together. It was one of the best days, up until the end. The bunch of us, sailing, swimming, running around town. Zero cares, zero worries. We enjoyed ourselves the way that only kids who believe they're going to live forever and that all's right with the world can. Then the day stopped being fun. Then, bam, like that, we grew up."

Love's Labor's Found, Episode 180, The Reunion, Audio Livestream:
"Welcome back, sweeties, to our one-hundred-eightieth episode. You're listening to *Love's Labor's Found*, the podcast that's all about second chances. If you listen regularly, you know this is part three of three in Eileen's search for Ned. You met Eileen in part one and Ned in part two and now, it's time to bring them together. If you're joining us for the first time, tender heart, ordinarily I'd advise you to go back and listen to the previous episodes before tuning in to this one. However, if you do that, you'll miss the excitement of a live broadcast. That's right, I'm audio livestreaming here in Newport, Rhode Island, waiting with Eileen for Ned to arrive, all the way from Kansas City. This episode will be recorded so you can listen to it later, but a replay can't match the excitement of being there as events unfold. So, grab a seat and a glass of whatever beverage makes you happy, and come along with me. That clacking sound you hear is my footsteps on Newport's, er, charmingly eccentric cobblestones. Eccentric, as in, not a level stone in sight. Ignore the occasional engine roar in the background. Extraneous noises are a livestreaming hazard. They're also one of the reminders in this town, like this basketball hoop in front of me, that we're in the twenty-first century, not the eighteenth.

"Let me set the scene for you, sweeties. Picture a pocket park, a charming bit of greenspace tucked under the trees along the edge of a stately residential neighborhood filled with houses that pre-date the founding of this nation. Look out at the harbor and see a lighthouse at the end of a little island, highlighted against the backdrop of a resort hotel. Beyond that, a majestic suspension bridge stretches to the horizon. Look the other way and see a smaller bridge, utilitarian instead of majestic, connecting the little island with its larger neighbor. See a shipyard, its gritty industrial quality a contrast to the glamor of the multimillion dollar boats it services. Walk to the foot of this little bridge and see a long, down-sloping wooden pier with a gabled gazebo at its far end. A ladder, fixed to a platform near the gazebo, descends into a channel of water between the pier and the bridge—a channel just wide enough to tempt daring teens who think the world is theirs to conquer.

"Walk back to the park, to a wrought iron bench with a view of the nearby street in one direction and the lighthouse in the other. A well-dressed woman sits, dark hair styled short, handbag in her lap, chocolate brown eyes filled with anticipation. Hello, Eileen."

"Hi, Rona."

"Eileen, you look nervous."

"Silly, huh? Gosh, I've known Ned my entire life. You wouldn't think I'd be anxious about meeting him again, but my heart's pounding louder than the waves in the harbor."

"That's your heart telling you it's ready to be whole again. And you're allowed to feel anxious. It's been two decades since you last saw Ned. You suffered a lot during those years. Anxiety is expected. Do you think he will have changed much?"

"I don't think so. I'm betting he'll be the same old Ned."

"We'll find out soon enough. He'll be here in a minute or two."

"Before he gets here, Rona, I want to thank you again. Thank you for this second chance."

"Here he comes. Sweeties, picture a tall man with a bit of salt-and-pepper at his temples, approaching from the street. He's well-dressed, too, in khakis and a collared shirt. Hello, Ned."

"Hi, Rona."

"You know who this is, of course."

"Hi, Eileen."

"Hello, Ned. It's been a while. Too long."

"Twenty years. Hard to believe."

"You still look good, Ned."

"How does Eileen look to you, Ned?"

"Like the same, sweet, beautiful girl I fell in love with, oh so long ago."

"I'm not quite the same, Ned. I'm not as sweet."

"Eileen! What's that? What are you doing?"

"Put the gun down, Eileen. Calm down and put the gun back in your bag."

"I'm calm, Ned."

"Eileen, please, do as he says."

"I'll handle this, Rona. Put the gun down, Eileen."

"You're still bossy, Ned. See, Rona, I told you he wouldn't have changed much."

"Eileen, are you insane? Have you lost your mind?"

"Actually, Ned, I'm quite sane. I did almost lose my mind with grief after you let my baby brother drown. I almost killed you then, at Stevie's funeral. Remember the commotion when my dad and Father Paul dragged me out of the nave? I'd grabbed a brass candlestick from the chapel and was coming after you. They sent me away for a while, after you'd left for Chicago. I had plenty of time to calm down."

"Eileen, please, I'm begging you. If you ever loved me—"

"You son of a—You killed my brother, and you had the nerve to come here to meet me, on a podcast, for chrissakes, because what? You thought I'd forgive you? Or that I'd forgotten what you did? That I wanted you back? Bastard."

"Oh, my God, no! Eileen, what did you do?"

"I shot Ned, Rona. Dead, I think."

"Ohmigod, ohmigod, ohmigod. How could you—"

"Do what I should have done years ago? Easy."

"No, please, Eileen, no, don't shoo—"

"To all you sweeties out in listener land, this is Eileen. I'm afraid *Love's Labor's Found* will be on hiatus after this episode. Rona's not, um, up to recording any more. Nothing to tune into next time. No more second chances. Those sirens you hear are coming my way, so I've got to go. If you enjoyed this episode of *Love's Labor's Found*, please leave a five-star rating and a review on your favorite podcast listening platform."

EVERYBODY'S GOT A COUSIN IN MIAMI
ALEX SEGURA

"You know anybody that can get me a passport right quick?"

Carlos gave his friend Hambar a quizzical look before taking a long sip of his Cuba Libre.

"What the fuck for, man?" Carlos asked. "And how quick?"

Hambar frowned.

"No sé, Carlito, but they need it fast." He looked away then turned back to Carlos. "They're coming in hot. Like, tonight. They need some kind of paper trail, you know?"

Now it was Carlos Trelles's turn to frown. He'd come to this shithole Keys bar—Lorelei's on Mile Marker 82—to avoid situations like this. Trouble. But he knew it was all gonna be sour when Hambar walked in. Hambar was trouble, whether he wanted to admit it or not.

"Who needs it?" Carlos said, lowering his voice. "And how much are they willing to pay?"

"You sure you wanna know, bro?" Hambar asked, giving Carlos a lingering sideways glance that said *after last time?*

"Wouldn't ask if I didn't," Carlos said. "Why?"

"No, nothing, Carlos—it's just, you fucked up big time on your last job. Wasn't sure if you were retired or what. I mean, didn't Pete Fernandez retire?"

Carlos shook his head.

"Fernandez? Fuck that guy. He had a kid and went soft, that's it," Carlos said. "More work for me."

"Right, right, but still, you messed up pretty bad on that delivery," Hambar said, looking at the bottles displayed behind the bar, unable to meet Carlos's eyes. "Word gets around, man. I can't believe you let that happen."

Carlos took another sip of his drink before responding.

"Tejedor had it coming to him, all right?" Carlos said. "He didn't pay what he said he would pay, so I did what I had to do."

"Bro, let's be serious—you dumped the guy's entire fucking supply in the Miami River, like it was no big deal," Hambar said, his words hissing out of his chapped lips. "Of course his bosses are gonna want payback. You're lucky they didn't know it was you who did it. But now Tejedor's six feet under and word is going around that you're hot because the Echevarrias want your ass fried."

"Shut the fuck up with that shit," Carlos said, waving Hambar off. He didn't have time for this. He didn't need a lecture from a two-bit junkie about his problems. "Do you have a job for me or not, cabrón?"

Hambar scooted his chair closer to Carlos, the loud Buffet playing in the background drowning out most of the crowd. Carlos hoped it went both ways. He didn't need people over-hearing this.

Carlos hated the term "private investigator." That wasn't him. He wasn't cut from the same cloth as people like Lupe Solano or that Pete Fernandez guy. No, Carlos was a fixer. He made problems go away. You had a problem? Okay, sucks to be you. You had some money? All right, now we can talk until the money's gone—and your problem, too. Carlos didn't have a license and didn't want one. He was a bail bondsman when he needed cash. And if he needed cash, something had gone wrong—and the fixing wasn't going so hot.

"Fine, fine, yeah—so these people, they got nothing in terms of cash, Carlos, claro—how can they? They're coming from Cuba, hombre," Hambar said, as if trying to reason with Carlos. But he noticed Carlos' expression was frozen, so he didn't press it. "But the guy—Tino is his name—yeah, Tino, he has a cousin in Miami. That guy—that's the money, my man. That's the hook up."

Carlos nodded slowly and let his eyes scan the bar. It was getting late. Not past-dinnertime-late, but around the time most of the working stiffs went home to their wives or snuck off to a hotel to fuck their mistresses. This was when the dregs, the drunks, and tourists stuck around to get sloppy—their bodies getting a little too close, the shots going down too fast, the smiles happening too easily. It was a good moment to be here, Carlos thought, if it meant he'd get paid. He settled his gaze on Hambar's gaunt face.

"Everybody's got a fucking cousin in Miami, bro," Carlos said, his tone flat. "Everybody. You gotta do me better than that, acere."

Hambar feigned offense.

"C'mon, bro, you know me, man," he said, pleading now. "I just need to get this guy to his primo's house in Little Havana. Then you get paid, he gets gone, and we all walk away."

"What's your cut, huh?"

"My cut?"

"Yeah, did I stutter? Your cut," Carlos said, his tone still dry and emotionless, as if he were reading the weather report aloud. "You expect me to believe you're here out of the kindness of your heart? Look at you, bro. You look like you haven't eaten in months. Coke alone doesn't do that."

Hambar cursed under his breath.

"Well? What is it?" Carlos said. "I'm not judging you—I just want to know."

"Fifteen," Hambar said with a pout.

"Fifteen Gs or fifteen percent of something?" Carlos asked. "Be specific, man."

"Gs, bro, Gs," Hambar said, his annoyance level rising. "I get you in on this, I get fifteen clean—you get the rest."

Carlos nodded, sliding a toothpick into his mouth. He was a stocky man, late forties, fit but not built—big but not fat. His thick black mustache made it hard to read his lips or gauge his response. He ran a hand through his close-cropped black hair.

"You tell your guy that I'll do it for fifty," Carlos said slowly. "No less. If that's too much, fine—no skin off my ass. I'll keep driving south and have my vacation. Fifty plus expenses, none of that 'take it off the top' shit, okay? Half up front."

Carlos pulled out a small notepad and jotted something down, sliding the sheet over to Hambar.

"My cell. Have them call me with the info," Carlos said. "I'll be staying nearby."

It was around two in the morning when Carlos pulled his black Accord into the Grand Cafe parking lot on Duval Street. He saw the van in the far corner, the streetlight's pale-yellow light shining brightly on its black exterior. Carlos took the Glock out of his glove compartment and slid it behind his waistband as he got out of the car. He was sure whoever was behind the wheel of the van saw him do it. That was the point.

A foot away from the black van, before Carlos could get a good look at the driver, he heard the rear doors swing open. His right hand instinctively moved toward his back. But before he could do anything there was someone standing near the van. It was not what Carlos had expected.

She was tall, her hair coffee brown. She wore a frumpy gray hoodie that couldn't hide her shape. She was fit and closer to twenty-five than thirty. She looked tired and didn't have a drop of makeup on her. Carlos still considered dropping to one knee and proposing. Before he could, though, she spoke.

"Señor Trelles?" she asked.

Carlos nodded, his hands back at his sides.

"I'm Ana," her accent was heavy, but her English was solid. She pulled her small tote bag close to her. "You're my ride?"

Carlos tried to look past her, but couldn't make out anyone else in the van—or around. The directions had been clear: meet at the parking lot, pick up the visitor, bring them to Miami. The exact address would be texted to him as soon as his tires hit Homestead. Simple enough. *But where was Hambar?*

Carlos shrugged it off. Ana followed him to his car. He opened the passenger side door, but she made for the backseat. He walked around to the other side and opened that door— moving a few boxes of files and some takeout containers. She didn't seem phased. Did she think Carlos was some kind of armed car service? Though the woman looked tired and uninterested in talking, she didn't have the wear and tear Carlos would've expected from someone who'd just fled Cuba and made it across the Florida Straits. Another question to ponder on the two-hour drive back to Miami.

"Ana" didn't say a word as Carlos pulled out of the parking lot and turned onto Duval Street. She wouldn't start talking until the shooting did.

After two hours of silence, the shots almost seemed louder.

Carlos had just pulled past West Palm Drive in Florida City, was just about to make a snide comment to the knockout sitting in his backseat when the front windshield shattered and his car started to spin.

It was late, the streets were empty, but her scream was loud. Carlos gripped the steering wheel and tried to move the car off the street. More shots. The car shuddered as bullets hit the exterior. Carlos crouched down.

"Duck, lady, get down," he yelled. She complied.

The shooting stopped as quickly as it'd started. The quiet that had enveloped the night just moments before returned, and Carlos could hear the crunch of boots on glass and asphalt.

Whoever had been shooting was coming their way.

He snatched the Glock from the glove. He met Ana's eyes. She was crouched in the backseat, clearly frightened, but doing her best to hold it together. He didn't think he could like her more, silent treatment or not.

"Any idea who these assholes might be?" Carlos whispered, as he tried to slide back toward the driver's side door.

"I have an idea."

Carlos ignored the comment. The last in a series of mistakes that would mark his troubled life.

He rolled out of his battered car, trying to keep quiet—still listening. The footsteps had stopped. Not a good sign.

He sprung up over the car's bullet-riddled hood, Glock drawn. He was met by four figures standing a few feet away, their guns also drawn. They were decked out in black, including balaclavas over their faces. He was outnumbered, but Carlos wasn't a tactician. He'd been in tougher scrapes before. He could figure his way out of this.

But what the fuck was going on?

"Yo, guys, for real—this bitch isn't worth it, all right? You want her, take her," Carlos said, motioning toward his car. He wasn't kidding. This was already more expensive than the fee he expected to collect. "I got no skin in this game, okay? A buddy tells me his friend needs a passport, all I need—"

One of the four stepped forward and removed their mask. That's when Carlos knew he was well and truly fucked.

Rene Echevarria gave Carlos a huge, shit-eating grin.

"Carlos Trelles, it's good to see you," he said, gun still trained on Carlos' head. "Didn't think you'd fall for this."

"Fall for what, you smarmy piece of shit?" Carlos spat back. Rene Echevarria was the worst of the bunch. A hair-gel coated Fredo Corleone with half the brains. He was probably a big part of why the Echevarrias were losing ground to the Mujica cartel. "Can we just put our guns down and call it a night? You guys take this girl—whoever she is—and I get in my car and drive home. No harm, no foul."

Then he felt an odd, cold sensation in the back of his skull. Most people that felt it didn't have a chance to describe what it was like. Carlos was smart enough to figure it out, though. The barrel of a gun. But who'd snuck around his car?

He didn't dare turn around. He didn't need to, though. Not when he heard that voice.

"Not gonna be like that, Carlos," she said. The accent suddenly gone. The flirty lilt imagined. Ana's voice was clear and confident. That's when it all seemed to make sense. Ana. Why hadn't he looked at her more closely? Past the looks and into her eyes? Ana. She looked familiar, but Carlos had just chalked that up to being another Cuban girl in Miami, even if she was fresh off the island. But she wasn't, was she?

"Ana Tejedor," Carlos said, his voice a croak of defeat. "So what, you went all in with your husband's old bosses to get ol' Carlos?"

He never got a response.

He heard the *shunt* of the silencer a split second before it went dark. His last memory was the world flipping sideways as his face crashed into the mist-soaked Miami asphalt.

OUTSIDE
EDWIN HILL

The pranks start small. No one knows what we plan, heads together, whispering, the weirder amid the weird. At the premiere, Allen, the leading man, gets caught between scenes. Someone sewed his coat sleeve shut. During the matinee, a baseball cap hangs with the bowlers on a hat rack, a bright red dot against all that black. On closing night, a teacup shatters to the stage floor. A dead mouse peeks from behind the shards.

Who did it? they ask.

They wait for the five of us to betray ourselves, but we huddle among the others, fingers touching, safety in numbers.

You betrayed us, they say.

We don't say a word.

Later, we skip the cast party. On the beach, we run into the dark, the surf pounding on the sand as we dive into frigid waves fully clothed, our bodies traced in phosphorescence. We emerge from the sea, coated in salt. Within the month one of us will be dead. The rest of us will spend our lives knowing what we've done.

In the afternoons, we meet in the darkened auditorium. If an outsider comes close, we stop our whispers, our stare collective. What they don't know is that we spend time on the outside, too, turning on each other, four against one. The reasons are mundane and random and impossible to predict.

Kevin eats egg salad.

Lisa takes Latin.

Seth wears brown.

Today, it's Polly's turn. She's a Virgo. The virgin.

We chase her up the aisles and through the rows. *Virgo, Virgo, Virgo,* we shout no matter what she retorts. She puts her hands to her ears. We surround her. We make the word ugly, threatening, till Polly sits alone on the edge of the stage, numbed, and for a while at least the rest of us feel safe.

Days later, we arrive in a yellow Volvo sedan wearing baby-blue bowties, polyester waistbands, and yards of taffeta. In the gym, we dance to Janet and Sinead and Milli Vanilli, hands clasped, spinning, bodies entwined.

I dare to leave them. But only for a moment.

In the restroom, Allen stands at the next urinal. He's not one of us, and away from their stares, I laugh at his jokes. I consider telling him that sewing the coat sleeve shut wasn't my idea. We exit the restroom. He holds the door. We dance without touching at the very edge of the dance floor, only our toes moving, hoping not to be seen. He says he should leave, that he should find his own friends. He turns once and smiles.

They whisper as I return.

It's time to go, they say.

I follow as they pile into the car, and then into Seth's basement, the fancy clothes discarded, my bowtie tangled with the others. They eat Smartfood and green M & M's, and drink Bartles & Jaymes. They talk as though I'm not there, so I burrow into my sleeping bag to escape the outside. Polly sings Allen's name.

When I wake, I can't breathe. *Allen, Allen, Allen,* they say. I claw at fabric, at soft limbs. Dim blue light turns to darkness as the car engine starts, and I fight my way through sleep, through fabric, though panic, punching at the walls of the trunk till the brakes screech. Four toothy grins greet me. Four sets of hands lift me into the morning light and hurl me to the side of the road. I sprawl in the grass, still tangled in my sleeping bag.

Then they drive away.

Now, years later, I can't sleep. I lie in bed, lights out, and use my phone to search. I start with cupcake recipes or Wimbledon champs or kings of Sweden. Next come movies I saw long ago. TV shows, too. Who starred in what? How many Oscars has Meryl Streep won? What movie bombed and ended a career? You can find almost anything these days. Anyone. Or so it seems. Even things you thought you'd lost, like people you know you shouldn't find.

Allen is a pastry chef in San Francisco. Successful. Still a leading man.

Seth is in jail.

Polly died last year. Her obituary mentions three children and an ex-husband.

Kevin teaches history at a middle school in Ohio where he directs the theater program, and I wonder if he still eats egg salad, if he stays up at night and searches on my name, if he worries that those who know him now—the ones who call him nice, charitable, funny, whatever words they attribute to him—will find out who he was. I wonder if he hopes for a second chance.

With Lisa, I know what I'll find no matter how much I search. Her story doesn't change anymore. I remember her body by the river, her dark hair tangled with leaves, dried blood on her forehead, the EMTs lifting her onto a gurney. Her pale hand fell from beneath the tarp. One of the EMTs tripped on the steep bank, as Lisa had tripped, terrified, trying to escape. She could have been me. She could have been any of us, on the outside for the last time.

Who did it? they asked me later, waiting for a betrayal.
We did. All of us.
But I didn't say a word.

Beside me, Mark rolls over and mumbles something. I put the phone away, get out of bed, and patter down the hall to where our children sleep. We have a house with a backyard, a dog who barks at strangers, children who fight and make up. We lead an ordinary life. Most nights, Mark and I sit outside on the back porch and watch the children play with the dog. The kids chase each other and argue. That part I don't mind. It's when Mark joins them, when they bend their heads together, when they whisper their secrets, that I feel alone.

THE BODY
STEVE SHROTT

"Have you ever seen a dead body, Tim?"

"A dead body?"

"Yes."

"No. Have you?"

Penny paused, then nodded, tears rolling down her cheeks. She wiped them with a tissue and tossed it into her empty coffee cup. The restaurant had that interim feeling, too late for breakfast, too early for lunch. I could hear dishes clattering back in the kitchen.

This was an odd conversation. Especially as I hadn't seen Penny Winters since high school. Back then, ten years ago? She was the girl everyone wanted to date. But she was usually with some well-muscled football player. When she was single, I tried to ask her out once, but I stuttered back then and it didn't work out very well.

I was so hurt at the time that I lashed out and tried to spread a rumor that we had slept together. But no one believed that an awkward guy like me could possibly be with someone beautiful like her. I shouldn't have done it, it made me feel so much worse.

Despite all this, I always hoped that we would meet again in the future and I would get a second chance. Maybe this was it.

She'd messaged me on Facebook. So I agreed to meet. Who knew what would happen.

We met at Phil-osophy, my favorite coffee shop—owned by a guy named Phil—and though I was calm on the outside, inside I was jumping up and down like a five-year-old about to open his Christmas presents. It was May, but you know what I mean.

Phil's place was all dark red leather booths and dim lighting, but as soon as Penny appeared in the doorway, it seemed brighter somehow. I got to watch her as she'd ordered her coffee. She'd had cut her hair since the last time I'd seen her, but it was still blonde. And shiny. Her complexion glowed and her high cheekbones screamed model. She'd smiled at me as she'd headed to the secluded table I'd chosen in the back. When I stood up to greet her, she'd immediately wrapped her arms around my waist. It surprised me. She still smelled good.

I thought I'd been pretty invisible to her during high school. But after we sat down and stirred our coffees, she'd begun to recount all the things she remembered about me—how I'd been president of the magic club, that I'd worked at our school newspaper, *The Bugle*, and how my picture of a nearby farmer's field won an award.

Of course when she brought up the dead body, that really got my attention. She asked if I would come and see it with her.

This wasn't the experience I had dreamed about having with Penny. But I knew I'd go. "Sure," I told her. "If you need me to."

"I didn't finish telling you about it."

"You'll tell me on the way."

She got into my Toyota and we headed out to Rivera Park as she talked. Penny in my Toyota. Who'd have thought.

"I come out here each weekend," she said, as if we did this every day. "I'm an amateur photographer and love taking pictures of the old trees with their gnarly old branches. They really tell a story. But I'm sure you know all about that, since you won that award." She smiled. "Anyway there's a little stream beside this big oak and I usually sit beside it and read. To get some peace. That's when I saw the body face down in the water. It was horrible, Tim."

She looked up at me, tears in her eyes.

"Did you call the police?" I asked. I needed to know who else she'd told. Or who I should call.

She looked out the window of the car as if she thought the guy riding by on the bike might be listening. "No. I should have, but thing is, I have a bit of a record."

"A record?" The town going by had faded to suburbs, suburbs to woodlands.

I heard Penny take a deep breath. "I know I seemed like a normal kid back at school, but I kinda—ran with a rough crowd. I did things I'm not proud of. Small things. You know. No one got hurt, really, but I did spend time behind bars. I'm surprised you hadn't heard. So when I saw the body, I was afraid to call the police. I worried they might think…"

"You had something to do with it."

She nodded.

It was a lot to take in.

"To be honest that's why I wanted to see you." She seemed even prettier now, prettier than ever. "You always seemed to have this integrity. I have friends, but I don't trust them. So I wouldn't ask *them* to…"

"I get it." And I did, I guess. But as I stopped at a random stop light, no other cars in sight, I didn't think about that. My thoughts stayed focused on the fact that Penny Winters was actually in my front seat.

"I don't know if you remember," she went on, "but one time I lost my wallet and it had two hundred dollars in it. Money I was saving to buy my mom a new dress and shoes for her birthday. You found it and gave it back to me—all the cash still there."

I smiled, remembering I had hoped it would make her like me. It hadn't seemed to work.

"So I wondered if you could call the police for me." She

turned to me. "Say you found the body."

I kept my eyes on the road, thinking about that for a moment, not sure it would be a wise decision. But sometimes you want something so badly, you do the un-wise thing.

"Uh, sure," I said.

She reached out and touched my arm. For that fraction of a second, her hand burned through my skin.

"In here?" I asked, as I pointed to the park entrance.

Penny nodded. We left the car in the dusty front lot, walked silently past some empty metal swing sets and blue plastic slides, a deserted tennis court. We were too far out of town for any kids to be here. Maybe they were still in school. Who knew what kids did these days.

Penny pointed toward a narrow dirt path into the woods, and I followed her. The ground was still muddy from the morning rain, typical of May around here, so we had to be careful where we stepped.

I must say I loved the spring weather, the scent of new leaves and the promise of summer. But I especially enjoyed walking beside her, hoping that everything would work out.

"You okay?" I asked. We were going to see a dead body, I kept thinking. Maybe silence was easier.

Penny stopped. Pointed again. "We need to turn left onto that other path."

I nodded. I pushed the thorny branches of a locust tree out of the way, and they sprang back and hit me in the face. But I didn't care, I was on cloud nine.

"Are we getting close?" I asked.

"Just up ahead." She pointed toward a thicket of bushes. "Behind them."

I held Penny's hand as we crossed onto a muddier section of land. I could feel my heart pound.

A moment later, we were in front of the stream. That's when we saw it—the body. It was a man wearing a multi-colored shirt and blue chinos. He lay face down in the water, his arms outstretched as if he were making one last attempt to swim away.

I shook my head. "This is unbelievable, Penny."

"I know."

"Do you know who that is?"

"No. Do you?"

I shook my head. It was pretty disturbing, somehow, that one of his shoes had fallen off.

We both stood, staring.

In a softly apologetic voice, she told me she wished she had gone out on that date with me when I'd asked her so long ago. She said she remembered making fun of me about the stuttering and apologized, said she was too full of herself back then to appreciate a good guy like me.

I thanked her.

High school, you know? It was all we had in common. Except for the body.

"Want me to call now?"

She nodded. "Give me ten minutes. Then call."

"How will you get back to town?"

She held up her phone. "I'll be fine. Tim?

"Yeah?"

"Thank you."

And she was gone.

I waited, like she told me, then took out my phone and called 9-1-1. The lady who answered asked me to stay until the police arrived.

Ten minutes later, I heard their footsteps on the dirt path, and the undercurrent of their discussion. Two officers approached one chunky with a dour expression, the other smaller but also looking as if I was bothering him. Or maybe the body was bothering him.

"I take it you're Tim? You found this?"

"Yes."

"I'm Officer Walters. I need to ask you a few questions. But give us a minute."

They approached the body. Talked quietly to one another. I watched, riveted, as the shorter one began taking notes on a little pad. The other one turned toward me.

I glanced to my left. To my right. No sign of Penny.

"Do you come up here often, sir?"

"Yes, uh, I always walk this way. I'm a photographer."

"When did you get here?"

"Ten, fifteen minutes ago. I phoned nine-one-one as soon as I saw the body."

"You came alone?"

At this point I was getting uncomfortable with the questions and wanted to leave. But, of course, I couldn't.

"Yes. Just me." The officer stared at me a moment with narrowed eyes. "All right sir, I'm going to need your contact information. We'll probably need to talk with you again."

"Uh, sure." I wondered why there weren't any birds, or any bugs or anything. I wondered why it was all so quiet.

I tromped to my car. It was the only one in the lot. I went home, and immediately messaged Penny to tell her what happened.

She never got back to me.

The next morning Officer Walters came to my apartment. I'd just made the coffee, and was wondering about everything.

He'd stood in the corridor as I opened the door.

"Sir, I need to ask you a few more questions. May I come in?"

"Sure." *Here we go,* I thought.

The officer entered the living room and took a seat on my leather couch. It had seen better days, but I didn't care if he didn't care. I sat on my old ottoman a little distance away. The officer opened a leather pouch, and took out a copy of the Crestview High School Year Book—just like the one I had on my shelf.

"We now know the identity of the dead man." He held up

the yearbook.

"Good." I nodded. I guessed that was good.

He opened the yearbook to a page I'd seen many times. The Prom queen and king. The queen wore a rhinestone tiara and blue eye shadow. It was Penny. I never went to prom so I didn't get to see her in person looking so beautiful.

"Do you know him?" He pointed to the broad-shouldered king, a gold paper crown askew on his blond hair.

I nodded. "Yes, that's Don Lemmings."

"Were you friends?"

"Not really. He hung out with the popular kids."

"Any reason you would want to hurt him?"

"No, no, of course not."

He gave me a quizzical look. "Are you sure about that?"

"What do you mean?"

"We have a witness who says that you *did* want to hurt him. Apparently you were obsessed with his girlfriend, Penny Winters. The prom queen," he said, tapping the photo. "For years."

"What? That's ridiculous. I hardly knew her."

"I need to show you something." The officer stood up and moved close to me. He turned to another page in the yearbook showing a smaller photo of Penny. On it were words written in ink. "Stop going out with Don the doofus or you'll regret it." It was signed by me.

I had forgotten all about that, and the memory made me cringe. "Yes, I wrote it, but that was a long time ago. I was just a stupid seventeen-year-old kid."

"The witness can also place you at the crime scene during the time of the murder."

"What? I had nothing to do with this. You've got to believe me." I saw my life flash before my eyes. Sounds dumb, but I did. "Something is wrong here."

"You're right, sir, there *is* something wrong. You're in the woods the same day that a body turns up, and it turns out you went to school with the deceased. We have a witness saying you were obsessed with his girlfriend, Penny. Finally, we have you writing a threatening message to her about seeing the boyfriend. So yes, there is definitely something wrong here. High school is never over, I guess."

The officer handcuffed and arrested me.

Two days later, I was released.

The officer informed me that the truth had come out. Apparently Penny had been their witness, as well as the one who had killed Don. She had been trying to frame me for the murder because I had ruined things for her in high school. She deeply loved Don, but when he heard those rumors that I had slept with Penny, he didn't trust her anymore and he left. She blamed me for the downturn in her life.

She fed the cops all that hooey about how I was obsessive. Then she pointed them to the comment I wrote in the yearbook.

It all would have been a done deal except she had changed her story so many times that the cops now believed she was the murderer. The charges against me were dropped.

She was definitely not the person I thought she was. Putting it mildly. And that surprised me, as I had been watching her for years. I even saw how she reconnected with Don and met him every Friday at the stream—even though *he* was now married. She had him back, sure, but apparently her revenge burned deep and she still wanted to take me down.

I was sympathetic, of course. I'd had vengeful thoughts about her as well. I never forgave her for making fun of my stuttering. That ruined me. I lost the little confidence I had in myself, and my life consisted of a series of dead-end jobs and relationships.

Eventually, I'd gotten my life together by doing something I was good at. I called Don and told him I knew about the affair and I was pretty sure his wife would want to know, too. We finally settled on a price and a few hours later he was at the stream—where I took the money and stabbed him.

As a final touch I stashed the bloody knife in the undercarriage of Penny's car. Luckily the cops were smart enough to find it. She's going to be in jail a long time.

It had all worked out. Sure, my first attempt at revenge—spreading the rumor about sleeping with Penny—had caused some "issues" for her. But we all have issues, don't we? And "issues" weren't punishment enough for what she did to me in high school. My first try had been pretty good. But not good enough.

Sometimes you need a second chance.

THE UNAPPRECIATED WIFE
ELISABETH ELO

Polly moved some flowers aside to make room on the narrow window ledge for the new arrangement sent by Harold, Clancy, and Stearn, her husband's law firm. The window overlooked the packed parking lot of Massachusetts General Hospital, and her husband, Martin, was lying nearby in a bed, asleep now, hemmed in by metal rails and monitored by various machines.

The last few days had seen a steady stream of visitors. Martin's best friend and closest colleague at the firm, Frank Armistead, with his ruddy complexion and booming voice, had visited several times, grasping her hand in his sweaty grip. Their minister, Reverend Arnold Cabot, had appeared unexpectedly, his cold, limp hand slipping instantly out of her own in what was supposed to pass for a handshake. Martin's tennis buddy, Jim Patrone, didn't shake hands at all, just clasped her in a warm tight hug. And others, of course. Many others. Martin was a highly respected divorce attorney in Boston. He was a public man, loved by the many he had helped, hated by those he had screwed. Yesterday, Polly had noticed his assistant, Leila McIntyre, falling into tears in the corridor, only to be offered a carefully antiseptic hug by her son, Ronnie, who also worked at the firm. Ronnie's wife, Estelle, had been standing next to her husband, still as a statue, in a camel cashmere coat that Polly knew she wouldn't take off, no matter how long they stayed or how hot Martin's room became. Estelle struck her as a very closed-off person, almost secretive, and Polly had been disappointed to see Ronnie become more closed and secretive, too, during the years of his marriage.

Their daughters, Livvy and Tegan, were seven and five—two little poking, kicking, grabby monkeys who seemed to have been fed on nothing but stimulants since birth. Polly dutifully babysat whenever she was asked, and always did her best with the girls. Some nights she got them interested in a story and was gratified when their little monkey brains quieted into rapt attention.

The extravagant floral arrangement felt heavy in her arms. It easily dwarfed the other vases, as if the firm just couldn't forgo one more opportunity to prove its status, even in this somber situation. She almost hoped Martin wouldn't notice all the flowery support he was receiving, lest it remove any doubt in his mind that he was on death's door. Which he was. His cancer had spread, he was on a steady morphine drip, and there was talk of moving him to hospice soon.

Where was she to put it? The windowsill hadn't been wide enough, even after she had moved some things aside. She would have to make room on the bedside table, a blond formica thing on rolling casters, already crowded with what looked like an adult sippy cup, a telephone, a box of Kleenex, and what she had come to think of as a lawyer folder—marbled brown, able to expand like an accordion, with an attached elastic strap to keep it closed. She sighed. Had Martin really been working during his transient lucid periods? It wasn't unthinkable. He had worked like a Trojan all his life, racking up the billable hours with the best of them year after year. The law was his greatest love, he had once told her, with no apparent concern for how this news would affect her. Not that it had come as a surprise.

She moved the brown folder to one of the two chairs in the crowded little room and set the flowers down on the table, feeling mildly disappointed that her husband continued to sleep. According to the nurses, he had been his old self—alert, demanding, and sharp as a tack—for several hours this afternoon, when Frank Armistead, Leila McIntyre, and a third person stopped by to visit. Since she had arrived, he hadn't opened his eyes.

She sat quietly, keeping wifely vigil, until Ronnie and Estelle showed up. She wanted them to have the chairs, thinking they might sit with Martin longer if they were comfortable, so she moved the brown folder to the floor and put her purse over it, then folded her puffy down coat neatly over them both. Martin woke up obligingly, perhaps on hearing Ronnie's voice. He smiled at his son, and asked Polly for more pillows to prop himself up in the bed.

The conversation centered, as usual, on the firm. Eventually, Martin thought to ask about his granddaughters. Estelle gave the required answers, and the conversation swung back to the firm. Polly's mind wandered, as it usually did whenever Martin and Ronnie conversed. Over the last few months, as she had cared for Martin without complaint during his progressing illness, she had been increasingly haunted by a simple fact: she didn't really love her husband. Hadn't for a good, oh, twenty years. Frankly, the seventeen before that hadn't been ideal either. But there had been plenty of things to distract her from the state of her marriage: their growing son, Martin's demanding career, her job as a third-grade teacher's assistant, and endless community events. Later, Ronnie's marriage to Estelle, and the happy arrivals of Livvy and Tegan. Still, all that activity had not completely quelled her personal loneliness, and she had sometimes found herself dreaming of another love, a better love, that might be out there for her somewhere. But when she looked around at the men she knew—the doctors, lawyers, teachers, and so on—there wasn't a single one that attracted her. She supposed she'd had her chance at love and it had failed—or, rather, neglected to succeed—and she simply needed to make peace with a life that wasn't so bad, all things considered. Indeed, given all the suffering in the world, her portion of unhappiness was decidedly minimus. Just a quiet chronic aching of the heart.

Now Martin was dying. She was sad about that, though less sad than a happier wife might have been. She felt bad for him, because he didn't want to die, and she knew he felt hurt and betrayed, unfairly singled out by mortality, which had arrived prematurely, like a gauche guest at a dinner party. He was only sixty-seven. He was scared, too, as anyone would be. As she herself would be when her time came. To let go of your life...of your loved ones...of yourself...How were you supposed to do that? Life's last lesson was undoubtedly its most difficult, and perhaps its most bitter, depending on your spiritual condition. She wasn't sure she wanted to know what her disposition would be, didn't want to face that final test when the true state of her soul would be revealed to her at last. Better to be hit by a bus.

Martin was nodding off again, having spent himself in conversation, and Ronnie seemed unusually restless. He cruised around the room inspecting the cards and flowers, then darted out to the nurse's station, asking after Martin's condition probably, though nothing had changed for several days. Martin was sailing into his own private sunset on the wings of Morpheus. Feeling no pain, she had been told. Was that good? Shouldn't you feel the pain of your own passing? Or the joy of it, if such a thing were possible? Shouldn't you at least be alert long enough to say something meaningful to the spouse dutifully hovering at your bedside?

"I wish they wouldn't pump him so full of morphine," she told Ronnie a little plaintively when he returned.

He glared at her in irritated horror. "He needs it for the pain, Mom."

She felt chastened by his tone, then a bit resentful. Did he think she didn't know that? Did he actually believe she wanted the poor man to be howling for her convenience? "Of course," she said mildly, her voice trailing off. It wasn't worth trying to explain what she meant. She didn't trust herself to find the right words, and she didn't trust her son to have any interest in them should she succeed.

Ronnie disappeared into the corridor again. Perhaps it was sinking in now: his father would not recover. He would be transferred very shortly into another wing of the hospital that specialized in palliative care. The last stop in the first world's assembly line of death.

When Ronnie returned with one of the nurses in tow, both of them looking harried, Polly leaned over to peck Martin's cool, papery cheek. She said her good-byes to her son and daughter-in-law, and, rather than leaving the brown folder on the floor where it might be stepped on or tripped over, she tucked it to her chest with her winter coat and took it with her. She would bring it back tomorrow. In the meantime, it wouldn't hurt Martin to take a little break from work.

The brown folder sat on her kitchen table as she fixed her dinner— a frozen cod fillet with rice and frozen peas. A limp, unappetizing meal. She wondered what she would do when she was a widow. Would she still fix Martin's favorite—bland—foods, or would she order delivery pizza or burritos or Indian food every night, cost be damned? Or would she morph against all odds into a gourmet chef? Or finally get serious about her health and starve off the twenty pounds she clearly didn't need?

She absentmindedly opened the folder as she ate, pulled out some legal-looking documents, and skimmed the top sheet. *Last Will and Testament of Martin R. Clancy*. She was surprised. They had executed their wills together a decade ago. But this one bore today's date. She frowned, unable to imagine what had necessitated the making of a new will.

A sense of foreboding crept over her.

It didn't take long to notice what had changed. Whereas the last will had named her as the sole beneficiary, that honor was now bestowed on Ronnie. Martin was leaving his estate to Ronnie. She didn't grasp the implications for a few seconds. Then it sunk in: *Martin was leaving his estate to Ronnie.* His entire estate. Nothing was going to her.

Rising abruptly from the table, she stared around the kitchen with wild eyes, as if searching for a way out. It was impossible. Surely Martin didn't *mean* what the new will clearly specified. It was too much, too extreme! It couldn't be true.

What if it *was* true? What if, in some terrible error of judgment, he *had* intended to make such a drastic change? In that case, he surely would have discussed it with her first. She would have been perfectly amenable if in his last days he wanted to pass *some* of his estate directly to his son. Or even if he wanted to split the estate equally between the two of them. She wouldn't have *liked* that, but she would at least have understood it.

But this was something else entirely, something very different, for which there could be no rational reason. He was deliberately cutting her out.

She sank to her seat again, flipped hurriedly through five or six pages of legalese until she came to the last section, which was described as a non-binding addendum. Here she read that Martin "expected and advised" his sole beneficiary—Ronnie—to set up and manage a trust fund for the benefit of his surviving spouse—her. Polly was to be allotted a monthly sum sufficient to cover her needs—the amount to be adjusted at Ronnie's discretion as conditions changed. There was no indication of what this sum would be. No indication of how her "needs" would be calculated. What was quite clear to her was that these needs of hers could legally be determined without the aid of input from her.

Her sixty-five-year-old heart started hammering with alarming rapidity, as if she'd been injected with a strong dose of adrenalin. Her head seemed about to fly off her neck. She lowered it into cupped palms that also mercifully covered her eyes, obliterating the offensive document from her sight. She began to feel ill, as if a toxin were spreading through her body, beginning in her tightly wound intestines and creeping out to her curled fingertips and even into her eyes, which burned, as if she were going blind.

Her breathing was rapid and shallow. She needed to regulate it mindfully, as she had been taught in yoga class. *Breathe, Polly. Breathe.*

Thirty-seven years of marriage. Thirty-seven years of marriage. Those words kept repeating in her brain.

She was being fired. It was almost funny. Fired as a wife and mother, without so much as a cheap gold watch. Martin's wealth—it had always seemed like his, and indeed he had underscored her financial dependence on him many times—would not in the end be shared with her. She was not worthy of it, apparently. Not a blood relative like their son. Just a person to bear and raise a child, a burdensome necessity. Now she recalled a long-buried incident: Martin had taken her to a Clancy family gathering, and she had just been introduced to his uncle, a very successful, impressively smug lawyer with horn-rimmed spectacles and thick lips. Pulling her aside, this man had informed her that Martin, to whom she was recently engaged, was one of the most influential lawyers in Boston. *Stay out of his way*, he had whispered harshly in her ear, his strong fingers digging into her upper arm. He hadn't needed to repeat himself. The words, which she took to be a warning of some kind, were seared instantly onto her heart.

And hadn't that been Martin's attitude as well? She was expected to stay out of his way. And she did. Occupying a small space, a small life, while his was grand and influential. But hadn't she helped build his life? By doing almost all the childcare. Young Ronnie rarely saw his father, a fact she had continuously smoothed over. Not to mention everything—yes, *everything*—else. She had been fully employed as his at-home secretary, and she had worked as diligently as anyone could.

Oh, it was an old story, wasn't it? The unappreciated wife. She was embarrassed that it was so obviously *her* story now; ashamed that, on some level, she had known all along that that tired old shoe fit her quite well indeed. Yet instead of facing that fact and taking decisive action as a stronger woman might have, she had chosen to waste decades of her life blustering cheerily along, outwardly insisting on her happiness, while feeling small and scared on the inside, forever trying to bail out the swamped rowboat that was her marriage.

That *was* her marriage. It was clearly over now. For her, it was done.

She wiped away a single paltry tear. She wasn't sad enough to cry outright. She was just sadder than usual.

Wait. She had forgotten something! He couldn't leave the *house* to Ronnie, could he? The property had been paid off years ago, and surely the title was in both their names. She could check quickly enough. Martin was a stickler for organization, and something like that would be easy to locate. The file in his office was kept locked, but the key was stashed in the back of his desk's top drawer. She had used it a few times when he had asked her to dig something out for him. She ran down the hall to his book-lined study, found the key, and opened the top file drawer. She rifled through the hanging folders and pulled out one labeled "Titles." Sure enough, the property title was snuggled there alongside the car titles. Perched on the edge of his deep leather reading chair, she skimmed it eagerly, then sank back against the cushion, stunned.

Martin was the sole owner of the house. Her name was nowhere to be found on the document. Her home would go to Ronnie, too.

Gripped by sudden, acute nausea, she ran to the bathroom and heaved her dinner into the open toilet bowl, one hand pressed against the tile wall to hold herself steady. Afterward, rinsing her mouth at the sink, she declined to gaze at her reflection in the mirror. She knew it would be ugly. She was ugly. She stank of fish and frozen peas and bathos. If she could, she would crawl out of her scaly husk of old dry skin and leave it lying on the bathroom floor.

Plodding resolutely back to the document, she flipped to the last page to make sure it had been signed, notarized, and witnessed as required by law. Indeed, it had. Martin's scrawling signature was there in fresh black ink, just as pompously undecipherable as ever. The notary's seal was duly embossed in the appropriate place. The two witnesses—no surprise—were Frank Armistead and Leila McIntyre. The will had been executed that very day, then slipped into the brown folder for someone to pick up.

Ronnie, obviously. That was why he had been so restless, snooping around the room and badgering the nurses. If he had simply asked her if she had seen some paperwork lying around, she would have gladly handed it over, enjoying her own helpfulness. Why hadn't he asked? Was it because he'd felt guilty? Because he wasn't enough of a cad to make his mother innocently deliver her own financial death sentence to the aptly named executor?

No. It was because she wasn't supposed to know about the new will until after Martin's death. So she wouldn't make noise, or put up a fight, or *get in the way.* The new will was Martin and Ronnie's explosive little secret, to be sprung on her when it was too late to be altered. When her power, always slight, had been effectively zeroed out.

There were three copies of the will on her kitchen table, each one signed, notarized, and witnessed. Three official copies. One no doubt for Ronnie, another probably for Martin's office files. Who was the third copy for, she wondered? The judge who would sign off on the case, if judges even did that kind of thing? It obviously wasn't meant for her.

Feeling hot and shaky, she moved around the large kitchen, throwing open one window after another. Each time, a frigid blast of air hit her like a slap across the face. Good. She needed the bracing winter wind to lift her out of self-pity and clarify her muddled thoughts. This was war. A kind of war, anyway. Like a field marshal about to engage the enemy, she needed a clear strategy and tactics. Later, if she still wanted to, she could fall apart.

Ronnie would probably be here soon. Unable to locate the

freshly executed documents at the hospital, he would have to consider the possibility that his mother had picked them up by accident and taken them home, and he would be left with no choice but to ask her directly. Poor boy, at this very minute he was probably frantically worrying that she had read the new will, recognizing that, if she had, he would be facing a truly terrible night of potentially futile damage control.

Of course—and this idea blossomed slowly and beautifully in her mind like a newly opening bud in spring—this most recent will would be unenforceable if it wasn't found. She wasn't so stupid that she didn't know how at least a few things worked: a document that wasn't physically present at an official legal proceeding could not be assumed to exist. Any online copy, provided there even was one, would not have been duly notarized and witnessed, and thus would not be binding.

She smiled slyly as her luck dawned on her. Martin and Ronnie's bomb had slipped into enemy hands.

Headlights shone through her open windows. He was here, driving faster than usual up the driveway. She stuffed the documents hastily into the folder, affixed the elastic strap, and jammed the folder behind a nest of saucepans in one of the bottom cabinets.

She was smiling serenely when he blew in the door, his long wool coat flapping, his suit jacket open, his tie off. "Did you happen to see any paperwork in Dad's hospital room? Like, a folder or manila envelope? Anything like that?"

He wasn't bothering with pleasantries, she noted. "No, dear. Why? Have you lost something?"

"Not lost, exactly. Just...Dad was supposed to leave something for me, and I can't find it anywhere. He said it would be waiting for me at the hospital tonight." His eyes darted around the kitchen.

"Let's see..." She pretended to think. "I'm sure I'd remember if I saw a legal-looking folder or envelope. Hmmm. Have you asked Leila? She usually keeps track of things like that."

"She doesn't have it."

"Frank then?"

"He doesn't have it either."

"In that case, I'd try the nurse's station. They may have put it aside for safekeeping."

"Nope. Not there either. Well, no worries. I'm sure it will turn up," he said in a measurably lighter tone. He was undoubtedly relieved to think she didn't have it, and therefore couldn't have read it, and now he wanted to make the problem seem less important, so she wouldn't feel obliged to involve herself in the search.

She puckered her lips sympathetically, like she used to do when he was a child with a scraped knee. "I'm sorry, honey. I wish I could help." Bravely, she added, "Is it important?"

He threw back his shoulders and shrugged—a weird combination of movements. "Yeah, sort of." His eyes narrowed. "Sure you didn't find anything?"

"No, but I'll keep an eye out, I promise. Can you tell me what it was? Just so I know what I'm looking for?"

"It's nothing you'd understand. Just a case Dad and I were working on together."

"You don't usually work on the same cases, do you?"

"No, but this was a special thing. Not important, though. I'll figure it out."

"I'm sure you will. Can I get you some coffee?"

"Thanks but no. I've got to get back. Actually, Estelle's in the car."

"Really? You left your wife out in the cold?" She barked a strange-sounding laugh. "Does that seem fair to you?"

He grimaced at the suggestion that he might be less than a sterling gentleman. "The heat's on, and the babysitter's waiting at home. I've got to go."

He was about to sweep out the door the same way he had come in, on a jet-stream of urgency that moved too fast for her, when he stopped in his tracks and seemed to sniff the air.

"Mom, why are the windows open?"

"Oh, I felt a little feverish. I might be coming down with something. All the stress around Dad, I guess. I'm sure with Tylenol and a good night's sleep, I'll be fine tomorrow."

He shot her a disapproving glance. "Your electric bill's going to be sky-high."

"You're so right, sweetheart. I'll close them the minute you leave."

She waited by the front window as his car backed down the driveway and the red tail lights disappeared down the street. Then she waited five minutes more, in case he came back.

Folding her arms tightly across her chest to warm herself in the cooling air, she returned to the kitchen. It was all so sad, really. If only Ronnie had been *halfway* honest with her...if he had simply admitted that he was looking for a will...or mentioned that Dad was considering making a new one...then she might have handed the brown folder over with a measure of relief, even knowing full well what it contained, because in truth she wanted nothing more than to believe that her husband and son loved her and meant to take care of her in their own loving way, which might not be what she would choose for herself, but might not be as bad as she imagined.

Except he had not been honest with her. He had stood right here in her kitchen, the place where she had cooked and served him literally thousands of meals. He had stood directly in front of her, looking straight into her eyes, and he had lied.

She pulled the brown folder out of the cabinet, overturning some saucepans, which clattered onto the floor. She turned the dial of the gas burner to high, and held each page of the three official documents over the orange flame, watching each one singe and curl into blackness and fall as ash. She felt that these were Martin's ashes, not whatever would be left of his body after cremation. This was his real funeral. It was her family's funeral, too, though she and Ronnie would survive to possibly try again someday, after a major attitude adjustment on her part.

When the last page was destroyed, she swept the charred remains into the sink, stuffed the whole mess into the disposal, and flipped the switch. She let the disposal churn for a long time. Then she shut the windows and went up to bed.

She arrived at the hospital the next morning at eight. Visiting hours didn't begin until noon, but when patients were as near to the end as Martin was, the nurses allowed immediate family members to come and go as they pleased. Leaning over his bedside, she pecked his cheek. "Martin, dear, wake up," she said in a wifely musical lilt that nevertheless contained a thread of steel. Martin's eyelids fluttered. "It's morning, dear," she sing-songed, egging him into consciousness, and eventually his eyes opened and achieved a hazy focus on her face.

"How are you feeling today?" she asked. "Are you in pain? Yes? Terrible pain?"

He shook his bone-colored head, nearly bald now from the chemo. He was still too groggy to form words.

"Oh, you poor thing. Don't worry, darling; I'll let the nurses know."

She walked briskly along the gleaming hospital corridor, until she got to the nurse's station, where she rapped her knuckles on the counter sharply like a hotel guest demanding service. "My husband's in pain," she informed one of the nurses. "Terrible pain. For all I know, he's been in pain all night. How could you let that happen?"

"Hold on, Mrs. Clancy," the nurse said, pressing a flat palm onto Polly's rapping knuckles. She was obviously adept at soothing anguished spouses. "He's been stable all night. Let's take a look."

The nurse proceeded quickly to Martin's room, Polly following behind. When they arrived, Martin was fully awake. His eyes glared out of his oddly shrunken-looking skull the way they must have when he was attempting to intimidate an adversary in court.

"Mr. Clancy? How are we feeling this morning?" the nurse intoned in a volume generously adjusted for the possibly hard-of-hearing senior lying in the bed.

He swept his hand in an imperious gesture that Polly knew meant *go away*. To a stranger, it could have meant anything.

Catching the nurse by the elbow, Polly whispered urgently in her ear, "See? I told you. He's in the most awful pain."

"Are you having any pain right now, Mr. Clancy?" the nurse all-but bellowed.

"No," Martin managed to utter, enunciating so poorly that the *n* was inaudible, and his denial sounded more like a groan. Truly, he did seem less well than yesterday.

Polly floated to his side, raised one of his limp, withered hands off the folded sheet, and held it to her lips. "Darling," she murmured tenderly, "the nurse is here now to help you. You'll feel much better soon."

The nurse, who had been checking various readouts and dials, emitted a loud tetchy sigh. "I can adjust the drip a little, I guess. He seems otherwise fine."

"Oh, more than a little, please," Polly insisted with the all the ardor of a determined patient advocate.

The nurse obligingly turned a dial. "There. That's as high as we're allowed. Let me know if he needs anything else, Mrs. Clancy," she said on her way out.

When the nurse was gone, Polly leaned over the bed and said quietly, "Martin, can you hear me?"

An irritated stare replaced the pompous glare as he muttered, "For God's sake, Polly, what are you whispering for?"

He was obviously still annoyed by the nurse's fussing, she thought. Nurses annoyed him on principal. Or maybe it was

Polly. *She* annoyed him. Her very presence. Had she always annoyed him? Of course she had! Hadn't he always annoyed her?

"Now, dear," she said conversationally, settling her haunch cozily on the mattress by his side. "I know about the will. You know, the one you signed yesterday and left for Ronnie to pick up? The one that cut me out completely? I found it, sweetheart, and I burned it over the gas burner on the stove."

Martin's wiry gray eyebrows pinched together over his bony nose. His gaze shifted furtively in the direction of the bedside table.

"It's not there. I took it home and burned it. Don't you believe me?"

He blinked a few times. She watched his irritation gradually shift into wariness and then into something else, an emotion she hardly ever saw on his face. His body shifted, too, under the blanket, but he was too weak to move very far. She felt his hand, the one she was still holding, try to tug away, so she tightened her grip.

"I have no idea what you're talking about," he finally croaked.

She pressed her index finger against his dry lips to shush him. "Listen, please. We've got to move quickly now. Knowing our son—how resourceful and determined he can be—I think we have to assume he'll arrange to have fresh copies of the new will executed sometime today. He thinks the other ones were lost, you see. He doesn't know I found them. I'm not sure how he'll arrange it with the notary and witnesses and so on, but that doesn't really matter. The main thing is…" Here she made an exaggerated sad face. "…you need to be gone before he arrives."

Martin's eyes widened dramatically, a ring of bloodshot white appearing around the irises. Polly couldn't recall seeing that particular expression before either. His eyeballs rolled to a disturbing sideways position. He seemed to be desperately searching for something out of his field of vision. Glancing up, Polly saw it before he did. The red call button that summoned the nurses. It was on a cord draped loosely over the corner of headboard. A bit jury-rigged for a world-class hospital like Mass General, she thought disparagingly.

Rising a little and reaching across his chest, she flicked the cord off the headboard, and the call button fell somewhere behind the bed. "Always scheming, aren't you, darling? Always one step ahead. No one will ever convince me that my husband wasn't a *very* intelligent man."

She stacked his hands on top of the folded sheet, one nested neatly on top of the other, as she had seen the hands of the dead arranged at open-casket wakes. "There, let's leave these where I can see them." She placed one of her own hands firmly over them both.

His eyelids were in a constant flurry now—first drooping, then flying open again. She got the feeling he was struggling against the effects of the increased morphine dose, valiantly trying to keep himself awake. Good. She wanted him conscious a while longer. She had more to say.

"I'm sure you can appreciate the position you've put me in," she said in a practical tone. "This would not have been my choice, I can assure you, if things had gone as planned. I have no desire to...ah..." She searched for the right word. When she couldn't find it, she went on, "You're going to die soon anyway. We just need to move that timeline up a bit. Whatever the difference is—a couple of days at most, probably—it won't mean anything to you when you're gone, and, frankly, it shouldn't mean much to you now either, given the state you're in."

Remembering the various humiliations the poor man had had to endure in the last few months caused her to choke up a little. One awful indignity after another. With her free hand, she stroked his stubbled, sunken cheek. "I know how much you've hated becoming so helpless, Martin. You might want to thank me for saving you the last little bit."

She sighed deeply and a little sorrowfully, realizing the grave enormity of the task in front of her, but she remained undaunted.

She had no real choice in the matter, not if she cared about herself. And since no one else was doing the caring for her, she *had* to do it for herself.

"There's still so much I want to experience, you see," she explained.

His eyes had become almost perfectly glassy. There was just the smallest wince of discomfort or resistance in them.

"Travel, take an art history course, learn photography," she continued, warming to her subject. "Move to a new house or an apartment in the city. Make new friends. This should be one of the loveliest times of my life, Martin, when I'm free of responsibilities and can do whatever I wish. I can't have someone telling me what my allowance will be, as if I were a child. I *need* your money, darling—*our* money, actually—so I can try to be happy before I die."

Just the word itself—*happy*—began to lift her on wings of newfound joy. A hologram image of her future self wavered on the other side of the bed, just out of reach: Polly Clancy—confident, peaceful, self-possessed—a woman entirely capable of giving and receiving love. "Oh, my dear Martin," she gushed, transfixed by the vision, "I know you want that for me, too!"

The joy crashed into something hard and immoveable, and fell abruptly to earth, like a flying bird smacking into a clean glass window.

"Oh, gosh. What was I thinking?" she muttered. "Of course you don't want me to be happy. Oh, well. At least we can finally drop the facade and say exactly how things stand between us: We were never right for each other. We should have divorced years ago." She was amazed at how utterly easy it was to tell the truth. Why had she been so afraid of it?

Martin was tranquil now. His skin had a milky undertone, as if the blood had moseyed somewhere else. She leaned close, her lips at his ear. She hoped he could hear her. Despite everything, she didn't want him to go alone. "You had a full life, my darling, and you will be missed. Not by me, at least not very much, but you weren't expecting that. Other people will miss you. The ones you cared about, if you cared about anyone. Did you, darling? Did you care about anyone?"

There was no motion in him now, other than the very shallow rising of his lungs, and a drop of spittle trembling at the corner of his mouth.

She scrunched even closer to his side. Checked the slice of hallway she could see through the open door. Made sure her body blocked the view of his face should someone enter. Then, clamping one hand tightly over his mouth, she pinched his nostrils with the fingers of her other hand. "Good-bye, Martin Clancy. God speed," she whispered tenderly.

There was some awkward twisting in his neck and fitful kicking in his legs. His hands flapped weakly for several seconds against her solidly tensed forearms. One of them tried unsuccessfully to scratch her face. It felt more like involuntary muscle spasms than purposeful resistance.

She looked over at the heart monitor when his body had fully quieted. The fluorescent green blips were still making their way across the black screen, spurting upwards at regular intervals, but the peaks were getting shallower, and the pulsing beeps of the machine seemed to be getting softer. She began to feel tired— this was difficult, lonely work—but she kept her hand pressing down as hard as she could, and her pincer fingers tightly squeezed. Soon the green waves looked like rolling speed bumps, which gradually deflated. The flat line was accompanied by a sudden screech like a detonated smoke detector.

"Nurse!" she yelled frantically, jumping to her feet. She ran to the door, stuck her head into the corridor. "Help, please! Something's wrong!"

Two nurses were already running. A young man in scrubs—a doctor or an orderly—was coming from the other direction. The three huddled at the end of Martin's bed, whispering among themselves. The young man grabbed Martin's chart and flipped through it, before turning to Polly with a tense, solemn face.

"You're the patient's health care proxy?"

Polly nodded, authentic tears pooling in her eyes. "Is he...?"

"Shall we resuscitate?" he asked.

It was just after noon. She was alone in the waiting room, sipping the last of some bitter coffee from a paper cup, when the elevator doors retracted like theatre curtains, and Ronnie stepped out in his dark wool coat, a brown folder tucked under his arm.

"Ronnie." She waved him over. "I tried to call you."

He sat in the chair next to her, concerned. "I didn't get any message. Something wrong?"

"He passed."

Ronnie dropped his gaze to the floor, and stayed completely still for a long time. Nothing moved except his jaw, which slid back and forth almost imperceptibly. When he finally looked up at her, she noticed gray sacks under his eyes, suggesting he had been up half the night.

"Was it—?" he asked.

She nodded. "Painless."

He breathed out heavily, chewed his bottom lip.

They were both silent.

"You found the folder," Polly finally said.

He glanced at her in surprise. "What?"

"The one you were looking for. You found it."

He raised the brown folder in a half-hearted, fumbling way, as if it were a strange object he had just been made aware of. "This?"

"Yes, isn't that the one you so urgently needed? Last night, when you came to the house?"

He didn't answer.

"I'm so sorry you and your father never got to discuss it, whatever it was." She crumpled her empty coffee cup, tossed it into the trash container. "I'm afraid it's too late for that now."

She started for the elevator, pleased to leave him alone to

wrestle with his disappointment, when a sharp sense of maternal duty brought her to a sudden halt. A mother owed her son her best advice at all times, she believed, whether he valued it or not. Turning to face him, she said, "You ought to be very careful how you treat Estelle, dear. You just never know what a person is truly capable of."

KILLING CALHOUN AGAIN

ALAN ORLOFF

The first time I killed Royce Calhoun I'd been floating on three Wild Turkeys and a raft of rage. We'd been drinking at a dive bar south of the Stockyards in Fort Worth, and I made out like it was pure coincidence that we found ourselves bending elbows there together, but I'd been hunting him for the better part of a week. I'd discovered he'd been doing the nasty with my gal Angela May and, well, a man's gotta do what a man's gotta do when it comes to things that gotta get done.

So I shot him. Twice. Once square in the chest and once just above his butt-ugly brass belt buckle in the shape of Texas, and just a smidgen smaller. He went down, and I went over to where he sprawled on the dusty barroom floor. Took a gander to see if I'd accomplished my mission. Those cold black orbs of his stared back at me, unseeing.

I had.

Unwilling to end up in prison, and unwilling to patch things up with Angela, I left town without looking back.

Now, three years later, I spoke into the phone from two states away. "You sure?"

"Pos-o-tive. A few years older and a whole lot grayer, but sure as shit I spotted Royce Calhoun, back in town," Mouse Honeycutt said, adding, "And he was canoodling with none other than your Miss Angela."

I had no reason to doubt Mouse, not about this anyhow. He spouted some conspiracy nonsense at times, and he had trouble always knowing right from wrong, but when it came to something like this—ratting someone out—he was usually dead on. Least he had been back when we stirred up trouble together. Still, it didn't add up. "But I killed him. Shot him dead."

"Well, you *shot* him, yessir. After you left, some of his boys came and retrieved the body. And I'd swear he was dead, too. But judging by his recent appearance, I guess he really wasn't."

"Doesn't seem possible."

"Well, Boyd Gillen and I were talking, and he said that Calhoun must have recovered somehow, then him and his cronies kept on faking his death so he wouldn't have to face up to Xavier Daniels. And now that Daniels is dead hisself, shot by one of his own crew, in fact, I guess ol' Royce felt it was safe to show his ugly mug again."

"Makes sense, I suppose." And it did sound like something Calhoun would have orchestrated. Rumor had it that he was up to his Stetson in debt to Daniels, and Mouse was probably right—with Daniels no longer on this side of the dirt, Calhoun had come crawling out of his hidey hole.

"Just thought you should know," Mouse said.

Thinking about Calhoun again had spiked my anger. "Him and Angela, huh?"

"Yep."

"See you in a couple days, Mouse. And there's no need to say anything to anyone about my return, is there?"

"No need," Mouse said. "No need at all."

Not always a man gets to kill his enemy twice.

The first time I killed Royce Calhoun I had Mouse by my side, watching my back. We'd been drinking buddies, carousing buddies, brawling buddies, and now I sat with him on the porch of his shotgun shack catching up on what I'd missed since I'd been gone, in general, and with Calhoun's resurrection in particular.

"Sure glad to see you again." Mouse tossed me a beer from a small cooler he kept at his feet and popped one open for himself. Then he leaned back in his rocker and gave me a several-gap-toothed grin. He'd never been a fan of the dentist, and things hadn't changed none in my absence.

"Glad to be here." I opened my beer and took a sip. Tepid.

Mouse squinted at me. "Come back to finish the job?"

He knew me too well. I didn't answer.

"And to see Angela again, too, I reckon." He raised his beer in the air in a mock toast.

I held my can up in response, then took a healthy gulp. "Need your help, Mouse."

"If I can, I will."

"Need your help flushing out Royce."

Mouse's face darkened. "Don't know if I can help with that. He's got some ornery friends, and I gotta live in this town." He shook his head somberly.

"You had my back before. Don't think I wasn't thankful then. Help me now, and I'll be sure to repay the favor. This time, in cash. Say five hundred?" Mouse's loyalty wafted on the wind, and I wanted to stake my clear claim to it now. Calhoun was bound to hear I was back in town, and if *he* dropped some incentive in Mouse's path, no telling whose side Mouse would play for.

"Not sure helping you take out Royce Calhoun is in the best interest of my long-term health," Mouse said.

"With Royce gone, I think his posse will stand down. Hell, half of them only do what he says 'cause they're afraid of him. With him gone, things'll be different around here." I eyed Mouse and watched his mouth pucker. "Okay, make it a thousand bucks."

Mouse downed the rest of his beer, crushed the can in his hand, then tossed it in the general direction of the front door. It bounced off the door frame and came to rest at my feet. I kicked the crushed can off the porch into the front bushes with the toe of my boot. "That's exactly what you and I will do to Royce Calhoun."

Mouse sighed. "Okay, I'll help you. But I'm not going to be the one to do the dirty deed. I merely despise the man, and that ain't no reason to actually kill him."

Mouse always did have squirrelly logic. "But it's reason enough to *help* get him killed?"

"When we're talking 'bout Royce Calhoun, it damn sure is." Mouse grinned. "Plus, I could use a thousand bucks."

The first time I killed Royce Calhoun, I'd been head-over-spurs in love with Angela May. We'd met doing the two-step one night in a crowded honky-tonk, and we quickly became a couple. That lasted until about two weeks before the incident, when we'd had a massive blow-up and had *un*coupled, going our separate ways. I'd thought it was just a temporary tiff, something lovers endured from time to time, something that'd get smoothed over before we rushed back into each other's lives, swearing it'd never happen again.

Evidently, she'd seen it as something final and had sought comfort, first in Royce Calhoun's arms and then in his bed. Although I'd wager a large sum of money that it had been mostly Calhoun's idea, probably something he'd been plotting the minute he'd seen me and Angela hitting it off so well.

Now, Angela and I sat in her kitchen, at a rickety table in rickety chairs, the sounds of a TV on somewhere in the house providing a faint soundtrack. She had a cat now, and it sashayed around, every so often rubbing up against the legs of my jeans. A stack of old newspapers rested on the floor, in the corner, perfectly folded, as if she'd never even read them. A few dirty dishes soaked in the sink, and a smattering of pizza boxes and empty liquor bottles were strewn about like accent pieces. None of that mattered to me. I was a slob, too. Two peas in a pod, two pigs in a sty, and all that.

"I'm glad you came back, Jake Pardee. I've missed you." The time I'd been gone had been good to her. She'd grown her hair out and sported freshly done nails, trimmed and tapered and painted a nice shade of red. Seemed sexier, somehow, in a more mature way. But maybe it was just absence made my heart fonder. Maybe I was just picturing her and me in bed, writhing and moaning, like back in the good ol' days. Before the break-up. Before I killed Calhoun the first time.

"I've missed you, too." The absolute truth. After my initial anger had subsided, and I figured that skunk Calhoun had coerced her into cheating, I *had* missed her. "But what's this I hear about you and Royce?"

A flash in her big brown eyes. "Who told you that?"

"Don't matter."

"We had a beer together, that's all. I was kinda shocked when I saw him, you know? Him being *dead* and all." She shook a cigarette out of a crushed pack and lit it with a shaky hand.

"Just a beer?" I asked.

"Maybe two." She took a long drag, then tilted her head and slowly blew the smoke up toward the ceiling. "Nothing going on there, Jake. I swear."

"And I'm supposed to believe you?" I loved her, but Angela sometimes only had a passing acquaintance with the truth.

She pointed her cigarette at me and a bit of ash dropped to the table. She raised her voice a bit, even though I sat only three feet away. "First of all, you and me? We ain't together no more. Second of all, you should believe me because I'm telling the truth. Third of all…" She stopped and choked up a little. Wiped a tear from her eye. "…you broke my heart when you took off. Sure, I'd slept with Royce, but that was just to make you jealous." One side of her mouth curled upward. "Guess it worked, too, dinnit?"

"Are you saying you weren't mad at me for shooting Royce?"

Her features tightened. "Oh, Jake, I don't get mad."

I waited for her to add, *I get even*, but she kept her lips pressed together.

"So now what?" I asked.

"Dunno. *You* came back to town. *You* called me up. Seems like the next move is up to *you*." She softened and hit me with one of her pussycat smiles, the kind that turned my insides to oatmeal. "But if you could see clear to give me a second chance, I'd gladly take it. And this time, I think we could make it work. I really do."

Now my *stomach* did the two-step. I hadn't been sure how I was gonna feel seeing Angela in the flesh again. Wasn't sure if I was going to be able to forgive her. But being here was just like I hadn't left. From all indications, she felt the same way. Could we pick up where we left off? Could we make it work this time?

After all, I believed in second chances, I did.

Most of the time.

For most people.

The first time I killed Royce Calhoun, I'd been blind with anger about him stealing my girl. We had a history, me and him, and that had been the goddamn last straw. As I'd tracked him down that first time, I'd pondered ways to learn him his lesson. A fistfight? I'd gone at it with Calhoun before, on several occasions, and a whipping hadn't ever been enough to change his ways. Thick, that one. Torture? Not my style. I'd come up with only one way to dislodge the thorn from my side named Royce Calhoun.

Thought I'd succeeded, in fact. Was wrong.

Now, me and Mouse asked around, checked with our friends and family, close and extended. We put the word out, on the down low, that we were looking for Calhoun, and in short order, we'd been tipped off to some of his new hangouts and watering holes. The quick response told us there were a whole lotta folks anxious for a final solution to the Royce Calhoun problem.

Looked like I was going to get my second chance to finish what I'd started.

We'd come up with a plan: corner him at a bar, then I'd pick a fight with him and kill him, claiming self-defense. I had no desire to get locked up over someone as insignificant as Royce Calhoun. But the more Mouse and I talked it out, the more we discussed the possible outcomes, the more nervous I became about getting railroaded. About getting a raw deal from the local law. About getting fingered as the aggressor, perhaps by someone who had an axe to grind with me, and there were a fair number who qualified, I feared. Too many things out of our control that could go wrong.

After knocking it around for the better part of a six-pack—each—we decided that offing Calhoun in a deserted location, without witnesses, would be our ticket to success.

We identified an abandoned warehouse on the outskirts of a lightly-trafficked industrial park.

"How are we going to get him there?" Mouse asked.

"Tell him that you heard about a lucrative job, and that you need a partner. Tempt him with tales of riches."

Mouse's eyes bugged out. "Me? You want *me* to call him?"

"If I called him, he'd be suspicious, don't you think?" Mouse wasn't the sharpest nail in the box.

"Okay. But I'll say it again. I'm not pulling the trigger. Not even showing up."

"Fine. Just arrange the meeting. I'll take it from there."

Mouse made the call and arranged the meeting for tonight at eight o'clock sharp.

I took a shower, grabbed some grub, and cleaned my pistol, counting down the hours.

At twenty minutes past seven, I pulled up to the abandoned warehouse in Mouse's truck. We wanted to set the trap right, and if Mouse was supposed to meet Calhoun, we needed to make it look like he was there.

No other vehicles were in sight, and from where I'd parked, you couldn't see any others in front of the neighboring warehouse buildings about a quarter mile away, neither. The place was perfect. No one would be able to hear Calhoun beg for mercy. No one would be able to hear the gunshots.

I circled the warehouse, getting the lay of the land, just to make sure there'd be no surprises, then entered through a back door that had been pulled halfway off its hinges. I waited a moment for my eyes to adjust. There were plenty of shadowy corners to hide in, but a row of busted windows lining one wall would allow enough light in for me to get a good bead on Calhoun when he arrived, even as the sun was beginning to set.

It took a few minutes to find a decent hiding place near the front door, and as I squirmed into it, I felt the reassuring weight of my pistol in its holster. I'd say what I had to say to Calhoun, then I'd give him lead poisoning.

I settled into my crevice and tried to control my breathing as I waited.

Half an hour passed, then the front door swung open on creaky hinges, and Calhoun stood there, a dark silhouette. "Mouse?" he called out as he stepped into the warehouse proper. He, too, paused. "Mouse? Where you at?"

Calhoun's voice echoed in the cavernous space. He walked farther inside, slowly, cautiously, as if maybe someone had set a trap for him. A sickening thought struck me. Had Mouse tipped him off? I noodled it through and relaxed. If Mouse had blabbed, then Calhoun would have come in, gun drawn. He'd probably bring back up, too. I exhaled and quietly pulled out my pistol.

Calhoun had drifted to the other side of the large room, and I seized that opportunity to slip out of my hiding place and creep a few steps closer. When he turned around, I sprang out at him, brandishing my piece. "Don't move a muscle, Royce.

Unless you want to be dead before you hear what I got to say to you. And that'd be a true shame."

Calhoun jerked back in surprise, but recovered quickly. Laughed. "Well, lookie who it is. Jake Pardee, come to finish what he started. You know, being a dead man had its privileges. Didn't have to watch out for critters sneaking up on me from behind."

"Ain't right going after another man's girl."

"She came after me. Didn't seem like she was satisfied with what she had. Fact is, I could hardly have stopped her. If I'd wanted to, that is."

My finger caressed the trigger. "You're full of shit."

He shrugged. Casually. Too casually. The hair on my forearms bristled. Something was—

"Lay down your piece, Jake. Nice and slow," a voice commanded from somewhere off to my right.

I froze. Calhoun cackled.

Mouse stepped out of the shadows, not twenty feet from where I stood, gun aimed directly at me. "Do it now. Drop it on the floor."

I held onto my gun. If I was going to get gunned down, might as well get off a shot of my own. "Ah, Mouse. Betraying an old friend?"

"Since you left, me and Royce have gotten tight. Fact is, it was his idea for me to call you. Lure you back to town. He didn't want to be looking over his shoulder the rest of his life. Wanted to settle things. After all, you tried to kill him. A man don't usually look kindly on that."

"Shut up, Mouse." Calhoun drew a gun from his waistband. "Pardee don't need to know all the details. Pardee just needs to know that he'll be drawing his last breath real soon."

They say time slowed when you were facing death, and it did for me. I glanced back and forth, from Calhoun to Mouse and back to Calhoun. Both men had their guns trained on me. I might be able to get a shot off at one, but I'd be dead in my boots 'fore I got off a second.

While I was contemplating my move, a shot rang out.

Mouse crumpled where he stood.

I hit the deck, rolled, came up shooting at Calhoun. Fired once. Twice. Thrice. He dropped like a sack of feed. He'd been too surprised at Mouse getting shot to even think about pulling the trigger on me.

I kept low, not knowing exactly what was going on, but I figured anybody shooting at Calhoun and Mouse might very well be someone I'd like to buy a drink.

After a few moments, Angela May emerged from a dark corner.

"So, how about that second chance, Jake Pardee?" She grinned as she holstered her gun. "I think we could make it work. I really do."

Three minutes later, Angela and I were in her truck, headed west, destination unknown.

I liked to take full advantage of second chances.

The second time I killed Royce Calhoun was even sweeter than the first.

And much more permanent.

Three years later

Now, lemme tell you about the first time I killed Angela May...

CODA

G. MIKI HAYDEN

The piano tuner ran through the usual succession of ascending chords, enjoying the touch of each gently yellowed, ivory key. His ear sufficed to find the flaws, but he had left none here. He was well familiar with the instruments in the recital hall near the Old Market Square—the concert grands he had guarded respectfully during many of Warsaw's economically and politically difficult years.

Lojek smiled to himself, but a moment later stopped his work in response to the unwelcome shouting of the crowd in the square. Lech Walesa, the electrician from Gdansk, was out there speaking, inciting change with his Solidarity movement. Not that the piano tuner cared one way or the other. Politics, which pervaded every aspect of Polish life, had been a matter of great indifference to him for the last several decades. Lojek classified his concerns in very different terms than political ones. The issues that obsessed him he considered to be personal.

A concerto came to mind as he sat there, and his fingers followed.

With no more announcement than the creaking of the wooden doors to the hall, a man walked in while Lojek played. Lojek ought to stop, but, really, why? The white-haired man came to the front of the auditorium, and Lojek peered down at him.

"Good day, comrade maestro," Lojek called to the foot of the stage, recognizing the man from the posters.

"Guten tag," replied the honored guest conductor, and the man found the stairs and walked up to where the piano tuner sat.

Lojek nodded and smiled and finally stopped the music he made.

"You play Tansman, do you?" commented the maestro, still speaking German.

"My bad taste," agreed Lojek, for Tansman, the Jewish-Polish composer who had lived in France since 1919, wasn't acceptable in Communist Poland. Politics, politics. Lojek gave the maestro a smile that bespoke some irony. "What do we musicians give our devotion to, music or politics?" he asked. Of course, Lojek shouldn't classify himself as a musician before a conductor of such note.

The maestro shrugged. "You play well," he commented.

"I was trying to tune the piano for the concert tomorrow, but the noise from the square…"

Poland was on the verge of economic collapse, which the conductor from East Berlin surely knew. Economic collapse, rioting, chaos—all those meant the present government might crumble—yet the Communist regime itself would never fall. The people of Poland could indeed go hungry, but should they starve, they would do so under Communism, damn it.

Lojek let out a short laugh at his own inner dark humor and rose from his seat. "I'll go out for a while, maestro, and then come back," he said. "Will you be here when I return?"

"Possibly. I want to get the feel of the hall. The acoustics," the conductor answered. He glanced around.

Lojek walked down off the stage, and after he did so, the other man took the seat the piano tuner had vacated and began to play Chopin. Chopin had himself been an exile to France, but since the composer hadn't been a Jew, he was tolerated, even exalted, by the Polish Party.

Once outside, Lojek found himself moving against the growing mob thronging into the Old Market Square. He squeezed his bulk this way and that and tried to flatten himself along the walls of the venerated Medieval buildings. The cafes and restaurants that usually made the shabby, impoverished old city center a place of escape were shuttered now for fear of damage by the masses.

Down a side street, and avoiding the increasing numbers of police, Lojek turned onto Grodzka, then made his way to the bank of the Vistula near the Slasko-Dabrowski Bridge. Even the river these days smelled of Poland's peculiar brand of poverty. Lojek sat on a piece of stone wall, lit a cigarette, and waited.

Itzkovich came out of the dark, approached, and leaned on the wall next to Lojek. This was only the third time Lojek had met with Itzkovich, and the piano tuner wasn't yet sure what to think of the man, but that didn't matter, really.

"It's him," said Lojek.

"Absolutely sure?"

"Oh yes, more than absolutely. Much more."

"Many years have gone by," said Itzkovich.

"Have they?" asked Lojek. "Not for me."

The foreigner slouched against the wall next to Lojek and looked around.

"Everyone's listening to Walesa," said Lojek.

Itzkovich nodded. He reached into his pocket, pulled out a semi-automatic handgun, and gave it to the Pole, who examined the gun, then simply stuck it in his pocket. "A Pistolen-08," said Lojek with a slight chuckle, using the formal name of the Luger pistol, a favorite of Himmler's Waffen SS.

"Did you think we wanted the police to trace the damn thing to us?" By "us," Itzkovich meant the people Lojek had contacted a month before: the Israeli Mossad.

Lojek didn't feel like answering. He got down from his uncomfortable seat. "No more Eichmanns," he said finally. SS Obergruppenführer Adolph Eichmann, responsible for mass deportation of Jews to the extermination camps, had been captured by the Mossad in Argentina and brought before an Israeli court for war crimes, then convicted and hanged.

Itzkovich gave a sign of agreement. "But you'd better be right," he added.

"Yes, yes," said Lojek.

Already tired of the Israeli, Lojek walked back toward the recital hall. He would try to circle around and avoid the police, the crowds. He could visualize truncheons coming down on necks, hotheads run over by official vehicles or trampled by officers on horseback.

Lojek admired the Mossad's tactic of refusing to do the job themselves but deputizing the local idiot, a man stupid enough, or desperate enough, or despairing enough to do the killing. Lojek could admit to being all of these, yet he would still confess his trepidation. He was nervous with a million ugly *what-if*s filling his head.

Fate favored him, however, and he knew it. How could he have predicted the congregation of so many radicals in one place and the convenience of the noise and the confusion they provided to hide what authorities would call the "crime." Lojek, of course, called what he intended to do *justice*.

Since he knew the square and his end destination well, he felt he could slip by quietly and without fuss. He should have reckoned with the determination of the Citizens Militia in countering the anticommunist Solidarity movement. Every byway Lojek sought seemed to be blocked by barricades and chanting workers. But Lojek had to return to the recital hall. He'd waited too many years for this moment, and he wasn't going to let either the strikers or ZOMO—the motorized detachments controlling the square—stop him now.

The piano tuner began to wiggle his way through the crowd, then under the barricades, and then forward. So many people were in the square already, he couldn't figure out why the police wanted to keep anyone out. But that was the present government for you. If the workers wanted to go north, the Peoples Republic of

Poland and Prime Minister Jaroszewicz must make them go south.

Scrambling over yet another barrier, Lojek just about fell into the arms of one of the very officers he'd hoped to avoid. Lojek quickly tried to appeal to him to understand that he was just the piano tuner and needed at the hall, over there. The man, an instrument of the state, was armed with a baton and not hesitant about using it.

Before Lojek even realized what he was doing, he had the gun Itzkovich had given him in his hand. He suddenly ceased all resistance and hugged the militia man to him as he might an old friend. He shot the Luger and felt the other man also give up his opposition—in fact, all life.

Dear God, thought Lojek. But he didn't mean God. God had vanished for him many, many years before. Still, he felt, if not bad exactly, perhaps that he'd wasted a human life.

The gun had issued no report or none that could raise its voice above the excitement of the crowd. And when Lojek released his victim and looked around, if anyone saw him, and a couple of men did, their reactions were of a different kind than might ordinarily be expected. One of the witnesses actually shrugged at Lojek as if to offer a commonplace, *In such times, what can one do?*

Lojek felt he had lived in "such times" all his life, and he continued on, around the least of the crowds in between two buildings until soon he was back at the recital hall. He put away the gun and pulled closed his cotton jacket, buttoning it, to obscure the bloodstains.

He stood a moment outside the tall, embossed wooden doors of the auditorium and tried to relax, then pushed them open. He locked the doors behind him and made his way up toward the stage. The maestro had taken a seat on a worn velvet theater chair in the front row. He looked up from his notes at Lojek who settled against the wooden lip of the stage apron that came to his upper back.

"All you all right?" asked the maestro. "You seem upset."

"Yes," said Lojek. "I'm fine. Quite a lot is happening outside, however. I think you may regret coming to Poland."

"We can't control these things," remarked the maestro. "The rabble…"

"Must be Jews," said Lojek. In the square, the shouting, brash, sincere, rose ever louder.

"Of that we can't be certain," answered the maestro. "Are you positive you're all right?"

Lojek stared at the man. He unbuttoned his jacket and opened it to examine the bloodstains. "I killed a member of the Citizens Militia on my way across the square."

"You must be kidding," said the maestro. "Why tell me?"

"I know who you are." Lojek's eyes remained on the man.

"I would hope so," agreed the maestro.

"No. I mean I really know." And Lojek took the long-barreled gun from out of his pocket. The gun, too, had blood on it for he had pulled the trigger while holding it tight against the officer.

Outside, a single voice could be heard over an amplifying system. Lojek was unable to make out any individual words.

"Who am I then?" asked the maestro. He leaned forward a little bit in his seat.

"You were there at the train station," Lojek said in Polish. "You were with the Judenrat, the so-called Jewish Council. You helped herd the rest of us into the cars. I remember very well."

"Not at all," objected Schmerling, or the man who now called himself Maestro Erik von Josephs.

Lojek noted that the conductor didn't pretend not to understand Polish.

Perhaps Lojek should have sniffed Schmerling out many years before. But how many conductors, how many musicians, were there on the European continent? Lojek had only had the realization when a poster picturing Josephs was put up both inside and outside the rehearsal hall. In coming to tune the piano for another concert, Lojek had been struck through the heart by the photo of the white-haired, genteel-appearing Schmerling.

Sadistic was the word that had been most often used to describe the maestro all that time before.

"I was ten years old," Lojek said. "They took me away with my father."

"Ah, so sad," Schmerling observed. "Terrible days. But that has nothing to do with me." The maestro had begun to sweat and he wiped a hand across his brow.

"You can't imagine how hot it was in the cattle cars," said Lojek. "So many crammed together in there. We had two dead already by the time we reached Treblinka."

"And your father?" asked Schmerling as if he were inquiring into an acquaintance's health.

"He went, as we said, up the chimneys." That was, his father, a lovely man, had been gassed and cremated to make way for others. Lojek's having survived was simply an oddity. The year 1942, when he'd been taken away, until the "liberation" of the camp by the Soviets in 1944, had been a lifetime. Yes, he remembered the short duration of the prisoners' revolt. Like a dream, a foggy episode in the midst of a nightmare.

Schmerling shook his head as a sign of great regret for something from which he was completely removed. Perhaps Schmerling even believed he hadn't been responsible.

But what Schmerling believed made very little difference to Lojek, who boosted himself upon the stage to wait more comfortably.

"What now?" asked Schmerling. "So many years later. Your memory has gone bad and you see those who once harmed you everywhere, a terrible, but perhaps understandable paranoia. A distortion."

Lojek laughed. These men had been insane at the very start of it all and they were insane now. Schmerling thought he could manipulate Lojek?

"What now? No 'man in the glass booth' trial for you," Lojek said, referring to Eichmann who'd been placed in a glass booth for his safety during his trial in Israel. "I'm simply going to execute you, Schmerling."

"Ich bin nicht Schmerling," the maestro denied, switching to German.

Lojek smiled.

"All right. Shoot me then," said Schmerling in Polish.

"Oh, I will."

"You won't get away with it."

"Why not?" asked Lojek. "You did. Until now." The shouting outside was that of a single, united voice. Angry. Enthusiastic. Seeking justice. Seeking revenge. "I will get away with it," he added. "But it doesn't matter. Any real life I had ended nearly forty years ago."

The two men sat there and stared at one another.

Schmerling squirmed in his seat. "What are you waiting for?" he asked after a while.

"The apex of the crescendo," Lojek said. "We will listen to the music of the chorus outside. We will listen for the crescendo. At the very top, I will shoot you, and you won't hear the tune descend."

Despite the noise on the outside, the interior of the theater seemed quiet, still...benign. Not a mouse stirred.

In front of him, Lojek saw the boxcars. He saw Schmerling, oh so clearly. But the sense that occupied him most right now was his hearing. When the crescendo came to its absolute high point, the sound of an explosion would tear through the theatre, a final note ending thirty-eight sad, lonely, agonizing, tormenting years.

Sad, lonely, agonizing, tormenting for the maestro as well? Lojek certainly hoped so.

A MATTER OF DUTY

CHARLES TODD

September 1919, London

"I always fancied tall men," she said, smiling coquettishly as she looked up at him. "Are you married? Not that it matters. I won't tell if you don't."

Rutledge threw a stern glance in the direction of the grinning constable, who flushed and quickly straightened his face. Rutledge turned his attention back to the elderly woman draped in an array of shawls and wearing a bedraggled cast-off hat, its feathers drooping sadly.

"I'm told you witnessed the murder?"

"Give us a kiss, and I'll tell you what I know." She lifted her chin, daring him.

"You'll tell me now, or at Scotland Yard," he retorted,

Pouting, she said, "I pity your poor wife, I do." But as he gestured the constable to come forward, she quickly added, "I didn't see it, like. I did hear someone cry out. By the time I found him behind yon crates, he was gasping his last. But the lady was still there."

"What lady?" Rutledge asked sharply.

"She was tallish, slender. Veiled. She smelled of sandalwood— I caught a whiff as she turned to go. Which was as soon as she saw me. She dropped the knife in her hand, and I could see the blood all over her white gloves."

"You're sure they were bloody?" The lighting here was dismal.

"They were splotched, black."

Rutledge looked around, ignoring the small crowd of dustmen who had come to clear away and stayed to gawk.

Covent Garden drew large audiences when there were performances. He'd been to more than a few. Tonight the building was dark, and back here, where produce was brought into the city in bulk, there were more shadows than light.

He walked back to the victim, trailed by his witness. The dead man lay behind two barrows, sprawled now on his back, where Constable Higgins had turned him over to look for signs of life. The gold watch chain across his vest stood out against the dark cloth of his evening clothes.

Not robbery, then.

"How was the lady dressed?"

The old woman described the lady's clothing with the eye of a connoisseur. "Long dark evening cloak, lined with silk, a pale blue evening gown beneath, and feathers in her dark hair, which was pinned back to show off diamond earrings. No idea why they should choose to meet here. She'd have dirtied her skirts in the muck."

He'd been asking himself the same question as he sent Constable Higgins running to find any hansom cabbies on the street. Although it was more likely that they'd come, the man and the lady, by private carriage.

"Were they together? Have you seen them before?" he asked.

"Buy my violets, and I'll tell you."

Sighing, he bought the remaining bunches, and she said cheekily, "You might kiss me too." But the expression on his face wiped the grin from hers.

"Oh, very well. I've seen him a time or two. But not her. They must have been together, else why would she suddenly take a knife to him?"

"Why was he here?" A sergeant had arrived with the doctor and more constables. Rutledge moved away, letting them do their work.

"Love, he never said. But he was looking for someone, I expect. Sadly, not me. Distracted, like."

"In evening clothes?"

"Never saw him any other way."

A private party, then? But why stop at Covent Garden on his way? Or returning home? It didn't make sense. Rutledge had heard a church clock chime two just as he'd arrived. The market was nearly deserted, at this hour there was little to bring a gentleman here. Much less a lady...

Constable Higgins came back, out of breath as he reported. "No one has seen the gentleman. One of the drivers thinks he saw a lady disappearing down that street." He pointed—it was one of the streets that led to the market. "But he's not sure."

The sergeant came up to speak to Rutledge. "He's dead. Knife's long enough to reach his heart." He handed Rutledge a man's wallet, then went back to the body.

Rutledge opened it, after elbowing the old woman away, as she tried to peer over his arm.

Money, enough for an evening of gambling, cards to several clubs, and his identification. *Edwin Marshall.*

Rutledge knew the name, although he hadn't recognized the face. But then he hadn't seen the man for ten—twelve years? Marshall had come to his father, a solicitor, to ask about a divorce from his wife, claiming that she had lied to him about who she was—her family was in trade. Whether he'd pursued the divorce or not, Rutledge didn't know. He'd only heard part of the conversation while waiting for his father.

He turned to Higgins. "Take three or four men and comb every street leading into the Garden. Look for a gambling den, a house of prostitution, or even a private party. Wherever a man might walk from here." As soon as the constable had left, Rutledge said to the old woman, "Leave your name and address with the sergeant. He'll want a statement from you."

She started to argue with him, but he shook his head. "I have other work to do."

He conferred briefly with the doctor and the sergeant, then left. His own motorcar was standing at the entrance to the market, and he drove through the quiet streets of London toward the elegant world of the wealthy and influential.

Marshall's house was on street lined with plane trees, their peeling bark visible his headlamps as Rutledge slowed to look for Number Seventeen. Except for the numbers by the door, it was impossible to tell one house from its neighbors, for they were all painted white, with a black door, an expensive brass knocker, and a pair of potted trees on the doorstep.

He got down and went to lift the knocker.

When at last a middle-aged woman wearing a heavy wool dressing gown opened the door a crack, he held up his identification so that she could see it in the light of the lamp on the table behind her. "Inspector Rutledge, Scotland Yard. Is this the home of Edwin Marshall?"

"It is, sir, but he's asleep in his bed, and I shouldn't like to wake him. Could you come back in the morning?"

"I'm afraid it can't wait."

"But, sir—"

"I'm sorry to be the bearer of this news—"

He was cut short by a cross male voice from the top of the stairs. "What is it at this hour, Mrs. Tremayne? Send him off, he has no business waking decent people."

"It's—he says he's Scotland Yard, sir. I think you'd best come down."

Angry footsteps on the staircase, and then a man in a dressing gown came stepped in front of the housekeeper.

"Well, speak up," he said brusquely "What is your business here? Be brief, or I'll report you for this disturbance."

It was Edwin Marshall—changed with age, but clearly recognizable. "I think it would be best if I came in," Rutledge said, and as Marshall and the housekeeper stepped back, he moved into the handsome foyer. "There's been a death," he said abruptly. "And the murdered man was carrying your identification."

"Murdered—what's this?"

"Can you tell me why such a victim was carrying your identification?"

"Possibly because I was pickpocketed last week, and you lot did damn all about it."

Hamish, in the back of Rutledge's mind, said. "He's no' the first, ye ken?"

And it was true. Sergeant Gibson had been complaining about the number of cases in the last six months.

Men, all of them—middle-aged, respected, well-to-do...

"Where did this happen?"

"The Opera House, of all places. Didn't know my wallet was gone until I had to pay the cabbie for taking me home afterward. Bound to have happened there, but the manager told me it was the cabbie who brought me to the Opera, or even the friend I was with. Anyone but his people. Damned fool."

Rutledge went next to the morgue to look at the victim in better light. There was a passing resemblance to Marshall. But not as strong as he'd thought there was at the scene. The same graying hair, the same Edward VII beard—middle-aged, portly...

He looked at the body again. *Thin.* "Where are his clothes?"

The attendant showed him the lot. "And he was wearing this, oddly enough." He held up a stomach pad, such as actors wore. "He was wearing grease paint as well. Changed his appearance with it. That's been washed off."

Rutledge swore. "You should have informed me straight away."

Stopping by the Yard, he spoke to Sergeant Gibson.

Putting aside the file he was reading, Gibson said, "We've had men watching when there was a performance. But we never caught the pickpocket."

"Because it was probably a woman, dressed to attend the opera. His killer, in all likelihood. And she passed the wallets to someone else—our victim. But why kill him?" He gave the matter some thought as Gibson waited. "Marshall's wallet had money in it. What if it wasn't money our man wanted—but a different identity?"

Gibson considered the question. "Shall I look through the fraud inquiries, sir? He might have wished to withdraw a larger sum by pretending to be someone else."

"Possibly. Still, none of the pickpocket victims have reported other losses, have they? Just their wallets. Look at unsolved murders. What do we have in that file?"

Gibson took it from a drawer in his desk and began to thumb through it, reading the particulars of each murder to Rutledge. And each time Rutledge shook his head. "Cast your net wider, Gibson. An inquiry where a gentleman might have been involved."

"Well, there's the prostitutes, sir. That could be a gentleman. Ten of them reported missing in the last six months. So far only three bodies found, each on Hampstead Heath. Two identified, third hasn't been. He beat them to death with a Malacca cane, so the surgeon says. That's the only clue we have—"

"Did he indeed?" He thanked Gibson and left.

At the next performance at the Opera, Rutledge was there. He'd purchased a few odds and ends, borrowed a few more items from the morgue and his sister, and dressed with care.

Hamish said, as Rutledge left his flat, "Your ain brother wouldna' know ye." For Rutledge had greying streaks in his dark hair, an Edwardian beard that itched from the glue required to keep it in place, a visible paunch that he'd had more than a little trouble buttoning his own clothes over, and faint lines on his face that aged him, as long as he was in dim light.

Wearing evening dress, carrying an ivory-headed cane, he summoned a cabbie and was driven to Covent Garden. He had his ticket for a box and was early enough to enjoy the bar before lights dimmed and he headed to his seat. No one paid him any particular attention.

An attractive young woman appeared in the doorway of his box just before the curtain went up. She ignored him until the interval, seemingly absorbed in the music. And then she stumbled over her own skirts as she was leaving to join the rest of the audience, making their way toward the bar.

Rutledge moved quickly to keep her from falling, and she smiled up at him as he caught her and set her on her feet again. The scent she was wearing was sandalwood...

"Thank you," she said huskily, turning her head away in embarrassment. "I would have been hurt, if you hadn't acted so promptly."

"Could I bring you something?" he asked.

"How thoughtful of you. But I think I shall sit here and catch my breath. I feel rather shaken."

He left her there, and when he returned, the attendant informed him that the lady had requested a cab, telling him she was feeling unwell.

The constable, a young man in dressed in workman's clothing, whom Rutledge had posted outside, came up just then. "I helped her into the cab," he said, "and I heard her give the cabbie her direction, sir." And he handed Rutledge a slip of paper.

Rutledge had already looked in his pocket. The wallet that he'd prepared for the evening was gone.

He found a cabbie to take him to the address given him, close by the British museum. It turned out to be a lodging house for actors out of work.

Showing his identification to the woman who answered the

door, he described the young lady.

"There's no one here by that description."

"A cabbie put her down here not fifteen minutes ago."

"That was Tommy," she said, grinning. "My lad. He loves to dress and attend the opera. No harm done."

"Then it's Tommy I wish to see."

She argued with him, but after he threatened her with obstructing the police in the course of their duties, she went to the stairs and shouted for her son.

A tall, slim boy of fifteen came down warily, eyeing his mother and then Rutledge, who hadn't changed out of his evening dress.

Tommy had removed the pale blue dress he'd worn under his cloak and the pretty blonde wig. But the face powder and rouge as well as the sandalwood scent he'd worn earlier gave him away.

"My wallet," Rutledge ordered harshly.

"I—I don't have it," the boy said. His voice was light, refined. "I gave it to Mum."

Rutledge turned on the woman, who began to back away.

"I need the money," she began. "He never paid the rent, that man, and I was terrified of him. I was glad to see the end of him." She began to cry. "I think he killed the young woman who had lodgings next door. She was no better than she ought to be, but she didn't deserve to die."

"Why do you think he killed her?"

"Look in his room," she said, pointing to the top of the stairs. "There's things there that frightened me."

"What was his name?"

"Bertie Sommers. He said. He never got any letters. So I couldn't be sure, could I?"

Rutledge went up the stairs, trailed by mother and son. The door to the room she'd indicated was locked.

"I never had a key. He kept it. I only saw in that once, when he forgot to lock it."

"Stand away," Rutledge said in resignation, and broke down the door.

He stepped inside, but the woman and her son stayed in the passage, peering into the room.

There was a white coverlet on the bed against the far wall, and all along the side were locks of hair—brown, red, blonde— each tied with a ribbon that had been carefully sewn into the cloth of the coverlet itself.

"Why didn't you call the police?" he asked, turning away in disgust. "After you'd seen this?"

"I daren't. He wasn't a man you'd cross. I was afraid he'd kill us too." She pointed shakily to a red lock of hair. "That's Jennie's—I'm sure of it."

"Was her body ever found?"

"They found something. They can't be sure it's her."

He was walking around the room, opening drawers and finding pots of makeup and a variety of beards, as well as a box full of wallets. Opening the first two or three of the ten or twelve in the box, he saw that they belonged to different men, all of them with street addresses in squares like Edwin Marshall's.

"That's them," the boy exclaimed. "He wouldn't even let me keep the money."

"Is that why you killed him?" When the boy looked alarmed, Rutledge added, "You were seen behind Covent Garden, dressed as you were tonight, and standing over the body, the knife you'd used still in your hand."

"But I never did! I always met him outside the Opera House and handed him the wallet I'd taken. He didn't trust me, he was always *there*." He was pleading now, fright in his eyes, looking frantically from Rutledge to his mother. "Ask anyone—ask the flower lady who sits by the steps."

"What flower lady?" Rutledge asked.

"She's old—older than my mother. She sells flowers for the ladies. Men buy them from her. She's always there, chatting up the men."

But she hadn't been there tonight...

Rutledge gave them a stern warning not to leave the house until he came back. And then he left them standing there beside the broken door. He went back to the market behind Covent Garden.

A lorry had just arrived, and porters were unloading it. But the old woman wasn't there, although he made a thorough search. He finally stopped a porter carrying cabbages in the sack over his shoulder, and asked about her.

"The one selling violets? That's Lettie. She wasn't here tonight," the porter said. "Or for the last few nights, come to think of it."

"I must find her," Rutledge said affably, "There's a lady who prefers Lettie's violets."

The porter grinned. "Then you're out of luck, sir. At least tonight."

But Rutledge spent over an hour searching the market, looking in stalls and under piles of sacking. And he found a tray, a dead violet leaf caught in one corner. Lying in the tray was a knife, and he studied it with interest. The Yard already had one, covered in the victim's blood.

He ought to return to Sommers' room, to look for any clues to where more bodies might be found. Instead he went to the Yard. Gibson wasn't there, but the file he'd shown Rutledge earlier was still in the stack on his desk.

He opened it and scanned the list of bodies found on the Heath. Of the two who had been identified, one had lived with her grandmother in Bloomsbury. The file also described how she had been beaten to death. It was ugly. But the name given for the grandmother was not Lettie.

Still, it was the only clue he had. He noted the address and left the Yard.

* * *

It was just after dawn when Rutledge drew in his motorcar within view of the small house sandwiched between two larger ones, where the dead girl had lived. There was a chill in the air this morning, but he ignored the rug in the rear seat, where the voice of Hamish MacLeod so often came from. Folding his arms across his chest, he waited. The hours crept by.

At length she came out, although he barely recognized the person dressed in sober black and pulling on black gloves as she walked down the street, hurrying a little as she saw the omnibus in the distance.

He got out and followed her, calling to her as she paused at the corner.

"Lettie?"

She turned, unable to hide the dread in her face as recognized him. But she said nothing. Waiting.

He brought the knife out from behind his back, and held it out.

Sighing, she said, "My name is Helen Jordan. My granddaughter Lily's funeral is today. I wanted very much to be there. Will you let me attend? And then I'll tell you whatever you wish."

"Why did you kill him?"

"They wouldn't let me see her body. But they told me how she had suffered. 'You're to blame,' the attendant told me, 'letting one so young walk the streets.' But she hadn't. She'd sold violets at the Opera House, to make a little money. And when he came up to her and offered a different life, she believed him. I took her place, and I twisted a note in every bunch I sold to men like him. Just her name. I waited—and finally he appeared at the market, looking for me. He told me he could take me to Lily, but of course he was lying. He had a knife, but I had one too. He didn't expect that. I was quicker, because I already knew what I wanted to do. He died easily. Not like Lily. But I left him where he fell. Among the boxes and sacks and filth of the market. Just as he'd abandoned Lily when he'd finished with her."

"He killed others. Not just Lily."

"That's what the policeman told me when he came with the news she'd been found. I asked why her killer hadn't been stopped. And he told me that they had nothing to go on. She lay in the morgue for three weeks before they identified her from the report I'd made in *June*." Her voice nearly broke on the last word. But she looked up at him and said, "I should be given a medal for doing your work for you. I won't mind hanging. I don't have anything to live for now. But I'd like to go to the service for Lily."

He heard himself saying, "I'll drive you there."

Nodding, she quietly followed him to his motorcar.

They were the only two mourners at the sad little service.

Afterward, Lettie said, resignation in her voice, "You kept your promise. Now I'll keep mine."

He helped her into the motorcar.

By the time he'd turned the crank, he'd made up his mind, although Hamish was not happy with it. "Ye must do your duty," he reminded Rutledge. "You're a policeman, no' a judge."

As Rutledge got into the motorcar, he said to her, "I'll make a bargain with you. I'll take you home. But I'll keep the knife. If you come to the notice of the police again, I'll see you are charged with the unsolved murder at the market and tried for it. Do you agree?"

She cried then, although she'd sat dry-eyed throughout the service. "I thought—I was resigned—there would be no one left to put flowers on her grave every year."

He gave her his handkerchief, and when she was a little calmer, he asked, "As a matter of curiosity, the woman you described as his killer—was *she* there?"

"I'd seen her several times at the Opera. I never expected anyone to believe me anyway. And so I described her as the killer." She looked at him through her tears. "Lily thought she would have clothes like that, and a carriage. He deserved to die, if only for breaking her heart."

Rutledge thought of the locks of hair sewn into the coverlet of Sommers' bed, and silently cursed the man again.

But he said nothing of that to Lily's grandmother as he drove her back to Bloomsbury.

STRANGE THINGS IN THE NAME OF LOVE
HEATHER GRAHAM

The body was in pieces.

Several of them.

Limbs had been spread over several sarcophagus-style graves, while the head and feet had been placed as if they sat on welcome mats in front of the family mausoleums in the old graveyard.

Alex LeBlanc looked at Officer Andrew Smith, the first man from the NOPD on the scene.

"The medical examiner is on the way?" she asked.

He nodded and grimaced. "I thought it was a prank at first. Some kid chased me down on the road, screaming there was a dead man in the cemetery. I said, 'Hey, kid, there's lots of dead men in the cemetery.' Then I realized he was serious. You know, there's a reason we ask for people to have guides into the cemeteries—not to mention the folks who want to write on the Marie Laveau tomb and act like fools and rip stuff up. Or the drug deals that sometimes go down. Anyway, the kid was—as you can see—right."

"Thanks, Andrew," Alex said. "Please make sure it's closed off. See that the gates are locked—no tours anywhere in here. We don't need anyone but those who need to be in here walking around. This will hit the media in a big way, and we don't want details out."

"The kid will talk to the media," Andrew said, shaking his head sadly.

"Yes, but he was freaked out, and we'll keep details from him. And when we've got something to say, we'll call a press conference."

"Okay, well, reporters are already gathering at the gate—"

"Right. You can tell them we have found remains in the cemetery, but we don't know anything else. We don't have an identity on the body, and when we have something, we will talk. Where's the kid, by the way?"

"He ran. I told you. He was terrified."

"Ran—"

"Alex, I couldn't stop him. He was yelling hysterically at me, and then he took off and ran toward Rampart Street." He hesitated. Andrew was nearing retirement. He was a good cop. He had turned down a few promotions. He told her once that he loved New Orleans and people. He did not love paperwork—and did as little of it as possible.

"We need to find that kid," Alex said. "Andrew, please, see that our officers are out looking for him."

She started to walk away, but Andrew called her back, saying her name softly.

"Alex."

She turned to look at him.

"He's back."

She frowned. All she could think of from his words was the Alice Cooper song, "The Man Behind the Mask."

"Who is back?" she asked him.

"I guess it was what? About fifteen or sixteen years ago now? You were probably just in middle-school back then," Andrew said tightly. He let out his breath. "It happened soon after Katrina and everything was a mess and...I was a beat cop and it might be why I stayed a beat cop."

"What happened?" she asked.

Andrew extended an arm. "This," he said. "Body parts. In

two of the cemeteries. And by the time anyone got to them... well, we couldn't tell much of anything. And in trying to get the city back up after the storm, it went cold-case without anyone finding out much of anything. You need to remember, some people were loving the cops then, some were hating the cops, people abandoned the city, some came back, new people came in..."

She shook her head. "How many bodies?" she asked.

"Uh, I believe they found parts to one body. One male."

"And that didn't become major news because—"

"Katrina. Bodies everywhere," he reminded her.

She nodded. "Thanks. So, let's control this with the press. I can't imagine the same killer went dormant for almost twenty years and suddenly started up again, but this time, we will investigate until we find out what's going on."

Andrew smiled at her. "I believe you!"

Alex nodded and smiled back, then left Andrew behind and began to investigate the crime scene, drawing out her smart phone, starting to make notes. She was careful—not wanting to trample any little bit of evidence the forensic crew might find— and watched the ground as she walked first to the tomb where the head lay in waiting.

The victim had been a man. She had no idea of how he had died, but his eyes were open, giving the real human head the look of a Halloween prop set in front of a "tomb" at an amusement park. He'd been in his forties, she thought, with thinning, gray-ing hair and a face showing lines that suggested he wasn't too old but wasn't too young. His hair had once been dark; his eyes a powdery blue.

She frowned, noting a little patch of dirt and grass near the tomb. She tried to decide if a few lines there were natural from rain and the elements, or if someone had tried to write some-thing. She studied the little area, and then snapped a photo of it. Looking at her photo, she shrugged. Rivulet lines from rain, she decided.

"The torso is in a little strip of flowers over there," someone said in deep tones.

She was startled by the sound of the voice, so close to her when she hadn't heard anyone approach. Of course, several people were on the way. The medical examiner and his assistants, the forensic team, and her partner, Steve McKinley.

But the speaker was not NOPD or from the morgue or the lab.

He was a tall man in a plain blue suit. He had a headful of hair so dark it appeared to be black, and even a few feet away, she could see his eyes were the color of steel. He was, perhaps, in his mid to late thirties. He was a fit and striking man and had an air of authority about him, but she still wanted to know what the hell he was doing in her crime scene. He wasn't looking at her; he was staring at the head.

"And you are?" Alex demanded.

He turned to her. "I'm sorry. Detective LeBlanc, is it? Special Agent Jack Walker."

"Well, thank you," she said, "Yes. We will need the torso. But this, this is New Orleans. I'm with the NOPD. And this is the first—"

"The first you've seen," he said, interrupting her, his voice quiet.

He looked at her.

"But it happened before."

She was startled. Whoever he was, he knew about body parts in her city that she'd never known about.

To be fair...

She'd been in middle school, just as Andrew had suggested, when Katrina had come through; and the levees had broken and the city had been devastated.

With the schools down, she'd been sent to live with a family in Richmond, Virginia, for the following year. They had been nice people; she still loved them. Her parents had come often, but she had begun the year there and she had finished it there.

"I was called within minutes of Officer Smith who was alerted to the...situation. How did you get here so quicky?"

"Quickly? I'm out of the New Orleans field office."

"I see," she murmured. "So, you're about to tell me I'm in the middle of *your* crime scene. I'm still not sure why the FBI would—"

"It has happened before."

"But—"

He shook his head and extended an arm, indicating the way the body parts were strewn about.

"Why don't we think of it as *our* crime scene? We've got enough gruesome to go around."

As he spoke, her phone rang.

She never challenged him; it was her lieutenant on the line.

According to him, the FBI would be taking the lead. Of course, the NOPD would still be on the case.

She ended the call, smiling.

"All right. I agree. Plenty of gruesome." She was still puzzled. But at least he wasn't being a jerk, telling her it was his crime scene and police were secondary.

Agent Walker nodded and said, "So, let's treat this as if we aren't both here. We'll investigate the crime scene separately, and then get together and compare notes."

"Okay," Alex said.

She turned away from him and continued investigating. It was not going to be easy for the forensic team to find evidence—the cemetery was visited by tours every day.

She made notes as to where each of the body parts was lain, along with the family name on every tomb and the individual names on the single tombs. She looked for any little piece of evidence, knowing the crime scene forensic crew would be on it as well. As she worked, the medical examiner and the forensic people arrived, and in the end she stepped back, letting them work.

She was maneuvering around carefully and greeting the forensic crew when her phone rang again.

It was her partner Steve. A great guy and great cop.

"Alex," he said.

"Steve, there's an FBI agent here, and—"

"Oh, thank God! Then I can leave you to represent the NOPD."

"Steve—"

"Alex, I'm at the hospital. My dad was just rushed in. I think he's going to be okay—they caught the problem quickly enough. I'd like to stay here but I didn't want to leave you with such a horrendous crime on your own. If the FBI is taking over—"

"Steve, stay with your dad. I'm on this. I don't understand why this guy is going to be lead on the investigation. It's New Orleans."

"Hey—just be thankful, huh? Won't be our fault if we don't find the killer."

It occurred to her then she wasn't sure if there was a killer—or if the body parts had been stolen from a mortuary, of if the person had somehow expired of natural causes before being cut up.

"Stay with your dad. Give him my love." She hesitated. "I can't let it go, Steve. It's our jurisdiction. I guess I'm going to go get warm and cozy with the FBI guy."

"I'll have you get me up to speed later, okay?"

"Sure."

Steve sighed softly over the line. "Blue moon," he told her.

"What?"

"Last night was the blue moon. People get crazy during the blue moon."

"Okay, thanks. I'll use that," she said, shaking her head as she ended the call.

She saw Dr. Gerard, an experienced medical examiner she had worked with often, hunkered down by the torso.

Dr. Gerard fit his role well, a studious looking man with

white hair clipped short, a serious face, and dark brown eyes that seemed to see all. He was a detail man, something she appreciated.

Details often brought them where they needed to be.

She started toward him, noting the FBI guy had already gotten there.

"Alex," Dr. Gerard said in quiet greeting. "Well, this is a hell of a mess. Photographers have captured all the parts in situ as they were discovered. With your blessing, I'll be moving the body. Pieces."

Alex glanced at the agent. The one having the lead on the investigation with no reason.

He nodded. She did the same.

"Did you find any identification on him?" she asked.

"No. But we'll be on it with prints and dental as quickly as possible," Dr. Gerard assured her.

"Thank you. We'll need anything and everything you can get to us as soon as you can," she said.

The body was being removed; the forensic crew was busy.

She could leave. Head back to her office and see what she could discover about the body found after the levees had broken in the aftermath of Katrina.

"Hey."

Jack Walker was addressing her as Dr. Gerard walked away.

"I really don't like stepping on toes," he said quietly. "Come with me. I know a great place. Coffee Science. Sure, they do the fancy stuff, but they also make a great cup of plain old coffee. I can explain why I'm here and…well, I can explain."

She was tempted to argue, but that would be counterproductive. And of course, she wanted to know what he knew.

"Sure."

"We can take my car and I'll bring you back to yours," he said, and then added, "or you can drive and bring me back."

She smiled. Yes, she'd been touchy. She had been born and bred in New Orleans. It was her city. She was a cop because she wanted to be a good cop, because her city was historic and unique and wonderful—and not without crime.

"Sure. Coffee. And what others know that I don't. Except, you're not that old. You couldn't have been that much older than I was when Katrina hit."

"I was twenty-two, not long out of college, and I'd been with the NOPD about five months when the storm came, the levees broke, and the city was in the middle of disaster. I wasn't with the homicide detectives on the case—I was the one who came upon the pieces. Coffee?"

She nodded. "Coffee! And I don't care who drives."

He drove. The drive was short. They were seated and munching on the best avocado toast she had ever had and drinking coffee—it really was excellent—when he explained the rest of what had happened at the time.

"As you know, looting was a problem. I was chasing two men who had hit one of the antique shops on Royal Street when they leapt over the wall into the cemetery. I followed, naturally." He hesitated. "It was the same scene," he said quietly. "The head was in front of a family mausoleum while the limbs and torso were elsewhere. The pieces were so badly decomposed the medical examiner could never pinpoint a time of death—except he thought it had been before the storm. I believed the killer had planned the murder before Katrina hit, and then...well, bided time to place the body parts. Anyway, detectives were brought in. But there was so much else going on their investigation was hampered at every level. No witnesses to the body parts being placed. No tangible clues whatsoever." He hesitated with a rueful grimace. "We were still trying to save the living," he said.

"So, the case went cold. And the media was—thankfully in a way—obsessed with people needing rescue off their roofs that the case went cold with no fanfare."

He shrugged. "Took a ghost tour once—and the guide mentioned the mystery of the body parts. But no date, nothing else was mentioned. You know—if you see a floating head, that's kind of a thing."

She shook her head. "I still can't believe it. And it's so many years later…"

"Right. But you understand I can't let it go." He hesitated again. "I could swear I heard something when I first got into the cemetery—before I saw the body parts. Somebody whispered, 'In honor of you, my love.'"

"It might have been someone bringing flowers," Alex murmured.

"It might have been. But the words have haunted me."

"Did they ever discover the identity of the body?"

He shook his head.

"I stayed with the NOPD another year and then applied to the FBI. I worked up at the NYC offices for a few years, and then I transferred back here. And my supervising director knew about the past, so here I am."

"Well, we'll see what the M.E. and forensics can tell us," Alex said.

He nodded. "You understand. I can't let it go this time."

"I do understand."

He leaned back, studying her. It was okay; she was accustomed to people studying her and wondering about her. She thought she'd just tell him about herself and get it over with.

"Yes, I'm a walking testament to the United Nations," she said. "My mother's mom is African American and her dad was of Japanese descent. My father's dad was a Cajun, born and raised right here in the south, and his mom was Choctaw."

"Beautiful," he said.

"Pardon?"

"Beautiful. And it always is, I think, when we mix things up. I didn't want to say this at a crime scene, but you really are stunning."

"I—uh—thank you. Well. I guess we should get back."

"Yes. We'll keep in touch, I promise."

Jack took Alex back to her car. Left her there. The cemetery remained closed. It would stay closed until the forensic team was certain they had covered everything.

But Alex didn't head back to the office; she went home. It was easier to work on her computer there. She looked up cases of dismemberment, profiler versions from officers and agents who had interviewed such killers.

She looked up the cemetery, and the families of all those who had been noted on the tombs where the body parts had been left.

She spoke with her partner later and assured him everything they could do was being done. He should stay with his father.

She also found herself wondering about her accidental partner on the case—and avoiding returning calls from her friends.

She wasn't up to a night out with anyone.

This time, of course, the body parts hit the news. They hadn't found the kid who had first come running to Officer Smith, but somehow the word had gotten out on the streets, and the media had gotten wind of it.

She watched the news as Jack Walker spoke, saying that, yes, a body had been found in the cemetery—one that hadn't belonged. The police and FBI were involved in a joint investigation, and there was nothing else they knew or could tell at the moment. More information would hopefully be forthcoming when the remains were identified and next of kin notified.

He looked good on TV. And he handled the press smoothly.

She was surprised to receive a call from him soon after the briefing.

"Hey. You have something?" she asked him.

"The deceased was a man named Timothy Morgan. The man's fingers were badly mangled, but they managed to get his prints. And he was in the system. He'd been arrested for kidnapping and rape, but he'd beaten the rap at trial."

"I'm looking him up right now...revenge? Someone who thought justice wasn't done?" Alex suggested.

"Possibly. But his victim was a young woman named Shelley

Fontenot and she died of cancer two years ago. She was an only child and her parents are deceased. She wasn't originally from the area."

"She must have had friends."

"I have all the records pulled. Feel free to meet me at the office."

"I'll be there."

She left her home in the Irish Channel section of the city and made her way quickly to the FBI offices.

It was quiet at night; she was quickly led to the room where Jack Walker was working.

He greeted her with satisfaction.

"Thanks for coming."

"Of course."

He sat behind his desk; she took the chair in front of it and set up her laptop.

He handed her a stack of files. They went to work in an oddly comfortable silence.

"Shelley Fontenot was a waitress—and druggie," Alex said quietly. "She'd been picked up for prostitution, which is probably how Timothy Morgan managed to get off, despite the fact he probably did assault her."

"Possibly," Jack murmured.

She looked up, frowning. "But...Timothy Morgan was arrested just four years ago. You found the same thing right after Katrina. Doesn't add up!"

"I know."

"Hm."

She looked back at the files again.

Then she hit a key on her laptop, looking for the sketch of the kid that was drawn after she'd asked Officer Smith to get an APB out on him.

She studied the picture.

Flyaway hair, an oval face, large eyes wide apart. A kid? He might easily have been in his twenties.

"We still haven't found Andrew's 'kid,'" she said thoughtfully. "I don't think he's a kid—I think he's older."

"Still, he'd be really young to have murdered and chopped up someone right after Katrina," Jack said.

"Right. But..."

She started wondering again about the pattern of lines in the grass and dirt by the tomb.

She looked up at Jack and started to speak.

And they spoke at the same time.

"What if we're looking at this wrong—" he said.

"What if we should be looking at this from a different angle—" she said.

He smiled. "From the past. A wrong done...well, we'll need to dredge up more files. And it's past midnight. And as much as I want to keep going—"

She pulled out her phone and showed him the picture she'd taken of the grass and dirt by the tomb where they'd found the head.

"What do you make of this?" she asked him.

"It's uh—dirt. And grass."

"But there are lines in it."

"There are. Send me that?"

"Sure. It's probably just dirt and grass, the stuff in the few feet between tombs. But it bothered me, so..."

"So, we look at it. Although right now..."

"Yes. We should get some sleep and start fresh. I guess your wife will be wondering where you are."

Whatever made her say that?

"I'm not married, but my cat will be waiting," he said with a grin. "You?"

"I don't even have the cat," she told him.

He smiled. "I'd have thought you'd have...sorry. Not my business."

"Work," she said. "And...I don't know. I was engaged once." She winced. "He, um, wanted me to quit my job."

He nodded. "I know. It's hard to get...close. And I admit to being obsessive. Well, I guess we all get second chances somewhere. Anyway, sleep is necessary—while a decent outside life might not be."

They walked out together, agreeing to meet in the morning at the morgue and find out what else the medical examiner could tell them before delving back into old files.

Alex was heading home. She really was. But she found herself driving back to the cemetery instead.

An officer was at the gate but he quickly stepped aside when he saw Alex.

"Working late!" he told her, grimacing. "I guess it's a 'haunting' case.'"

"You could say that, I suppose," she told him. "Anyway, I want to take a look at the scene again."

He nodded and she walked in.

The "Cities of the Dead" New Orleans was famous for the moody and haunting places, beautiful in their atmosphere, truly chilling by night with their renowned "decaying elegance."

She'd been a street cop for years before earning her detective's badge; she'd seen a lot. New Orleans was wonderful and historic, offering stunning streets and wonderful tales, music, museums, great food, and more.

And she loved it. She'd seen the grandeur—and the underbelly.

She wasn't easily frightened.

And yet that night...it was dark in the cemetery, despite the moon and the glow from the small flashlight she waved before her.

She felt as if shadows followed her. As if the gargoyles atop tombs might move, as if...

Someone was watching her.

She shook off the thought. She wasn't afraid of the dark. Or a cemetery.

No matter how haunting and atmospheric.

She walked to the tomb where the head had been. The family

name "Cassidy" was etched into the stone that guarded the gated door.

She went to the little area of grass and dirt by the tomb, reminding herself it could be a fool's quest—the forensic team had been there all day.

But she pulled out a glove and gingerly touched her finger to the ground, deepening the grooves she had seen earlier.

She sat back stunned. She couldn't be sure of course. The power of suggestion was there in her mind.

But she could swear someone had written in the dirt, "In honor of you, my love."

She looked at the tomb again.

Cassidy.

Jack Walker might be asleep already. She thought she'd call him anyway. But as she pulled out her phone, she felt a whisper of air.

Then the cold steel of a gun against her head.

"You shouldn't have seen this. I never wanted to hurt a cop!"

"Then don't," Alex suggested.

She'd been a fool, so engrossed in the ground she hadn't realized someone had come upon her. How? Cops had been around the cemetery all day. There were officers out...

But maybe they weren't expecting a killer to return. Maybe they couldn't watch every inch of the wall. Maybe there had been an opened gate to an unsealed tomb and...

It didn't matter. There was a gun at her head.

"You don't understand. They deserved to die."

"Maybe."

"You're a cop; agreeing can't help you."

"Yes, it can. You can get that gun away from my head. I know what happened."

"You do?"

"A Cassidy was wronged—and the killer or abuser got away with it—"

"She was murdered!"

"Murdered. I'm so sorry. So, the body parts in the cemetery after Katrina belonged to the man who killed her, right?"

"Yes. My father...he had to do it. He had to kill him. My mom...she was in the wrong place at the wrong time, but... well, now you know who I am."

"A jury will understand that you killed a man who abused someone years earlier—and walked away just because she'd walked the streets sometimes. Everyone deserves justice. But if you kill me, it won't be in anyone's honor."

She twisted around. And she saw the face that had been in a sketch done by Officer Smith's description to the police artist.

"If you kill me—"

"I don't want to—I have to!"

Words suddenly rang out loud and clear.

"No, you don't!"

Alex blinked, incredulous.

Jack Walker was standing just feet away, his Glock aimed at the kid.

"I can kill her first—"

"And you die, too, having done honor to no one! Hey, I know lots of good attorneys," Jack said.

The kid was shaking. Alex was afraid the gun was going to go off.

She took a chance. She moved in a flash, setting her hand over the nose of the kid's gun, and pointed it to the ground.

The gun went off; the kid panicked and spun around to attack her with his bare hands. He never touched her.

Jack Walker had him down on the ground, cuffing him.

"Sorry, kid. I know how it feels when you watch the bad guy walk away. I looked it up. Today would have been your mom's fiftieth birthday. *In her honor.* I'm sorry. But..."

"Yeah."

The kid just stood there, looking at the tomb. Alex didn't realize she was still on the ground until Jack offered her a hand.

She accepted it and stood.

Suddenly, the cemetery was alive with light. More haunting in the harsh glare...

Decaying elegance. Death.

But they were alive.

And as other officers rushed in to take the kid into custody, she was eager to walk out into the night, into the sounds of the city.

Back to the land of the living.

There was paperwork. Tons of it. There was the press. The kid's name was Reginald Cassidy; his mother had been murdered.

Her killer had walked. His father had taken care of the killer.

And Reginald Cassidy had turned his life over to finding those who hurt women—and got away with it.

The press went wild with the story.

Back at Coffee Science a few days later, Jack and Alex talked at a corner table, across from each other on red leather benches. The sound of the expresso machine and the clatter of dishes mixed with soft jazz from somewhere.

"I don't think he would have killed me. But thank you—it is possible you saved my life."

"You had it under control."

"But he wouldn't have been distracted if you hadn't come. And I'm still wondering—"

"Your picture."

"Pardon?"

"When you left, I couldn't let it go. I had to see the patch of grass myself."

"It's the little things, huh?"

"Yeah."

"Well, here's the good...it's a solved case, and I won't be haunted by the past anymore."

"That's good. That's great."

Alex was startled when he reached across the table and touched her hand.

"Instead," he said, "I may be haunted by the present."

"Pardon?"

"Want to go...? Out? Friday night? Barring nothing else outrageous pops up?"

She smiled. "Um, yes! I'd love to go out Friday night, whether something else outrageous occurs or not."

"We're on." Then he frowned, serious. "You do like cats, don't you?"

Alex started to laugh.

"I like cats just fine," she assured him.

It was so strange, she thought. A gruesome and horrible case. A second chance for him on a murder that had haunted him through the years. And...

Yeah.

A second chance for them both.

NIGHT BUS
ELLEN CLAIR LAMB

Jodie was last in line for the cheap bus to New York. By the time she got on, only one seat was left—on the aisle, next to an old lady who wasn't asleep.

Damn.

"Sorry, it's the last one open," Jodie said as she took it, stuffing her messenger bag under the seat in front of her.

"Not at all," the old lady said. "Do you have enough space?"

"I'm fine," Jodie said. *Please, please, please don't talk to me.*

"I'm Barbara." She put her hand out. "What's your name?"

Shit, shit. shit. "Mary," Jodie said. It was the first name she could think of.

"Nice to meet you, Mary." The woman's hand was warm and dry, and squeezed Jodie's before letting it drop.

At least she doesn't smell bad. "Nice to meet you too," Jodie said. "I'm going to try to sleep most of the way, okay? I'll try not to lean on you. Just poke me if I snore."

The woman laughed. It wasn't an old lady's laugh. Now that Jodie looked at her, maybe she wasn't that old—she just had white hair.

One of those environmental types who doesn't believe in dye, Josie thought. *Or who's just given up.* She considered pushing the button to let her seat recline, but the knees of the passenger behind her were already jammed into her back.

"Not a lot of room on these buses," the lady said, as if reading her mind. "That's why it only costs fifteen dollars to go to New York."

"Only ten to Philadelphia," Jodie said, before she could stop herself. *Cut it out. Now she knows you're going to Philadelphia.*

The bus pulled out of the Union Station garage, and the darkness of the night settled in. A few overhead lights clicked on. Jodie was relieved that her seatmate didn't reach for hers.

"I don't mind if you turn the light on," Jodie said despite herself.

In the shadows, the woman—*Barbara, her name is Barbara*—smiled. "Yes, you do. Go ahead and sleep. I don't need light for this." She raised a circular knitting needle from her lap, with what looked like a blanket attached. "I'll try not to bump you with my elbows."

Jodie closed her eyes and took a deep breath. The woman next to her didn't smell bad, but the bus smelled like a subway car in winter: damp wool, old onions, unwashed gym clothes and the funk of last night's alcohol.

I'm probably no better myself. Didn't they say you could smell fear? What did fear smell like?

She had drifted off into something that wasn't consciousness, if it wasn't quite sleep, when the bus slowed, pulled over, and stopped. She opened her eyes and saw only darkness, then the flash of red and blue lights.

"Why are we stopping?" she asked.

"We've been pulled over," Barbara said.

"Speeding?"

"I think it's something else."

The rest of the bus was awake and talking. Someone said, "That ICE? *La migra*?" and someone else said, "Shit." Someone got up and went to the back of the bus, to the scary toilet.

They can't be looking for me. How? How would they know?

"I can't imagine they're looking for anyone in particular,"

Barbara said. She was still knitting. "These buses don't have passenger lists."

Jesus, lady, get out of my head. "What?"

"It's a bus full of people who paid cash," Barbara said. "We're all suspects."

"You make it sound like a TV show. Who are you, Jessica Fletcher?"

"Oh, because of the knitting? God, no. But people on an anonymous bus in the middle of the night are traveling because they have to, not because they want to."

Despite herself, Jodie asked, "Are you traveling because you have to?"

"I guess you could say so," Barbara said.

"What's in New York for you?"

"Another bus."

The driver had left the bus to talk to whoever'd pulled him over, leaving the door open and letting the winter air in. He returned with two uniformed officers and switched on the light strips on either side of the bus's interior.

"Please have your identification ready for inspection," one of the officers said, as the other moved to the back of the bus. Both held large flashlights. "Passports, if you have them."

Jodie pulled her bag up. Her wallet was zipped into a front pocket—*thank God*—and she extracted her license, then kicked the bag under the seat again.

Barbara already had her passport in hand, apparently from a pocket.

Who gets on a bus with a passport?

"I don't drive," Barbara said. "I have what they call a 'walker's ID,' but the passport is easier when I travel."

"And you never know when you might have to leave the country, right?" Jodie meant it as a joke, but Barbara gave her something that wasn't quite a smile.

"You never know," she said.

The officer who had called for ID had worked his way from

the front of the bus to their row.

"Identification, please?"

Barbara handed him her passport and he scrutinized it before handing it back to her.

"Where are you headed tonight, ma'am?"

"New York City."

"And the purpose of your trip?"

Barbara hesitated long enough for Jodie to notice. "I'm visiting family."

The officer turned to Jodie. "ID, please?"

Jodie handed him her license.

He barely looked at it. "Are you an American citizen, ma'am?"

"Yes," she said.

"Place of birth?"

"Fayetteville, North Carolina."

He grunted something that might have been thanks, handed the license back to her, and moved to the next row.

Jodie sagged back against her seat.

"You're all right," Barbara said.

This was starting to annoy her. "How do you know? Who the hell are you, anyway?"

Barbara was knitting again. In the light, Jodie could see it was something in shades of green and blue, ocean colors.

"Do you know the prayer to St. Michael the Archangel?"

Oh, for Christ's sake. She's one of those. "I've never needed it."

Barbara didn't seem offended. "Well, it doesn't come up much, outside of military parishes. Catholics in the military like it, because it's all about battle."

"My father was Army. I've never heard of it."

"Oh, Fayetteville," Barbara said. "Fort Bragg?"

"We moved when I was still a baby. I don't remember it."

"Not much to remember about it, though the river trail is nice," Barbara said.

"You've been there?"

"I've been everywhere." The needles clicked against each

other, new fabric flowing from them. Whatever she was knitting really did look like water. "Anyway," she continued, "St. Michael the Archangel."

"What about him?"

"The idea of St. Michael is that he fights the devil, specifically. 'Satan and all the evil spirits, who prowl through the world seeking the ruin of souls.'"

"Sounds like a movie."

"It does, doesn't it?" Barbara laughed. "With Gabriel Byrne. Or maybe he played the devil in that one. I can't remember."

"I don't believe in the devil." Jodie felt the need to get that out there.

"Well, no, of course not," Barbara said. "I'm not sure I do either, at least not as an actual creature walking around with a tail and horns. But I believe in the ruin of souls."

She raised her eyes to look directly at Jodie as the bus lights snapped off, plunging them all back into darkness. Whatever the officers had been looking for, they hadn't found. They'd left the bus and the driver was starting the engine again.

"People think what they do can't matter much to other people," Barbara said as the bus accelerated back onto the highway. "It makes them careless. People don't listen to each other. People don't see each other."

"But you do?"

"I don't know whether what I do matters. But I do look. I listen. You're running from something."

"How do you know?" Jodie asked.

"Because we all are," Barbara said. "Anyone who sat in your seat would have been running from something. The question is what."

"What are you running from?"

"That's not your business," Barbara said pleasantly. "But for most of us, you know, whatever we're running from comes with us, or at least is waiting for us when we get there."

"Get where—to New York?"

"Or to Philadelphia," Barbara said. "But sometimes, I can help."

"Help?"

"With whatever you're running from."

Jodie snorted. "You got a magic carpet? A get out of jail free card?"

"Are those what you need?" Barbara asked.

"For starters."

"What's in Philadelphia?"

"My job. My apartment."

Barbara reached into her knitting bag and pulled out a flask. "Bourbon? You can have the cap as a cup, I haven't drunk from it."

"I'm not drinking," Jodie said.

"Then I won't, either." Barbara dropped the flask back into her bag. "Are you in recovery?"

"No," said Jodie. "I'm pregnant."

It had been a shock. Jodie had been on the pill since she was seventeen. Who knew tetracycline made the pill less effective? She did, now.

She hadn't expected him to be happy about it, but she felt she had to tell him in person, instead of by text or over the phone. He had office hours on Thursday afternoons, so she'd taken the bus down that morning, and hung out in the library until fifteen minutes before his office hours were supposed to end.

"This is a pleasant surprise," he said when she knocked on his open door. "What are you doing in town?"

"I wanted to talk to you."

They hadn't touched each other until after she graduated. He'd been her thesis adviser, guiding her research on the influence of Novalis on the March Revolution of 1848. She stayed on through the summer, working at the library before going up to Temple for their History Ph.D. program on War, Empire, and Society. Somewhere in there he'd started coming by the library late in the afternoon, suggesting she join him for a drink. And the rest, as they said, was history.

Except he was married. Except he was up for tenure. Except he didn't love her, and she wasn't sure she loved him.

"I have a meeting at five," he said. "But I can meet you at The Tombs after. Six?"

"Okay," she said.

She waited for him in a booth on the bar side, where they were less likely to be seen. She ordered an iced tea and a bowl of artichoke dip, thinking of it as rent. She opened her satchel and pulled out a biography of Mansa Musa she was reading for an Empires of Africa course, but she couldn't focus. She opened her planner and traced the weeks on the calendar—ten weeks back, thirty weeks forward. Forty weeks altogether. Less than one percent of her life, if she lived to be eighty. Nothing, compared to the twenty-two months elephants spent pregnant.

He slid into the booth opposite her, briefcase first. "A short one, for once. Finals start next week." He looked at the dip and the glass of iced tea in front of her. "Do we have a waiter, or should I go to the bar?"

"I just ordered from the bar."

"Okay, that's what I'll do. Do you need anything?"

"No," she said. "And I paid, I'm not running a tab."

He returned to the table with his usual: bourbon straight, water back. She watched in silence as he scooped three ice cubes— always three, never more, never less—into his drink, then used a straw to add exactly twenty drops of water. He swirled it once and set it on the table.

"Let it open up," he said, as if she didn't know.

How had she ever thought that was charming?

"Hey, I got good news this week," he said. "*The Journal of Military History* accepted my article on the Polish Legions." He held his glass up for a toast.

She obliged, clinking her tea glass with his whisky. "That's great," she said. "I'm pregnant." It was the first time she'd said it aloud.

He bobbled his glass, nearly dropped it, and set it down without drinking.

"Well," he said. "Congratulations, I guess. Who's the father?"

She slapped him, grabbed her bag, and walked out of the bar.

He caught her on the stairs before she reached the sidewalk. "Jodie, wait. Wait. I'm sorry. Are you—are you saying this is mine?"

"Who else could it be?"

"I don't know. I don't know your life. For all I know, you've got a boyfriend in Philadelphia."

They were on the sidewalk, and night had fallen. It was cold, and 36th Street was almost empty of traffic, automotive or pedestrian.

"You know I don't," Jodie said. "Forget about it." She turned toward Prospect and the Exorcist stairs. She could walk to the Ballston Metro.

"Do you need money—you know—to take care of things?"

It stopped her. She'd assumed she'd have an abortion, of course. But somehow, his assumption that she'd have an abortion was outrageous. Enraging.

"Fuck you," she said. "No, wait—I already did that."

"Jodie," he said. "You're not going to do anything stupid, are you?"

"Like what?"

"I don't know, like—" He raised his hands.

"Like tell your wife? Like tell the dean? Like write a letter to *The Hoya*? Like stand in Red Square with a big scarlet A on my chest?"

His hands dropped. "Yes. Like that."

"No." She rummaged in her bag for her keys, ready to hold them between her fingers in a fist as she walked to the Metro.

"What do you want from me?" he asked. "What am I supposed

to do here?"

"I don't know," she said. "I don't know why I came here. I thought—I don't know what I thought. You're the adult here."

"You're not a child," he said. "You're a grown woman. What are you, twenty-two?"

"Twenty-one," she said. "I skipped a grade."

She crossed Prospect Street, and he followed her.

"Plenty of women your age have children," he said. "Or at least, they know what to do if they don't want them."

"You're right," Jodie said. "You're absolutely right. I shouldn't have come here."

"Wait," he said. "Wait. What if—"

"What if what?"

"My wife and I have been talking about adoption for a couple of years. If you're willing, I could pay you—we could even say you're a surrogate."

"Seeing red" was not a metaphor, Jodie discovered. With her keys in her fist, she punched up and at him, catching him just under the chin and knocking him back against the brick wall at the top of the Exorcist steps. His head made an audible *thunk* as it hit the wall, and he slumped to the ground.

He didn't get up.

Jodie didn't stop to check whether he was breathing. She ran down the stairs, to the traffic lights at the corner of M Street, and dashed across as soon as the light turned yellow. She ran across Key Bridge, bag slung over her shoulder, across more lanes of traffic and to the Metro station, where she scanned her card and disappeared down the long escalator to the subway.

On the train platform, she turned off her phone. She wouldn't turn it on again until she got home.

"So you don't know how badly you hurt this man," Barbara said, still knitting, knitting.

"No," Jodie said.

"What's his name?"

"Lester. Dominic Lester."

"Okay, then." Barbara laid her knitting on her lap and pulled a phone out of another of her pockets. She opened a news app and typed in the name. "Nothing so far," she said.

"What if—what if I killed him?" Jodie asked.

"What if you did?" Barbara said. "You probably didn't. It's not as if people don't walk by there all the time. I'm sure someone found him in time to get help. And he's hardly going to turn you in."

She was right, Jodie realized. He had nothing to gain and everything to lose by accusing her.

"But what if he's dead?" she asked.

"If he's dead, he's dead," Barbara said. "You can't fix that. You go on. Live your life. Have your baby. Be free. Imagine your best self."

I could do that, Jodie thought. She wondered what her mother would say when she told her about the baby. *The baby. My baby*. What was it her mother always said?

"Babies bring their own," Jodie said.

Barbara had started knitting again, but seemed to be closing off the row she was working on, dropping the blanket from the needles stitch by stitch. "That's exactly right," she said. "Here, I'm finishing this. You can take it with you for the baby."

"What if I'm a murderer?" Jodie said.

Barbara laid a hand on Jodie's. "It wasn't murder, it was self-defense."

"Self-defense," Jodie said.

"Self-defense," Barbara repeated.

The bus pulled up alongside Penn Central, and the interior lights came on again. Jodie took the blanket Barbara had given her and folded it over the top of her messenger bag, since it wouldn't fit inside.

"Good luck, Mary," Barbara said.

Mary? Jodie had forgotten she'd given the woman a fake name. "Thank you," she said. "Thanks for everything."

"And don't worry. Everything gets easier from here," the white-haired woman said. "Only the first murder counts."

ABOUT THE EDITOR

HANK PHILLIPPI RYAN is the *USA Today* bestselling author of thirteen psychological thrillers, and has won thirty-seven Emmy awards for her television investigative reporting. Her books have won five Agatha Awards, four Anthony Awards, and the coveted Mary Higgins Clark Award. Reviewers have called her "a master of suspense" and "a superb and gifted storyteller." *The Murder List* (2019) won the Anthony Award for Best Novel. *The First To Lie* (2020, with a starred review from *Publishers Weekly*) is now nominated for the Mary Higgins Clark Award and the Anthony Award. *Her Perfect Life* (with starred reviews from *Publishers Weekly* and *Kirkus*) will be published in September 2021. She lives in Boston.

ABOUT THE CONTRIBUTORS

SHARON BADER is a transplanted New Yorker-Floridian-Californian who lives and writes in North Carolina, where she is currently researching and writing a historical mystery novel. Her stories have appeared in two collections published by Anchala Press and the Triangle Sisters in Crime. She holds a Master of Science degree in geological oceanography.

DAMYANTI BISWAS is the author of *You Beneath Your Skin*, an Amazon-bestselling crime novel, now optioned for a major motion picture by Endemol Shine. She supports Project WHY, a program that provides quality education to underprivileged children in New Delhi. Her short stories have been published in magazines in the U.S., UK and Asia. She also helps edit the *Forge Literary Magazine*.

CLARK BOYD currently lives and works in the Netherlands. His short fiction has appeared in High Shelf Press, Scare Street, Havok, *After the Kool-Aid is Gone*, *Fatal Flaw Magazine*, and various Jazz House and DBND horror anthologies. Before turning to fiction, he spent two decades reporting, writing, editing, and producing international news stories for *The World*, a daily program produced at WGBH public radio in Boston. Clark's currently working on a book about windmills. Or cheese. Maybe both.

LUCY BURDETTE (aka Roberta Isleib) is the author of nineteen mysteries, including *A Scone of Contention*, the latest in the Key West series featuring food critic Hayley Snow. Her books and stories have been short-listed for Agatha, Anthony, and Macavity awards. She's a past president of Sisters in Crime, and currently serving as president of the Friends of the Key West Library.

KAREN DIONNE is the #1 international bestselling author of *The Marsh King's Daughter*, published by G.P. Putnam's Sons in the U.S. and in twenty-six other languages. Praised by the *New York Times* Book Review as "subtle, brilliant, and mature...as good as a thriller can be," *The Marsh King's Daughter* took home the Barry and Crimson Scribe Awards for Best Novel and is in development as a major motion picture starring Daisy Ridley. Karen's newest psychological suspense, *The Wicked Sister*, is also an international bestseller and was chosen by *Publishers Weekly* as one of the Best Thrillers of 2020.

ELISABETH ELO is the author of the suspense novels *Finding Katarina M.* and *North of Boston*, selected by *Booklist* as a year's best crime novel debut. Her Pushcart-nominated short stories have appeared in *The Gettysburg Review*, *Alaska Quarterly Review*, and other publications. She is a former magazine editor, high-tech project manager, and halfway house counselor. She lives in Brookline, Massachusetts.

A former English and drama teacher, **ELIZABETH ELWOOD** spent many years performing with music and theatre groups and singing in the Vancouver Opera chorus. Having turned her talents to writing and design, she created twenty marionette musicals for Elwoodettes Marionettes and has written four plays that have entertained audiences in both Canada and the United States. She is the author of six books in the Beary Mystery Series, and her short stories have been featured in *EQMM* and Malice Domestic's *Mystery Most Theatrical*. Born in England, Elizabeth lives on British Columbia's beautiful Sunshine Coast.

ALEXIA GORDON is a physician by day and an award-winning, own voices crime novelist by night. A Virginia native who grew up in Maryland, she's lived all over the U.S. and currently resides in New England with her cat, Agatha. She's into early American history, distilled spirits, embroidery, and good ghost stories. The fifth novel in her Gethsemane Brown mystery series, *Execution in E*, was published in March 2020. Alexia is a member of Crime Writers of Color, Sisters in Crime, International Thriller Writers, and Mystery Writers of America.

New York Times and *USA Today* bestselling author **HEATHER GRAHAM** majored in theater arts at the University of South Florida. After a stint of several years in dinner theater, back-up vocals, and bartending, she stayed home after the birth of her third child and began to write. Her first book was with Dell, and since then, she has written over two hundred novels and novellas including category, suspense, historical romance, vampire fiction, time travel, occult and Christmas family fare. She has sixty million books in print. Heather is the Chair of the 2021 Bouchercon Convention.

G. MIKI HAYDEN has published a steady stream of stories over the years and was the proud recipient of a short story Edgar. Miki's *Pacific Empire*, which garnered a rave in the *New York*

Times, was a novel comprised of interlinked short stories. She has published stories in both *Ellery Queen* and *Alfred Hitchcock*. Miki has published several novels and two writing instructionals. She has also been a Writer's Digest University instructor for more than twenty years and works freelance as a pre-publication editor in all genres, fiction and nonfiction.

EDWIN HILL's novels include *Watch Her*, *The Missing Ones*, and *Little Comfort*. He has been nominated for Edgar and Agatha Awards, featured in *Us Magazine*, received starred reviews in *Publishers Weekly*, *Booklist*, and *Library Journal*, and was recognized as one of "Six Crime Writers to Watch" in *Mystery Scene* magazine. He lives in Roslindale, Massachusetts, with his partner Michael and his favorite reviewer, their lab Edith Ann, who likes his first drafts enough to eat them.

CRAIG JOHNSON is the *New York Times* bestselling author of the Longmire series, the basis for the hit Netflix original series *Longmire*. He is the recipient of the Western Writers of America Spur award for Fiction, the Mountains and Plains Booksellers Award for Fiction, the Nouvel Observateur Prix du Roman Noir, and the Prix SNCF du Polar. His novella *Spirit of Steamboat* was the first One Book One Wyoming selection. He lives in Ucross, Wyoming, population 25. He is the American Guest of Honor at Bouchercon 2021.

ELLEN CLAIR LAMB is a writer, editor and researcher who has done many things for many authors over more than twenty years in the crime fiction community. She was assistant editor of the Agatha, Anthony, and Macavity Award-winning *Books to Die For*. She has been a lobbyist, an association executive, a bookseller, a stage manager in the NY Musical Festival, an unsuccessful *Jeopardy!* contestant and a winner of Ben Stein's money.

KRISTEN LEPIONKA is the author of the Roxane Weary mystery series. Her debut, *The Last Place You Look*, won the Shamus Award for Best First P.I. novel and was also nominated for Anthony and Macavity Awards. The second book in the series, *What You Want to See,* won Shamus and Goldie Awards. She is a cofounder of the feminist podcast Unlikeable Female Characters and currently serves as Chapter President for the Midwest region of Mystery Writers of America. She lives in Columbus, Ohio, with her partner and two cats.

ALAN ORLOFF's novel, *Pray For the Innocent*, won an ITW Thriller Award. His debut mystery, *Diamonds For the Dead*, was an Agatha Award finalist; his story, "Dying in Dokesville" won a Derringer Award; and "Rule Number One" was selected for *The Best American Mystery Stories*. His YA thriller, *I Play One on TV*, came out in July from Down & Out Books. Alan is currently the MWA Florida Chapter president. He loves cake and arugula, but not together. Never together.

MARTHA REED is the Independent Publisher (IPPY) Book Award-winning author of the John and Sarah Jarad Nantucket Mysteries and of *Love Power*, a new series set in the magically spellbinding city of New Orleans featuring Gigi Pascoe, a transgender sleuth. She's vice president of the Florida Gulf Coast Sisters in Crime and an active member of SinC's online Guppy chapter and of Mystery Writers of America. She contributes writerly insights on the revered Writers Who Kill blog and in a moment of great personal folly she joined the New Orleans Bourbon Society (N.O.B.S.) at Bouchercon NOLA 2016.

ALEX SEGURA is an acclaimed, award-winning writer of novels, comic books, short stories, and podcasts. He is the author of *Star Wars Poe Dameron: Free Fall*, the Pete Fernandez Mystery series including three Anthony Award-nominated crime novels, and the upcoming *Secret Identity* (Flatiron Books). His short story "Red Zone" won the 2020 Anthony Award for Best Short Story, and his border noir short story, "90 Miles" will be included in *The Best American Mystery and Suspense Stories of 2020*. He has also written a number of comic books. He is also the co-creator/co-writer of the Lethal Lit crime/YA podcast from iHeart Radio, which was named one of the best podcasts of 2018 by the *New York Times*. By day he is co-President of Archie Comics. A Miami native, he lives in New York with his wife and children.

STEVE SHROTT is an award-winning writer whose short stories have appeared in numerous print publications, such as *Sherlock Holmes Mystery Magazine* and *Black Cat Mystery Magazine*. In Flame Tree Press's hardcover crime anthology, Steve's story, "The House," appears alongside tales by Author Conan Doyle and Charles Dickens. Steve has two humorous mystery novels published—*Audition for Death* and *Dead Men Don't Get Married*. His comedy material has been used by well-known performers of stage and screen, and he has written Steve Shrott's *Comedy Course*, a book on how to create humor.

CHARLES AND CAROLINE TODD are a writing team who live on the east coast of the United States. They are the *New York Times* bestselling authors of the Inspector Ian Rutledge Series and the Bess Crawford series. They have published over thirty titles including two stand-alone novels, an anthology of short stories and over twenty short stories appearing in mystery magazines and anthologies worldwide. Their works have received the Mary Higgins Clark, Agatha, and Barry awards along with nominations for the Anthony, Edgar, and Dagger awards. They also happen to be mother and son.

GABRIEL VALJAN is the author of the Roma Series and The Company Files (Winter Goose Publishing) and the Shane Cleary Mysteries (Level Best Books). Whether it's a Cold War mystery, or Seventies Boston with Shane Cleary, he is known for a turn of phrase and crisp spare prose. He has been nominated for an Agatha Award for Best Historical Mystery, an Agatha, Anthony and Macavity for Best Short Story, and twice for the Anthony Award for Best Paperback Original. Gabriel is a member of the Historical Novel Society, ITW, MWA, and Sisters in Crime.

DAVID HESKA WANBLI WEIDEN, an enrolled citizen of the Sicangu Lakota Nation, is the author of the novel *Winter Counts* (Ecco, 2020), nominated for the Edgar Award, the Barry Award, and the Hammett Prize. The book was the winner of the Lefty Award for Best Debut Mystery Novel and the Spur Award for Best Contemporary Novel. The novel was a *New York Times* Editors' Choice, main selection of the Book of the Month Club, and named a Best Book of 2020 by NPR, *Publishers Weekly*, *Library Journal*, and other magazines. He lives in Denver, Colorado, with his family.

ANDREW WELSH-HUGGINS, a reporter for *The Associated Press*, is the author of seven Columbus-based mysteries featuring Andy Hayes, a former Ohio State and Cleveland Browns quarterback turned private eye, including the Nero Award-nominated *Fatal Judgment*. Andrew is also editor of the anthology *Columbus Noir*, and his short fiction has appeared in publications including *Ellery Queen Mystery Magazine*, *Mystery Weekly*, and *Mystery Tribune*. Andrew's nonfiction book, *No Winners Here Tonight*, is the definitive history of the death penalty in Ohio.

On the following pages are a few
more great titles from the
Down & Out Books publishing family.

For a complete list of books and to
sign up for our newsletter,
go to DownAndOutBooks.com.

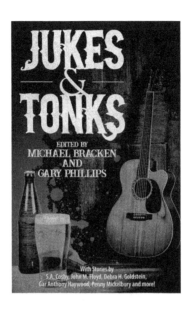

Jukes & Tonks
Crime Fiction Inspired by Music
in the Dark and Suspect Choices
Michael Bracken and Gary Phillips, editors

Down & Out Books
April 2021
978-1-64396-184-2

The stories in *Jukes & Tonks* introduce sinners and saints, love begun and love gone wrong, and all manner of unsavory criminal endeavors.

What they have in common is that they plop you down in worlds where the music pulsating from the stage provides the backbeat for tales that are unsparing, heartbreaking, twisty, and a few are as dark as the night.

Avenging Angelenos
A Sisters in Crime/Los Angeles Anthology
Sarah M. Chen, Wrona Gall, and
Pamela Samuels Young, editors

Down & Out Books
June 2021
978-1-64396-204-7

With an introduction by Frankie Y. Bailey and eleven original stories by Avril Adams, Paula Bernstein, Hal Bodner, Jenny Carless, LH Dillman, Gay Toltl Kinman, Melinda Loomis, Kathy Norris, Peggy Rothschild, Meredith Taylor, and Laurel Wetzork.

Dead-End Jobs
A Hitman Anthology
Andy Rausch, Editor

All Due Respect, an imprint of
Down & Out Books
June 2021
978-1-64396-212-2

A collection of eighteen short stories about contract killers by some of the hottest crime writers in the business.

"An incredible collection of powerful and haunting stories that exist in that shadowy realm between tragedy, nihilism and noir." —S.A. Cosby, author of *Blacktop Wasteland*

Houses Burning and Other Ruins
William R. Soldan

Shotgun Honey, an imprint of
Down & Out Books
May 2021
978-1-64396-115-6

Desperation. Violence. Broken homes and broken hearts. Fathers, junkies, and thieves.

In this gritty new collection, one bad choice begets another, and redemption is a twisted mirage. The troubled characters that inhabit the streets and alleys of these stories continually find themselves at the mercy of a cold, indifferent world as they hurtle downward and grapple for hard-won second chances in a life that seldom grants them.

CPSIA information can be obtained
at www.ICGtesting.com
Printed in the USA
BVHW030214041021
618082BV00006B/279